PRAISE FOR #1 BESTSELLING
AUTHOR KEN FITE AND PERSON OF INTEREST

★★★★★ "Heart-pounding..."

★★★★★ "The best Blake Jordan yet."

★★★★★ "Moves like a bullet train."

★★★★★ "Great characters and lots of action."

★★★★★ "I couldn't put it down!"

★★★★★ "Torn from the headlines..."

★★★★★ "Keeps you on the edge of your seat!"

★★★★★ "I loved the twists and turns."

★★★★★ "Ken Fite has done it again."

★★★★★ "The ending was very touching."

—Amazon reviews

D1295698

WANT THE NEXT BLAKE JORDAN STORY FOR $1 ON RELEASE DAY?*

*KINDLE EDITION ONLY

I'm currently writing the next book in the Blake Jordan series with a release planned soon. New subscribers get the Kindle version for $1 on release day.

Join my newsletter to reserve your copy and I'll let you know when it's ready to download to your Kindle.

kenfite.com/books

THE BLAKE JORDAN SERIES
IN ORDER

For the veterans who proudly served our great country.
You are not forgotten.

PERSON OF INTEREST

A BLAKE JORDAN THRILLER

KEN FITE

1

BOB MILLER DROVE INTO THE PARKING LOT AT WORK AND pulled into his usual spot in the back. He didn't park there for the exercise. He'd get plenty of that while he worked. Miller didn't have a new car he was protecting, either. No other cars would park nearby that could dent his old truck, anyway. Miller parked in that spot because he always had, ever since his first day on the job. And because he liked the sense of control that it gave him. He liked knowing that nobody else would park in his spot. It was one of the only things in his life he could control lately. Miller cut the motor and checked his watch. Then he sat in silence and closed his eyes for a spell. One last moment of respite before his eleven-hour day would begin.

He used the time to think. Another one of his rituals. He thought about his father's many sayings: If you're early, you're on time, and if you're on time, you're late. He always got to work early. He always sat in his truck before he had to head inside. He pulled a creased photograph from his shirt pocket and looked at it. Because he always did. And because it always gave him a reason to endure the grueling workday that was to come. After a long moment he slipped the picture back into his pocket, stepped out, and started moving.

The warehouse entrance was fifty paces away. Not forty-nine. Not fifty-one. Fifty. There was always a guy standing underneath the carport, directing drivers. He always said hello to him as he walked past. He always stepped inside to get that day's assignment from a man named Phil or from a guy named Dan. But Phil wasn't there. Neither was Dan. Instead, a new guy stood behind the desk, staring at him. *A bad omen*, he thought before dismissing it and forcing a smile as he approached the desk. "Where's Phil?" he asked.

"Out sick," the new guy answered.

"What about Dan?"

"Out of town, apparently. He wanted an early start to his weekend, so they called me in to cover for him."

Miller said nothing.

"Name?" the man behind the counter asked.

He paused a moment and said, "Bob Miller."

"Bob Miller," the man repeated to himself as he turned his gaze downward and picked up an old clipboard from the counter and flipped through the pages until he found the one he wanted. He pulled it loose and stared at it; then he set it on the counter and turned back to reach for the supplies. "You work here long?"

"Ten years," he said.

"Ten years," he repeated again, a habit Miller decided the man had. "So you know what you're doing."

Miller ignored the question and stared at the upside-down paper. "This isn't my route," he said to the man.

"It is today," the guy replied as he grabbed a scanner from a shelf and turned and set it on the counter.

"You don't understand, I always work the same neighborhoods. Someone else works this route, not me."

The new guy furrowed his brow and stared across. "You do *today*," he said, emphasizing the last word.

Miller stared back and held his gaze for a long moment. Then he looked away and nodded vaguely.

The guy took the paper and folded it twice. He stuffed it into a small sleeve and slid a company credit card inside and zipped it closed. He set it on the counter and pushed it forward. "Fill it up on your way back."

"Always do," said Miller as he picked it up and looked back at the man, feeling like his day was thrown off.

He grabbed the scanner and went into the next room. The instructions said he'd be taking truck number seventy-three. Miller walked to the wall where the keys hung. He found the keys for seventy-three and took them off the hook. Then he pushed open a door and stepped out into the fenced-in lot and found his truck, painted brown, a gold UPS logo emblazoned on the side, and opened the back door. Another habit of his. There was a lot of open space today. Which worried him. Miller turned and looked at the empty trucks at the far end of the lot for a brief moment; then he shut the back and said a quick prayer of thanks that he still had his job. One of the benefits of having ten years of seniority. Miller slid into the driver's seat, started the motor, and drove it forward, around the looping path marked with orange cones.

The same guy was at the carport, directing him. Miller didn't know his name or what the purpose of his job was. There was only one way out and only one way in. But he smiled at the man and thanked him anyway as he drove past and stopped briefly at the exit. He used the scanner the new guy behind the desk had given him to scan a QR code on the ceiling of the truck to sign in. Instantly, the handheld device he'd use all day to scan packages came to life and showed him his route. From that moment forward, the GPS in his scanner would be monitored. A lot of other things would be monitored, too. The man behind the desk would be able to see whether or not he was on schedule, how often he used his seat belt, how often he accelerated and braked. It tracked his turns and how many times he stopped his vehicle. The GPS on the handheld started navigating him to his first stop, and a woman's voice guided him toward the highway. Miller reached into his shirt pocket and took the picture out. He found a loose binder clip and lowered the visor and clipped the photo to it. He smiled and left the visor down so he could see it throughout the day. Then he checked the road for oncoming traffic and made a right turn, headed for the highway.

He turned the radio on and found his favorite AM talk station. The same one he always listened to. Another habit of his. The navigation told him to make the next turn, and he checked his mirror and saw a van, dark and hard to see in the early morning light. He made the turn. As he drove, he took a peek at the kind of deliveries he'd have to make throughout the day. They were all residential and mostly in Reston. It wasn't Fairfax, but maybe a change of scenery would be a good thing. Maybe the familiarity of his daily route had allowed him to think too deeply about his problems. Maybe the new route would be a distraction.

The monotone voice told him to make a right, and he obeyed. He took the on-ramp up to the highway and picked up speed. When the radio program went to a commercial, he turned the volume down and got ready to merge and checked the mirror. The van was still behind him and had pulled up close to his truck.

He merged. The van merged with him. Then a minute later the driver began flashing its lights at him.

Miller stared at it for a spell; then he turned his gaze to his dashboard, wondering what the problem was. He was going the right speed. There was no indication that anything was wrong. No warning lights were displayed. No alerts about low tire pressure or an overheating engine. He glanced at the mirror again and stared back at the head-lights flashing urgently behind him. An ominous warning. Something was wrong.

He drove on, and his mind raced. Had he left the back open when he looked over the packages? Had some of the boxes fallen out along the way? Had he left it ajar? He didn't think he had. He was always careful. But the flashing head-lights continued. So he punched a button, and the hazards came on. He looked for a clearing up ahead and found one and pulled to the side of the highway and carefully came to a stop. Miller glanced back and saw the van do the same. It slowed and pulled up close and parked behind him. He stayed seated and watched through his left mirror as the van's door pushed open, and a man stepped out and stared back. He was dressed in dark clothing. He wore sunglasses and moved fast. Cars sped by them. Miller stayed seated. "What's wrong?" he asked as the guy stepped closer. Then he heard a sound to his right. Another man appeared, hidden from the highway. He reached into his jacket and brought out a gun.

2

MILLER HESITATED FOR LONGER THAN HE SHOULD HAVE. IT took a second for him to understand what was happening. A man at each door. One to his left, inches from him. The other farther away, to his right, holding a gun, raising it quickly, aiming it directly at him. Another second passed, and his mind registered the gun and calculated his options as he stared at the moving weapon, his eyes growing wide, panic setting in. Then three things happened. First, the guy with the gun yelled for him to step out of the truck, a loud, booming voice cutting through the noise from the road as vehicles passed by, oblivious to the situation.

Second, the guy on Miller's left grabbed his arm through the open door and held on tight. The man with the gun yelled at him again, but this time Miller didn't register the words. He was focused on the guy holding onto him and what he was trying to do and realized the man was reaching for his seatbelt. Another second passed and Miller's fight-or-flight instincts took over, and the third thing happened. Without thinking, he stomped on the gas as he turned again and stared at the weapon. The truck moved, slow, loaded with a full day's worth of packages to deliver. The man with the gun moved with him as the guy to his left held onto him.

The truck picked up speed. The guy with the gun ran, struggling to keep up as he accelerated. Miller watched as the guy yelled some more, then started to slow, then fired two rounds. Miller flinched. When he opened his eyes, he saw the rounds had gone straight through the windshield, spiderwebbing the far side of the glass. He looked into the passenger-side mirror and saw the guy with the gun getting smaller as he drove, staring, watching him as he drove away. He turned and looked left into the driver's side mirror. The other guy was clutching the grab handle, very close, hanging on and struggling hard to steady himself.

"What the hell are you doing!" Miller yelled as he picked up speed, but the guy said nothing back.

Thirty seconds went by. Miller thought the man would let go, but he didn't and just kept holding on tight. Then Miller faced forward and noticed traffic up ahead was halted. Just a sea of red glowing brake lights as he drew closer to the bottleneck.

Which meant his truck was about to come to a grinding halt.

Which meant the guy hanging on wouldn't be struggling for much longer.

"Stop the truck," the guy yelled, sounding out of breath, speaking for the first time, struggling to hold on.

Miller stared through the spiderwebbed windshield as he slowed. Up ahead he saw room on the shoulder and figured it might buy him time. He looked out the passenger-side window and saw the lane was clear. He jerked the wheel right and navigated to the shoulder and glanced left as he drove, out the side mirror. The guy's body moved in response, pulling away from the truck through sheer physics, but the guy held on tight. At the shoulder, Miller straightened the wheel. Physics took over again, and the guy's body slammed hard against the side of the vehicle. Miller saw an exit a hundred yards out. Then he saw the line of cars stopped, taking the exit to avoid the bottleneck on the highway with a line of cars blocking the shoulder.

He was forced to stop. The guy let go and crouched for a long moment, catching his breath. Miller checked the mirror and saw the van, crossing lanes, getting closer, and it came to a stop directly behind him. The guy who had held on finally stood. He stumbled awkwardly towards the door and punched him in the face.

"You don't give up, do you?" the guy said as he punched him again. On the opposite side, the guy with the gun reappeared and stepped into the cab and jabbed the weapon into his side and stared down at him.

People in nearby vehicles seemed oblivious to what was going on. "What do you want from me?" he asked.

The guy with the gun smiled and said nothing. Just looked up and across at the other man as he grabbed Miller by the collar of his shirt and said, "We need you to do something," he replied, out of breath, panting.

"Do what?" asked Miller as cars buzzed past him, taking the exit as a light changed and the line moved.

The man with the gun reached into a pocket with his free hand and came out with a cell phone. He touched the screen with a thumb, and it came to life. He turned it around. Said, "Take us to this address."

Miller said nothing.

"It's not far away. You can be there in twenty minutes. Then you can be on your way."

He thought about that and said, "I know that neighborhood. There's a guardhouse at the entrance."

"You'll get us inside," the man to his left said, still holding onto him.

"I can't," he replied. "It's not my route. There's another guy who takes care of that neighborhood."

"So?"

"So the people in the guardhouse will question it. They know us by name. They'll know I'm out of place."

"You'll have to convince them, Mr. Miller," said the man with the gun after glancing briefly at his badge.

Miller shook his head.

Then the man to his left let go of his collar and glanced around the cabin. Miller watched him closely, desperate, trying to will him to overlook the one thing he didn't want him to see. But he found it anyway.

"Who's this?" asked the man, grabbing the small photograph clipped to the visor and holding it out.

Miller said nothing.

"I see a resemblance," the guy continued. "Let me guess. This is your daughter. Around six years old?"

Miller made no reply.

"You're not wearing a wedding ring. So I assume you're divorced. Or maybe you were never married at all. Either way, the mother isn't in your life. This girl means everything to you." He paused. "This is a hard job. You keep her picture with you, here where you can see it, to keep you going. How'd I do?"

"Leave her out of this."

The man to his left smiled. "We're running out of time, Mr. Miller. Help us, or we'll find her and kill her."

He looked up at the guy. Then he turned and glanced at the man with the gun. He thought about his options and noticed his scanner with the GPS, monitoring his truck's current lack of motion, monitoring his location, monitoring where he was according to where he was supposed to be, monitoring everything.

"I'll take you there," he finally said, turning back and glaring at the guy standing to his left.

The guy smiled again. He tucked the photograph into a shirt pocket and tapped it from the outside with the flat of his hand. "For insurance," he said and looked across at the man with the gun. "I'll follow you."

The man with the gun nodded his agreement. Miller kept his eyes fixed on the guy through the side mirror as he walked back to the van and climbed inside. Then he turned back and stared and said, "Now what?"

"Now you drive."

3

I STARED AT MY REFLECTION IN THE MIRROR AS I SPLASHED water on my face. The face of a man in his late thirties. The face of a man who'd seen more evil in this world than he cared to admit. The face of a man trying to start a new life, trying to forget his past and the scars hidden from others but not from himself.

I went downstairs and found Jami in the kitchen, watching the small TV on the counter set to cable news. She was pouring coffee into a travel mug. I stood in the doorway for a spell and leaned against it. Jami was the most beautiful woman I'd ever seen. Stunning in every way. She sensed me standing there and turned back and stared. Then she smiled and picked up the mug and handed it to me as she offered a little hug.

"Good morning," she said, yawning.

"Good morning," I replied. "They say a yawn is just a silent scream for coffee."

Jami laughed and said she'd already had some earlier. She looked up and gave me a kiss. Then she went over to the counter where I saw she was working as I took a long sip of the brew and stared at the TV. News anchors were discussing the overnight arrival of Russian president Aleksander Stepanov. They played footage of the man stepping out of a Secret Service vehicle, meeting President Keller, shaking hands, waving at cameras. Jami turned back and looked at me and asked, "Why do you think he's here?"

"I don't know," I said. "I guess we'll find out."

Jami nodded in agreement. She pulled out a barstool and sat down at the counter and went through her messenger bag, taking another look at paperwork she'd brought home from the Department of Domestic Counterterrorism. We had met years ago, when I ran the DDC field office out of Chicago. She was an FBI reject, like most of my best agents had been. After we married, Jami had transferred to the Washington, DC, field office to work for Lynne May, the special agent in charge. I'd tried to recruit Jami to DHS, where I headed up field operations for a man named Tom Parker, but she wanted to stay with DDC. Jami thought working for a separate agency was a good thing; plus she had a good working relationship with Lynne May. My best friend, Chris Reed, worked for the FBI. It proved to be a good way for us to stay in the loop.

"Don't forget about dinner. You made the reservations, right?"

"Right," I lied. My eyes grew wide as I took another sip of coffee and looked away.

Jami rolled her eyes and reached for my laptop on the counter and raised the lid. "What's the password?"

I stepped closer and set my coffee down on the counter. "I'll type it in."

"You don't trust me?"

I stood behind her and reached my arms around and typed my password on the keyboard and hit enter. She looked up. I gave her another kiss. "I love you," I said, stepping back and picking up my coffee again.

"Trusting someone is better than loving someone," she replied, unamused.

My phone buzzed in my pocket. I reached for it and glanced at the screen as Jami found and navigated the website for the restaurant we planned on going to after work. The phone call was from my boss at Homeland Security. "This is Jordan," I said, answering the call and setting my coffee down on the counter.

"Need you in the office today," Tom Parker said, road noise in the background. "Be here by eight."

"I thought you wanted me out in the field today."

"Change of plans. I'm setting up a joint meeting with Peter Mulvaney and Lynne May. I want you there."

I said nothing.

"Assuming Jami will be getting a call from May any minute now to represent DDC. Not sure who Mulvaney will bring in from the Bureau, but we're going to set up in the main conference room, okay?"

"What's this about?"

"I'll explain when you get there," he said and disconnected the line.

I brought the phone to my face and stared at the screen and watched it fade to black. I dropped it back into my pocket and stared across at Jami. She stopped typing and glanced back at me over her shoulder.

"Was that Parker?"

I nodded.

"What did he say?"

"He's setting up a meeting for eight with DDC and the FBI. You should expect a call from Lynne May."

"At the NAC?" she asked, referring to the Nebraska Avenue Complex, Homeland Security's headquarters.

I nodded again.

"Then I have a little time before I have to leave." Jami finished securing our dinner reservations and closed the lid to my laptop. "I didn't get to finish reviewing that file last night. I just need a few minutes."

I nodded again. "I think I'll head out now and help Parker set up. See you there?"

"At eight," she said, reaching into her messenger bag for the paperwork and keeping her focus there.

I grabbed my travel mug and headed for the door and turned to look back and told her I loved her.

She said she loved me, too, but didn't turn back. Just kept her gaze downward, studying the paperwork. I stared across at her for a moment; then I stepped outside and unlocked my SUV and climbed inside. I started the motor and just sat there for a moment, thinking. We'd rented the house after we married. It was small, but it was in a nice gated community. We felt safe here. Another moment passed; then I checked over my shoulder and backed out of the driveway and threw it in drive. I thought about her words as I drove, how she said it was better to trust than to love. I didn't believe that was true at all. I believed you could fully love someone even if they didn't know everything about you.

Jami wasn't my first wife. And I wasn't her first husband. Derek had turned to drugs before she decided to leave him, and my wife, Maria, had been murdered in Chicago. The pain was still there. It had never left. When you lose someone you love, someone who means the world to you, you never fully get over it. Even if you meet someone new.

Even if you love again, you still remember what you had. What was taken away.

I got to the front of the neighborhood and stopped at the gate and waited. The motion sensor triggered. The gate started moving. I pulled forward slowly, headed for the main road. To my left, at the entrance, I noticed a backup of cars with impatient drivers and security from the guard-house talking to a UPS driver.

4

EMMA ROSS SAT IN HER NEW OFFICE, READING A DOCUMENT referred to as the weekend package. A report that she, her boss, and other high-level people within the agency needed to review over the weekend. A report intended to catch everyone up with updates on various investigations and operations. The report always came out on Friday mornings. Enough time for it to be printed and packed away into briefcases and carry-on luggage for those visiting from satellite offices catching a flight home at the end of the workweek. Most would read the weekend package on Saturday mornings. A few, she assumed, would read it at the last minute on Sunday night. But she read it the moment it came out. Not because she wanted a promotion; being new to the job, she knew a promotion would take time. And not because she was kissing up to her boss. He hardly had any interaction with her at all and left her alone for the most part.

Emma Ross read the report as soon as it came out because she was a perfectionist. And because she wanted to be good at her job, whatever job that might be. And that meant knowing things as soon as they could be known.

Ross knew firsthand how beneficial it was to separate the learning from the thinking. Reading the report on Fridays was the first of her three-part approach to getting things done. Then she spent time thinking about what she'd read, which took up the entire weekend. In her experience, most people skipped the thinking part. They rushed through the reading, then focused on the doing, which was part three in her approach, what she did on Mondays —taking what she learned, fusing it with what she thought, then acting upon the connections she would have made on Monday morning. Three days from today. She grabbed a pen with red ink and underlined a sentence from the report as her desk phone rang, loud and shrill in the silence.

"Yes?" she said, answering it.

"Ms. Ross," her aide said from the lobby area just outside her office, "there's a gentleman here to see you."

"Who is it, Samantha?"

"Tom Parker with Homeland Security."

Emma said nothing back. Just stared out blankly at nothing in particular, thinking, her mind racing.

A long moment passed.

Then she heard, "Ms. Ross?"

She became fully present and blinked several times and said, "Yes, of course. Bring him to my office."

Emma gently set the phone down and stared at her office door. It was made of obscure glass. She watched as two blurred figures moved toward her and came into focus as they approached. Then the door was pulled all the way open. "Tom," she said as her aide stood in the doorway, gesturing for the man to enter.

The woman left, and Parker stepped inside. He stared across at her. "Would it kill you to call me dad?"

Emma tucked stray hair behind an ear and said, "Did you happen to be in the neighborhood?"

Tom Parker sat down in one of two chairs directly across from her desk and glanced all around. "Something like that," he said. "Glad to see they're treating you right. When do you get the corner office?"

"They have to give me some kind of incentive to do a good job, I guess." She paused. "Why are you here?"

Parker shifted his eyes to his daughter. He took a deep breath and said, "I've called a meeting for eight o'clock. Peter Mulvaney and Lynne May will be there." He breathed again. "I want you there, too, Emma."

She shook her head slowly. Lifted the weekend package and showed it to him. "I have some reading to do."

"You can read that later."

She dropped the report back on the desk. "I have no reason to be there if it's a domestic concern."

He tilted his head and crossed his legs. "I want you there," he said. "That should be reason enough."

"First off, I don't report to you. Second, unless it involves foreign interests, the CIA shouldn't be—"

Parker sat forward. "Damn it, Emma, don't do this to me," he said, cutting her off.

Her eyes grew wide as he stared across at her.

"I've missed out on so much of Elizabeth's life already. On so much of your life."

"So that's why you're here."

"Up until a few months ago, you lived hours away. Up in New York."

She said nothing.

"Now you're back. We work fifteen minutes away from each other. And we live even closer than that. This is crazy, Emma."

"It's not crazy."

"What did I do wrong?"

"I don't want to talk about it right now."

"Is this about your mother?"

Emma said nothing.

"She walked out on *me*, Emma. I didn't go anywhere."

"And why do you think that is?"

Parker made no reply.

Emma picked up the report from her desk again. "I'm very busy. And I don't want to get into this right now. We'll talk about this one day—just not today."

Parker sat back in his chair. He took a deep breath and let it out slowly and glanced away. Thirty seconds passed. Then a full minute. He said, "I've stopped drinking, Emma. I haven't had a drop in over a year."

She looked away and thought about that for a spell; then she glanced back at him. "I don't believe you."

"It's the truth. Whether you believe me or not." Parker checked his watch and sat forward again. "I miss you. Both of you. If you change your mind, come to the meeting. Eight o'clock sharp. I'll save you a seat."

Parker stood and went to the door. Emma watched as her father placed a hand on the door handle. "So after twenty years you stopped? Just like that?"

Parker glanced back at his daughter over his shoulder.

"You weren't the easiest person to live with growing up. My mom finally realized that. *That's* why she left. Okay? And that's why I keep Elizabeth away from you. That's why I avoid you. I don't want her growing up around that, in that kind of environment. It's just—toxic. So don't blame me for the relationship we have."

"I told you that I quit."

"And I told you I don't believe you."

He turned and lowered his gaze and gripped the handle tight. "Trusting me is your choice, Emma. Proving you wrong is mine."

Then he pushed the door the whole way open and left. She watched as it closed slowly on its hinges and his figure blurred through the glass as he moved away from her. Emma picked up her phone and dialed an extension. A purr, a click, a greeting. "There's a meeting at the NAC at eight; I want to know what it's about," she said as her boss opened the door and told her to go with him.

5

I CRANKED THE RADIO AS I LEFT MY NEIGHBORHOOD IN Reston, where Jami and I had moved to after getting married. It was a small house. A starter, as my dad would've called it. Fourteen hundred square feet. Perfect for newly-weds. Not so much for a family, but Jami and I figured we had a couple of years before we'd have to worry about that. It was located in a safe gated community, which was all we really cared about.

The drive was thirty minutes to DHS and about the same to DDC. Any closer and we'd have to settle for a condo or an apartment. Not a bad option, but we liked the separation between work and home. Even if the separation was only in miles. The drive into DC gave me time to think and plan my days. And the drive home gave me time to decompress. Jami and I both worked late nights and weekends and whenever our jobs needed us. We fit life in wherever we could, which wasn't ideal, but it never was in this line of work.

I approached an intersection and saw the light up ahead turn yellow, then red. I slowed and brought my SUV to a stop and checked my watch. Plenty of time to get to work. I remembered something my dad used to say to me: *The best way to be late is to have plenty of time*. It was similar to another saying I learned later in life after I enlisted in the Navy: *If you're early, you're on time, and if you're on time, you're late.*

The light was taking forever to change. A moment later, I understood why.

To my left, I saw movement out of the corner of my eye. I glanced across and saw an older lady crossing the street. Moving slow and steady and true. Constantly checking for traffic. Moving cautiously. I saw a countdown timer. She'd pressed the button for pedestrians, so the lights were giving her extra time to make it across the street. I checked the mirror for her. All clear behind me. Everyone was stopped. Same thing across the street. She glanced at each driver as she moved past them. She looked at me and smiled.

I smiled back. Then she faced forward and kept moving. As I watched her cross, something to the right of me caught my eye. I saw an older man on the sidewalk, wearing khaki pants and a tucked-in polo and a navy blue cap, pushing a walker slowly. I glanced back at the light and waited some more. Then something else caught my eye. Movement. To the right of me again, but up in the sky this time. I turned. Looked up and saw an American flag falling slowly to the ground. It tumbled down, folding over itself gently, almost like it was happening in slow motion. The old guy noticed it, too. He stood tall, turned his gaze upward, and gripped his walker tight and watched. The flag continued to tumble, and I watched it land on the lawn in front of the building close to him. He stared at it on the ground for a long moment and shook his head.

The woman made it to the other side of the street and

glanced at the flag, then turned and walked away. The old guy looked upward again, trying to understand why it had fallen off a flagpole. Then he looked back down, deciding what to do about it. The light was still red. The timer ticked on. Thirty seconds to go.

I glanced back and watched as the old guy made a decision and let go of his walker. He padded across the lawn slowly and picked up the flag. He stood up, careful not to lose his balance, and held the flag up off the ground. Trying to fold it by himself. Clearly struggling. A flag that size was hard to fold by yourself. Even harder with balancing issues, I guessed. The countdown timer got to zero, and the light turned green.

Do for one what you wish you could do for all, I remembered my father saying many times growing up. I wasn't sure if I wanted to run the risk of being late. Parker needed me. But maybe this guy needed me more. The driver behind me blew his horn. Loud and obnoxious. The old guy turned to see what all the commotion was about. The driver lost his patience. He pulled around me and sped off. The old guy was still watching. Then I accelerated and pulled to the side of the road and parked. I stepped out and jogged across the lawn. The grass was damp. It smelled freshly cut. Maybe it was. Blade clippings stuck to my shoes as I moved. The old guy watched me as I approached. I caught a faint smile as I got closer to him.

"Need some help?" I called.

"Don't we all?"

"With the flag."

"I know what you meant." He paused and looked me over. "Grab the end. Don't let it touch the ground."

I stepped closer and reached for the end hanging close to the ground and held it tight with both hands.

"Now walk backward," he said, steadying himself as I nodded. His voice was rough. Like he'd spent his whole life smoking. Or barking out orders. "Flag Code states it should never touch anything beneath it."

"Including the ground," I said.

"*Especially* the ground."

The wind picked up. I took three steps backward and looked up. Dark clouds were forming on the horizon. "They're supposed to take it down for inclement weather," I said. "Also part of the Flag Code, as I recall."

The old guy stopped and stared across at me. He smiled. The front of his cap had a patch on it that read *US Navy Veteran* and *Proudly Served* across the brim. He lowered his gaze and got back to work, keeping the flag taut, folding it once, bringing the stripes over the union. Taking his time. Being precise. Then we made another lengthwise fold. I followed his lead. "This one's okay to keep outside," he said a moment later. "It's all-weather. But I agree, they should've brought it in. We had a bad storm a while back. Woke up the next morning, and it was gone. What they need is a flagpole out here. Make it secure. Hang the thing by its grommets. Not by its sleeve on a damn stick." He paused again. "What's your name, son?"

"Blake Jordan," I said.

"Joe Nyland. Nice to meet you."

"You were in the Navy?"

"Thirty years," he said, pulling his end tight as we matched up the corners.

"Thank you for your service."

"Thank you for taking the time to help me. There are some things in life you just can't do on your own."

I nodded. Said nothing. I held onto the union side as

Nyland began folding the closed corner to the open edge, forming a triangle.

"How long were you in for?" he asked, glancing up at me for a brief moment, taking his time as he worked.

"How'd you know?"

He smiled again. Lowered his gaze and made no reply.

"Not anywhere close to you."

He nodded. "Some guys stay in their entire career. Lifers, they used to call us. Others enlist and stay long enough for their schooling to be paid for; then they bail." He eyed me briefly. "I think you were somewhere in the middle. Not a lifer. Not in it for the schooling." He made another fold. "How'd I do?"

"Spot on," I said.

Nyland nodded again. "Most men enlist so they can change the world. Few want to change themselves."

I noticed he was slowing down. Taking longer than needed. I realized maybe he needed the conversation.

"Do you have family close by?"

Nyland shook his head. "I have a son, but he's out of state. He's all grown up. Busy with his own family."

"Nobody looks after you?"

He nodded at the sky. "There's always somebody looking after me. But if you mean visitors, then no."

I glanced at my watch. Nyland caught me. He made another fold and stepped closer. "So what were you?"

"Navy."

"I figured that much, but what *were* you?"

"A sniper. With SEAL Team Three, stationed at Camp Rhino, Afghanistan. Operation Enduring Freedom."

He raised his eyebrows for a moment, like he was impressed. Made another fold. Said, "Learn anything?"

"Lots of things."

"Tell me."

I thought about it. "Focusing on the details, overcoming fear, leadership. Lots of things. What were you?"

"Captain."

"Wow," I said. "Learn anything?"

He paused a long moment and looked away, thinking. "Appreciating good food."

I laughed as I turned to look at the building to my right. "So what kind of rations do they have in there?"

"Oh, it's horrible."

"Worse than an MRE?"

"An MRE would be a treat."

He made another slow, careful fold. He took another step closer.

"What's your favorite meal?" I asked.

"Steak and potatoes. Without question." He laughed to himself. "My wife made the best. Absolute best. We used to grill out all the time. Years ago, after my son grew up and after I left the service. Back when it was just me and her. I'm not ashamed to say it. When it came to grilling out, she was way better than me."

"You want to give me your man card now? Or when we're done with the flag?"

Nyland laughed again. A smoker's laugh. "I like you, kid. So what about you? I see a ring on your finger."

"Newlywed," I said, checking my watch again.

He made another fold. The triangle was becoming thicker with each one. The stripes were all wrapped up. Now he was getting to the union. "All I can say is enjoy it while you can. And pray that you go first." Nyland told me he had a condition. And it was terminal. Then he went quiet for a spell. The man took another step toward me. He made another fold, taking his time. I glanced down. We were almost done.

"You know what to do?"

I nodded and lowered my gaze. I made a small fold on my side and made my own triangle. Then, with Nyland's help while keeping it taut, I tucked my side into the fold. Only the stars showed now. The stripes were hidden inside. Nyland let go with one hand and, with the other, handed the flag across for me to hold.

He stood up straight, balancing himself. Then his face changed. Sad eyes, remembering something. He kept his left hand at his side and brought his right up fast. The old guy stared down and saluted the flag, keeping his hand by his brow for ten long seconds. Then he lowered it slowly and became present again.

"Would you bring it inside for me?" he asked.

"Yes, sir."

He padded across the lawn a few paces, careful not to fall, and headed back to his walker on the sidewalk. Nyland gripped it tight and moved slowly, turning at the path that led to the nursing home's entrance.

"I'll have the groundskeeper hang it back up on Monday when he's back. And after the storm blows over."

"Okay," I said, walking next to him until we got to the door.

I opened it. Nyland stepped inside. Said, "Put it on the receptionist's desk. It should be safe enough there."

"Okay," I said again and did as he asked. Then I turned back and stood facing the man.

He glanced at my watch. "I'm sure you have to get to work. Best way to be late is to have plenty of time."

I nodded vaguely. My heart caught in my throat. "Maybe I'll stop by sometime," I said. "To check on you."

"I'm not giving you my man card."

I smiled. "You leave it in your other wallet?"

He smiled back.

"Maybe your son will surprise you one day. Maybe he'll show up with his family and take you out to dinner. Steak and potatoes. A meal fit for a king."

"Maybe pigs will fly out of my butt. I'm in powdered eggs and stale bread purgatory. But we'll see, I guess."

I nodded. "Nice meeting you."

"You too, son. MRE for the road?"

"No, sir. I like to enjoy my food."

Nyland smiled knowingly and nodded. Then he turned, headed for the cafeteria. I watched him until he disappeared. I glanced at the folded flag. I kept my left arm down and raised my right and gave a quick salute. Then I stepped outside, and I promised myself I'd be back.

6

I ARRIVED AT THE NEBRASKA AVENUE COMPLEX FIFTEEN minutes later. The large thirty-eight-acre complex looked foreboding against the dark sky and angry swirling clouds draped behind its many buildings. I pulled up to the guardhouse and rolled my window down. The security guy nodded and pushed a button. The gate opened. I drove to the building where Parker ran our black ops team out of, and I went upstairs.

But I couldn't find Parker anywhere. I checked his office. He wasn't there. I went to the conference room. Empty. Our head analyst, Simon Harris, was busy working. Simon was good, just not as good as other guys I'd worked with, guys like Morgan Lennox out of DDC's Chicago office. Well on his way, just not quite there yet. I checked my watch as I walked to Simon's desk.

He heard me approaching. Took a sip of Mountain Dew and turned to look at me. "What's up?" he asked.

"Where's Parker?"

"I don't know. He was here when I got in; then he got a phone call and left."

I glanced at Parker's office. The light was off. "When was this?"

"Maybe forty-five minutes ago."

"Who called him?"

He shrugged.

I turned and glanced at the sea of cubicles. "So do you know what this eight o'clock meeting is all about?"

"I think it has something to do with the president. Something big is going down today. That's all I know."

"Okay," I said as I checked my watch again. "I'll set up the conference room."

"Already done, but you're welcome to check it out."

I nodded vaguely. "Peter Mulvaney and Lynne May are coming in."

"I know. Mr. Parker asked me to add them to the list for security. I called down to the guy, so he's aware."

"Jami will be here, too. Parker said he thought Lynne May was going to be calling her."

"I'll call down to add her to the list."

I nodded again. Said, "Thanks," and headed to the conference room and stepped inside.

The main lights were off. Only the switch for the recessed lighting was flipped on. The lighting was dim. The window blinds were all closed. I went to each of them and twisted them partway open. Usually sunlight would stream inside around this time. But not today. I parted the blinds with my fingers. I saw the dark clouds in the distance. Still swirling. Moving closer. Soon there would be a light patter of rain hitting the windows, followed by a gradual shower, followed by a straight-out downpour. I checked the time. Ten minutes to go. Since Homeland was hosting the meeting, I figured Parker would arrive first. Peter Mulvaney was ex-military, so I decided he'd arrive next, followed by Lynne May, followed by Jami.

But Mulvaney got there first. I watched as he parked and stepped out of a black SUV. The man had graying, slicked-back hair and wore a suit. The passenger door opened, and Bureau agent Mark Reynolds stepped out. They closed their doors simultaneously and glanced up at the building. But before they headed in, another car pulled up. A black sedan. It parked two spaces over, and Lynne May climbed out. They all exchanged greetings. Mulvaney gestured for May to walk ahead, and they disappeared from view.

Two minutes after that, I met our visitors and walked them back to the conference room. Lynne May stepped inside, followed by Peter Mulvaney. Reynolds hung back and looked me over and shook my hand.

"Been a long time, man," he said.

"Too long," I said, thinking about the last time I'd seen the guy.

He stepped inside, and I followed him in, letting the door close behind me. There were eight empty seats around the conference table. Black chairs on swivels. Lots of padding. Executive style. Everyone left the seat at the head of the table vacant. That was for Parker. I glanced back at the door and checked the time. Five till eight. Parker was an Army guy, and being late wasn't like him. I glanced back. May took a seat by the window and left two spaces empty next to her. Mulvaney pulled out the chair across from May, and Mark Reynolds sat next to Mulvaney. I moved to the end and sat. An empty space to my right with Mark Reynolds next to that, and two empty spaces to my left with the seat next to May reserved for Jami.

A minute before eight, Tom Parker stepped inside, looking flustered as the door closed behind him. He nodded to his guests and pointed to the Polycom at the center of the table, and Mulvaney pushed it closer to him. Parker opened a line and dialed his conference number. The room grew quiet as Parker stared blankly at the empty chairs. Then a recorded voice announced there were two participants on the line, including us.

"Agent Rivera?" said Parker, lowering his gaze.

"I'm here," the president's head Secret Service man said from the line. "Who do we have in the room?"

"Blake Jordan and myself, Peter Mulvaney and Mark Reynolds from the Bureau, Lynne May with DDC."

"Should we begin?"

Parker glanced at me, then turned to Lynne May.

She checked her watch. Looked at me for a brief moment. Said, "Go ahead, Tom. I'll catch Jami up later."

I picked up my cell phone and looked for a missed call or a text message from Jami. There was none.

Parker said, "Then let's get started," and took a seat. He took a deep breath and let it out as he looked at each of us in turn. "This morning I received a call from the White House. From Agent Rivera, to be exact. As I'm sure you're all aware, President Stepanov arrived late last night, an unannounced visit to the US." He paused a long moment. "Agent Rivera, I believe you've been coordinating with the Bureau on this?"

"Yes," he said from the phone. "Stepanov isn't here for a casual visit. He's here to sign a peace treaty."

"That's unexpected," said May.

I glanced around the room, studying everyone. Silence. I spoke up and said, "That's a good thing, right?"

Mulvaney nodded. "He and Keller kept it under wraps. They didn't want fallout. But we have a problem. We believe there's going to be an attempt on the Russian president's life —and it's going to happen today."

7

I ASKED THE BUREAU DIRECTOR QUESTIONS. LOTS OF THEM. When was it going down? How was it going down? But Mulvaney had no idea. And that was the problem. He said the NSA had intercepted a communication and shared it with the FBI. Mulvaney had called Rivera about it earlier in the morning. Part of an exclusive partnership established between the FBI and the Secret Service many years prior. Mulvaney said that, although his predecessors held the agreement as sacred, he did not. DHS and DDC input was not only welcome, it was needed. Especially in today's world. And there was a reason why we were meeting at DHS's Nebraska Avenue Complex instead of the Hoover Building. "Want to explain?" Mulvaney asked.

Rivera replied from the speakerphone, his voice loud and commanding. It filled the entire room. He said after learning about the threat from Mulvaney, he'd pulled the president aside and told him what he knew. Keller in turn pulled Russian president Stepanov aside and shared the news with him and his security detail. Keller told Rivera to call Mulvaney back and ask for a meeting at the NAC. He wanted DHS to run point and act as a central hub for the operation. Keller said he wanted me involved and anyone I needed.

Rivera grew silent. Mulvaney said, "As I mentioned, my people are working on the communication the NSA intercepted. We're analyzing it, determining its legitimacy, its exact point of origin, everything else."

"What specifically did it say?" I asked as I sent a text message to Jami, asking if she was okay.

"It was a phone call. Initiated somewhere in Russia and answered here. In Washington, DC. Last night."

Lynne May asked, "But what did it say, Peter?"

Mulvaney answered, "It was spoken completely in Russian. A question was asked: *Are you in position?* And a moment later it was answered affirmatively." He glanced around the room. His eyes fell to the Polycom. "Then the caller gave the command. He said: *Take him out before he signs.* We didn't know what it meant at first. Then earlier this morning, when Agent Rivera told me about Keller's agenda for the day, we made the connection. Rivera told me about the peace treaty. How the two presidents have kept it secret for months. President Keller because of the perception that he's Stepanov's puppet. He's sick of the conspiracy theories and always playing defense. He wants to beat the news cycle for once and control the narrative. As far as President Stepanov's reasoning, he didn't tell his people simply due to safety concerns. Think about it. When was the last time a Russian president stepped foot on US soil?" Mulvaney paused. "Both presidents are hell-bent on signing this treaty. They're not budging at all. It will be signed —today."

I checked my phone. No reply from Jami. I glanced up and asked, "Where are they going to sign?"

"The Pullman House," Rivera said from the speaker-phone. "The Russian ambassador's residence on Sixteenth."

Parker furrowed his brow and asked, "But why does it have to happen today?"

Mulvaney cleared his throat. "Seventy-five years ago today, President Truman gave a speech marking the beginning of the cold war." He paused. "Today, President Keller, alongside President Stepanov, will give his own speech, marking a turn in US-Russian relations. Then they'll sign the treaty. So it's symbolic."

The room fell silent. Nobody spoke. Parker stared at the empty chairs as I checked my phone again. Still no reply from Jami. Then Lynne May said, "You have my support, Peter. Have your people send mine a sample of the audio file; we'll take a look at it. Maybe between the two of us, we can make some headway."

Mulvaney nodded. "Thank you, Lynne. I'll do that. Agent Rivera, I'm sending Mark Reynolds your way. We'll establish a perimeter around the building and cordon off the area to make it completely secure."

THE MEETING ENDED THE SAME WAY IT BEGAN, ONLY THIS TIME in reverse order. Parker pointed at the Polycom, and Mulvaney reached across and ended the call. Lynne May leaned in close to me while the others carried on a separate conversation. She asked if I'd heard from Jami. I told her I'd seen her before I left; I'd sent a text, but she hadn't responded. May nodded vaguely and stood and joined the others at the door. She excused herself and stepped out last, following Reynolds and Mulvaney. Parker said he'd be in his office if I needed him and left me alone in the conference room. I went to the window and parted the blinds again and watched our guests walk to their vehicles. May said something, and Mulvaney nodded. Mark Reynolds listened. They opened their doors and climbed inside. May left first, followed by Mulvaney.

There was thunder in the distance. It rolled in and rumbled for a long moment. No rain. No lightning. Not yet. I reached for my phone and looked at the text message I'd sent and stared at the screen. No reply at all. The message had been delivered, but it hadn't been read yet. I navigated the screen and dialed Jami. I brought the phone to my ear and listened to a purr as the call connected. One ring, two. Three, then four.

Then the call was answered.

"Jami, where are you?"

No reply.

"Are you okay?"

No response. I looked away and listened. I could hear road noise. I moved back to the window and looked outside. Listening hard. Then I heard her. Far in the background, away from the phone. A scream. Her voice muffled somehow. Then I heard a man's voice, also in the background. He was giving orders, telling someone to be quiet, grunting every few seconds, like he was delivering a beating and enjoying it.

Then a voice said, "Mr. Jordan, I'm only going to say this once, so you need to listen to me very carefully."

I narrowed my eyes and turned from the window and glanced around the empty room. "Who is this?"

"I'm the guy who just kidnapped your wife. And if you want her to live, you're going to do exactly as I say."

I stared at the door. Thought about getting help, but instead I just stood there, paralyzed, unable to move.

The voice said, "Don't even think about tracing this call.

I have people everywhere. Everywhere, Jordan. The minute you talk to someone, I'll find out about it. And a minute after that, she dies. Understand me?"

I said nothing. I heard Jami in the background. The screaming had stopped. Now she was talking to them. Her words were short and urgent but unintelligible. But one thing was very clear: they were hurting her.

"Who is this?" I asked again.

The voice said, "I'm your nightmare. I'm the worst thing that's ever going to happen to you."

"You sure about that?"

He laughed. "When people tell you who they are, believe them." A moment passed. He said, "I have a list. Specific tasks I want you to complete for me. Finish the list and she'll live. It's as simple as that. But first, you're going to wait. You need time to decide if you'll cooperate. I know people like you need convincing." He paused again. Longer this time. "And because she needs convincing, too."

Then the call was disconnected.

8

EMMA ROSS FOLLOWED HER BOSS DOWN THE LONG CORRIDOR of one of the CIA's two buildings in its large, secluded, sprawling campus at Langley. Her office was in the Original Headquarters Building. The one with windows, thick and dull and electronically shielded to prevent signals from passing through and being intercepted. A preventative measure. The New Headquarters Building on the other side of the cafeteria had no windows at all. She'd never been to that building. Not yet. But she was headed there now. Her boss led her down the stairs, through a courtyard, and swiped his badge to grant them entry into the NHB and brought Emma down a warren of corridors, then to a set of managerial offices and stopped at one of them. He gestured for her to step in first. She obeyed. There was a man in his early fifties in a dark suit. He looked up at her and narrowed his eyes. He didn't stand. Just stared and glanced over to her boss.

"David, this is Emma Ross," her boss said.

She extended her hand. The man stared at her briefly, but remained otherwise still. Emma lowered her hand and glanced at her boss, who nodded knowingly. "I'll leave you two alone," he said, excusing himself.

"Take a seat," the man said, leaning back and crossing one leg over the other as she stepped inside.

Emma furrowed her brow. She glanced over her shoulder at the closing door, then turned and sat down.

The man studied her for a long moment. Then he said, "My name is David Malone. I've worked for the CIA for a very long time, Ms. Ross. Longer than you've been alive, probably. So I've seen a thing or two."

Emma said nothing.

"I've been promoted many times. Too many to count. When you're trusted with little, if you prove yourself, you tend to be trusted with a lot more, eventually. Been that way since time began, I assume."

"Mr. Malone, where are you going with this?"

He forced a smile and nodded. He remained relaxed, looking across at her. "Ms. Ross, we know everything about everyone who steps through those doors out there. Just like any intelligence agency, if we can find something on the average American, you can be sure as hell we'll find even more on our own employees. We monitor every phone call, every text, every movement. We know everything there is to be known."

"Okay."

"But unlike other agencies, we take care of our own people. Once you're in, you're in. As long as you play by the rules, that is. So yes, we take care of our people. We protect them. But if you screw up, if you don't stay inside the lines, we'll send you down the ladder. You'll be working the mail room in no time. If you play along, maybe you'll have that corner office you were talking to your father about a few minutes ago."

Emma furrowed her brow and tilted her head to one side. "Excuse me?"

"Why do you think you're sitting here in my office right now, Ms. Ross?"

Emma fidgeted in her chair. She tucked a lock of hair behind an ear and looked away, thinking about it.

"That meeting at DHS you called your assistant to look into, the one that just ended, we already know what it's about. Keller and Stepanov are signing a peace treaty. Tonight, on live TV."

"How do you know about that?" she asked.

Malone thought for a moment. Said, "We've known for weeks. We have surveillance capabilities abroad. But the Secret Service only learned about the plans today. They phoned the FBI and your father at DHS. They don't have the full picture, Ms. Ross. They're all looking at things one-sided. From an American viewpoint, the impacts domestically if it's signed. In fact, they just had a conference call we listened in on. There's a fairly significant threat they're working together on, the Secret Service, the FBI, DHS; a communication we intercepted last night and told them about. A phone call from Russia to someone here, in Washington, DC, ordering their person over here to take out the president before the treaty is signed."

"Do we know who took the call here?"

"The Bureau's Cyber Division is tracking that down."

"Do we know who placed the call in Russia?"

"We're working with the NSA to figure that out."

"Okay."

Malone stared across at her. He said nothing for a spell. Just studied her. "And this is where you come in."

Emma fidgeted in her seat again. There was a long pause, and she suddenly became aware of the air conditioning blowing. The only sound she could hear besides her own breathing. "Explain," she said.

Malone nodded and sat up and leaned forward. He placed his hands on his desk, interlaced his fingers, and stared. "Ms. Ross, President Keller is going to sign that treaty tonight. And we can't let that happen."

"Because of the threat?"

"Yes and no."

"Explain," she said again.

"The venue isn't very secure. But Keller's well-being isn't our concern. Stepanov's is, along with our people around Moscow, along with the ambassador, should anything happen to Stepanov. Remember Benghazi?"

"Of course."

"Okay. If something happens to him, all hell is going to break loose."

"Then I suggest you stop talking to me and get your people overseas to a safe house."

"They're already there. Again, think about Benghazi. You're a smart girl. You know safe isn't safe enough."

Emma took a deep breath and let it out and said, "Why am I here, Mr. Malone?"

The man forced a smile and lowered his head and stared across at her knowingly. "I didn't think I'd have to say it, but apparently I do. I told you we know everything about our people. And we know everything about you and the president. And everything you don't want us to know."

She narrowed her eyes.

"You're one of the only people who can get to him. Maybe the only one. I need you to meet with him. Now. Without delay. Have him call this off. At the very least, change the venue. Help us keep our people safe."

9

JAMI JORDAN OPENED HER EYES AND BLINKED HARD, TRYING TO understand what was happening. She was facedown on the cold steel floor of a truck. A truck that was moving fast. Her face hurt. Then she remembered. The knock at the door, the punch to her face. Her arms were handcuffed behind her back. She turned her head. A man sat next to her. Not one of them. Someone like her. Taken against his will. That much was clear. She turned to look behind her. Another man sat alone on the floor, silent, holding a weapon, staring at her, contempt in his eyes. Adrenaline surged through her veins, but she realized there was nothing she could do. Not yet, anyway. So she lowered her head and rested it on the truck's floor. Then the pain took over. Fatigue washed over her, trying to take control of her body. She didn't fight it. She just closed her eyes and allowed it to take over as the truck drove on, and she drifted off to sleep again.

WHEN SHE OPENED HER EYES AGAIN, IT WAS BECAUSE something had changed. A sudden change in the environment. A shift from noise to silence. A motor had been cut. She closed her eyes again, but remained fully aware of her surroundings. A man sitting next to her. Another guy with a weapon, sitting behind her. A driver. Maybe a passenger with him. She focused hard and paid close attention to what happened next.

First the truck rocked from the front. But only on one side, left to right. So there likely was no passenger.

Then the back doors opened. She squinted as dull light streamed inside. *We're indoors.* The man in the back with the gun climbed out. The truck rocked again, back to front this time from the weight of the man. She figured he was a big guy. She hadn't caught more than a glimpse earlier. Then the driver spoke.

"Get out," he said. The man had a thick accent. Clearly Russian. The guy sitting next to her climbed out. The truck rocked again as he left. Then a moment later it rocked again. Someone was climbing inside. Likely the driver. There was a long moment of silence. She could sense one of the men looking her over.

Then she heard movement, and she was grabbed by the hair and pulled back. A big fistful of hair. It forced her upright and onto her knees. Her arms were cuffed and useless. It was the man with the accent. He turned back and spoke to the other guy, the big guy with the weapon. He spoke in a language she didn't understand, but understood the context of it. *Leave us*, the man had likely said. Because then she heard two sets of footsteps moving away as she stayed on her knees, faced forward, a knot of hair gripped by the man. The guy pulled upward and backward, and she got to her feet. She kicked backward and landed a blow against his shin. He took two steps backward as she spun around and stared. But the man just laughed and revealed a gun and stepped forward, grabbing hold of her shirt and pulling her closer to him.

He stared at her, face-to-face, as she avoided eye contact. The man was looking her over again, from up close this time. Like he was admiring his prize possession. She sensed things could get a lot worse for her. So she turned away. He touched the side of her face with his fingers. A gentle movement. Like he had thoughts she didn't want him to have. Then he stepped out and told her to do the same. Jami obeyed and moved cautiously. She got to the edge of the truck and stepped out and took in the expanse of a large warehouse. There was a black van parked to her right. Something stacked high along the wall. Jami located the exits and weighed her options and realized she had none other than to obey any orders given.

She shuffled forward and glanced back at her captor and got her first good look at him. She could see that the man had a shaved head. The front of his face was dark and silhouetted by fluorescent lights behind him. He moved closer to her. Stared at her. She narrowed her eyes and tilted her head as he approached.

"I know you," she said.

The man smiled as he stared back at her. "No," he said. "You don't."

10

I STARED AT MY CELL PHONE AND WATCHED THE SCREEN FADE to black. I tried calling back, but it went straight to voicemail. They'd turned Jami's phone off. I just stood there in the empty conference room, thinking, weighing my options, walking through each possible scenario and deciding what their outcomes would be.

I moved to the door and looked out across the floor. I could see Tom Parker sitting in his office. As the head of a new black ops unit operating within Homeland Security, I knew I could walk in there and tell him what had happened and I'd get whatever I needed. Anything I'd ask for, he'd give me, along with his support. I thought about Morgan Lennox in Chicago. I could call him, too. He could trace Jami's phone.

Then I remembered the man's words: *Don't even think about tracing this call. I have people everywhere.*

Who was this guy? Was he bluffing? How could he have taken Jami, someone I knew could hold her own?

My phone buzzed in my hand. I glanced down and saw

an incoming call from Chris Reed. I started weighing my options again as my cell continued to buzz. I could tell him what was happening. Ask for his help. The two of us could talk it through and come up with a plan. But there was something in the voice of the man who'd made the threats. He meant what he'd said. So I declined the call from Chris and dropped the cell back into my pocket, and I stepped out of the room.

SIMON HARRIS WATCHED ME AS I WALKED TO MY OFFICE. He raised his hand and motioned with two fingers for me to go to his desk. I slowed to a stop. Turned to face my office on the other side of the floor. Then I took a breath and let it out as I headed over to Simon's workstation and navigated the warren of empty cubicles along the vast open floor we hoped would one day be staffed with analysts just like him.

"What do you need, Simon?" I asked as I approached.

He turned and nodded toward the conference room on the other side of the floor. "What was that about?"

I glanced at Parker's office. The door was closed. I could see him through the blinds, sitting at his desk, a phone pressed hard against an ear, talking to someone, listening to their reply. Preoccupied. "Long story."

"Then give me the short version."

I nodded. "It was about President Stepanov's visit. He and Keller are signing a peace treaty."

"Are you serious?"

"Yeah. And it's happening today. I'm sure Parker will brief you soon. What are you working on now?"

Simon looked at Parker through the window and shrugged. "Nothing important."

Once again I thought about asking for help. I could pull Simon into a room and tell him what was happening. Tell him to do what Morgan Lennox could've done: track Jami and tell me where she was.

"Are you okay?" he asked as he turned back and looked at me. "You're sweating."

"Yeah," I said, becoming fully present and wiping sweat from my brow. "It's just hot in here."

Simon narrowed his eyes and glanced at the conference room again and asked, "Where's Jami?"

I said nothing.

"You had me call down to the guardhouse and get her added to the list, but I haven't seen her."

"She's at DDC," I lied. "Lynne May has her working on something else."

Simon stared at me for a moment, then looked away, thinking about that.

"I have to go. Tell Parker I had to run home for something, and I'll be back in about an hour."

Simon didn't reply. Just reached for his Mountain Dew and stared as I walked away and stepped into my office. I closed the door and locked it. I closed the blinds and went to a tall metal locker and punched in a code and opened it up. I grabbed a holster and strapped it on. I reached for my Glock and checked it. Found an extra mag and stuffed it into my pocket. I saw my bulletproof vest and stared at it for a moment. I left it and closed the locker and went to the door and moved back through the maze of cubicles again.

I glanced back over my shoulder and saw Parker through the blinds. Still on the phone. Still preoccupied. Simon noticed me and held onto his soda and swiveled his chair and watched me as I moved. I faced forward and walked toward the door. I pushed it open and waited until I heard it close behind me.

Then I ran like hell and took the stairs as fast as I could to the first floor. I climbed into my SUV and I left.

I MADE THE HALF-HOUR DRIVE IN TWENTY MINUTES. I RAN every red light I came to and glanced at the retirement home as I passed it. I pulled into my neighborhood and ran two stop signs as I approached the house. I made the last turn and stepped on the gas and drove the final stretch of road. Forty in a twenty.

Then I braked hard as I got to the house. Jami's vehicle was still parked in the driveway.

And parked right next to it, in my spot, was a black sedan.

I PARKED ON THE STREET AND STEPPED OUT. I FIGURED LYNNE May must've seen me because she swung her door open and stepped out and stood by the open door, watching me as I approached, concern in her eyes.

"She's okay," I lied.

"Where is she?"

"Inside, resting."

"What happened?"

I shrugged as I moved closer. "I don't know. She said she's just not feeling well."

"She didn't call me. And she's not answering her phone. Or the door."

I shrugged again. "She's probably sleeping, Lynne. I'll have her call you as soon as she wakes up, okay?"

She looked me over, thinking. "This isn't like her."

"I know."

"We don't take sick days, Blake. Especially on a day like today."

"I know," I said again. "Jami said she just needs to rest for a while. I'll make sure she makes it in, okay?"

May said nothing.

"How'd you make it past the guardhouse?"

"I'm on the list."

I nodded vaguely and looked away, wondering how Jami's kidnapper had made it through.

May tilted her head and stared. "Bring her up to speed, and have her call me, ASAP."

I nodded again as Lynne May climbed back into her sedan. She closed the door and started the motor. A minute after that she was gone. I turned and stared at the house. I went to the side corner and found the motion camera, still intact. I went to the front door. No sign of forced entry. I reached for my Glock and tried the door. It was unlocked. I stepped through. The lights were still on in the kitchen. So was the TV under the cabinet. I kept one hand on my weapon. With the other I turned it off. The house became silent. No sound at all. I cleared the first floor, then I took the stairs, and I cleared our bedroom and the office.

I holstered my weapon and sat down at my desk and moved the mouse. My desktop computer came to life. I navigated the screen and opened an application that recorded video from the camera outside the house. It showed me a view of my vehicle parked in the driveway. A live feed. I clicked and rewound the feed ninety minutes.

I watched as I climbed into my SUV and backed out of the driveway and drove out of view. Less than five minutes passed and a truck appeared. It took a wide curve around our cul-de-sac once and disappeared from view. A first pass,

I thought. Just to check things out. I waited two more minutes. I imagined the driver looking all around, making another wide turn somewhere, heading back to my house.

A minute after that, the truck reappeared.

It took another wide curve, but this time it backed into the driveway. It had a UPS logo on the side. My heart skipped a beat. I suddenly remembered seeing the truck at the guardhouse as I was leaving the neighborhood. The driver talking to security. A long row of cars behind it. Visitors waiting to get inside. "Damn it," I whispered, angry with myself for ignoring it and for leaving when I did. I watched as a man wearing UPS gear stepped out of the passenger-side door. He glanced back inside and spoke with someone. Unsure about what to do. Then he nodded and looked at the house. He stepped around back and pulled open the double doors. Then someone appeared to his left, out of view from my camera, giving the man additional instructions. The UPS guy nodded again and disappeared to the front door.

Nothing happened for a full minute. I imagined him knocking on the door, Jami answering. Then they both appeared. First the driver, then Jami with her laptop bag hanging from a strap on her shoulder. She was already heading out the door. About to leave. She followed him. I watched him move out of the way. Then a man wearing a black ski mask stepped out from behind the truck and rested his weapon against Jami's temple. He pointed inside the truck. Jami glanced right. Saw the UPS guy cowering. Not a threat. She turned back and, in one swift motion, pushed the gun away. But the guy was faster than her. There was a struggle. The guy in the mask punched hard. She went down. Then another man appeared. A third man. A big guy. They dragged her inside and closed the doors. Then they all climbed in and drove off.

My heart was racing. I clenched my fists. I was breathing hard. Then I heard the faint creak of a floorboard behind me. I felt the presence of someone. I reached for my Glock and stood and spun around.

11

————

Lynne May held two hands up slowly and said, "Put that away," as she stared across at me.

I lowered my weapon and holstered it. "I could've shot you."

"You wouldn't have."

"How'd you get in here?"

She lowered her hands. "You left the door wide open."

I said nothing. Just stared back at her from across the room.

"I know people. And I know Jami. She wouldn't miss a meeting or not return a phone call. Where is she?"

The minute you talk to someone, I'll find out about it.

"Blake, tell me what's going on."

May took two cautious steps forward and stepped farther into the room. "I don't know," I said.

"What do you mean you don't know?"

"I mean I don't know. Parker called as I was getting ready for work. He told me about the meeting, and I told Jami about it, too. I told her to expect a call from you. I said you'd probably ask her to join you there."

May nodded. She said nothing and took another step closer.

"Jami said she was finishing up with something she didn't get to work on last night. She said since the meeting was at eight, she had enough time to wrap it up, and she'd see me there. She was here when I left."

"Go on."

"You know the rest. She didn't show up to the meeting. And she wasn't answering her phone or her texts."

"So you came home to check on her."

"Yes."

"But I got here first."

I said nothing.

"You told me she was probably sleeping. Yet she's not here. Therefore you lied to me." She paused. "Why?"

And a minute after that, she dies.

"Lynne, please. You don't know what you're getting yourself into. I need you to trust me."

"Trust you? After you lied to me?" She took another step closer and narrowed her eyes. "Blake, you need to understand something. Right now, one of my agents is missing. And unless you tell me what's going on immediately, I'm going to have to escalate this. I need to talk with her. And if you don't know how to make that happen, if you don't know where she is, then maybe you need to trust *me* and tell me about it."

I remembered the phone call and the sound of Jami screaming in the background. A man's deep voice. An accent. The image I'd seen of a guy in a black ski mask with his partner. I put it all together. I clenched my fists again. May noticed it but remained silent. Just studied me closely, waiting me out, undeterred.

Ten seconds passed. Then thirty. My breathing grew heavy again as I thought through my limited options.

"I can't tell you, Lynne," I finally said.

"Why not?"

"Because if I do, they'll kill her."

May narrowed her eyes again. "Who is *they*?"

"I don't know."

"Why would somebody want to kill her?"

"That's what I'm trying to find out."

"Somebody took her?"

I said nothing.

"From here? From your home?"

I made no reply.

"Is that why you left the front door wide open?" Her eyes moved past me. She craned her neck slightly and saw my computer. I realized the camera footage was still up. I clenched my teeth as she put it all together. "Jami wasn't answering your calls or your texts. So you came home. Her car was in the driveway. You came inside and cleared the house. You watched a video from a camera outside." Her eyes moved back to me. "You saw how it happened. You don't know who they are. Not yet. But now you're going to find them."

I stared at her. Then I nodded. "If you'll let me."

She studied me some more. "But you're not telling me everything."

I said nothing.

"You told me she was okay when you got here. You lied to me. You wouldn't have said that if you knew she wasn't here. Therefore someone's made contact with you. Therefore they've already told you what they want. It was a call, wasn't it? They called you. Or maybe you called them. On Jami's phone."

"Lynne, I haven't talked to anybody."

We stared across at each other. Nobody spoke. Then my phone buzzed in my pocket, loud and urgent.

12

SIMON HARRIS TOOK A SIP OF HIS SODA AND SET IT DOWN ON the desk. He massaged the back of his neck. Then he got to work, looking into one of the daily routines Tom Parker had assigned to him. Parker was still on the phone, having a long conversation with someone. Simon paused from his work for a moment and straightened up and peered over the edge of the cubicle wall as he heard Parker wrapping up the call.

The conversation ended. Parker slammed the phone down; then he stared at it. He stood and paced. Simon sank down in his chair slightly, but kept his eyes over the edge of his cubicle, wondering what had happened. Then Parker opened his office door, and Simon dropped all the way down and started typing, looking busy.

He heard his boss walk around to the office next door. Heard the office door open, then close. Nobody was inside. Simon kept listening and heard heavy deliberate footsteps growing closer, approaching his desk. Parker moved past him, checking the conference room on the other side of the floor. Thirty seconds later, he came up behind him and rapped his knuckles on his cubicle. Two hard knocks. Two aggravated knocks.

Simon turned around and glanced at him and said, "What's up?"

"Where the hell is Jordan?"

"Blake stopped by earlier, but you were on the phone. He didn't want to interrupt you." Simon paused. "He said he needed to head home for something and wanted me to tell you he'd be back in about an hour."

Parker set his hands on his hips and glanced away, thinking about that for a long moment. Then he nodded to himself. "I need to make a few more calls. Send him to my office the moment he returns, okay?"

Simon nodded that he would.

Parker turned and headed back to his office as Simon stood and watched him go. He hesitated for a moment as he considered bringing up the discussion about Jami and her whereabouts to find out what his boss knew. But Parker was moving fast and was checking his watch as he moved. A man with somewhere to be. A man with calls he had to make. Someone with little time to deal with trivial things. And Simon didn't want his boss to think he was wasting time and not focused on the work he'd been assigned to do.

In the end, he said nothing at all and just watched his boss step into his office and close the door behind him. Simon sat back down. He thought about Jami and the conversation he'd had with Blake. Then he navigated his screen to an interdepartmental directory. He found a file for DDC's Washington field office. He found the cell number for Jami and jotted it down on a yellow pad; then he exited the program.

Then Simon accessed a system called Stingray, an application developed by the NSA and later rolled out to the FBI

and then to DDC and then finally to Parker's team at Homeland. An application that used cell tower data to locate
mobile devices. Officially, the DOJ required a warrant for its
use, but over the last several months, it had grown lax in its
enforcement. Simon navigated to a screen where he could
enter a cell phone number. He pulled his own cell phone
out from a pocket and found Blake Jordan's number. He
entered it into the system and clicked on a button. A few
seconds later, a map was drawn on his screen with a little
blue dot representing the phone's current location. Simon
studied it. He did a reverse lookup and confirmed it was
Blake's home address. He went back and saw another cell
phone in close proximity. Another government-issued
phone. He clicked another button to see whose it was. A
name appeared on his screen: Lynne May, DDC special
agent in charge for the Washington Bureau. Simon looked
away and furrowed his brow. He heard Parker back on the
phone. His voice unintelligible, in a heated discussion. He
just sat there, wondering what was going on. Simon glanced
back at his yellow pad. He went back to the spot where
numbers could be entered and cleared out Blake's number.
He typed Jami's number slowly and stared at the blinking
cursor at the end of the tenth digit. Then he ran the search.

13

─────

JAMI SAT ON THE COLD CONCRETE IN THE CORNER OF A makeshift cell. Her face was throbbing more now as the pain set in. She closed her eyes and thought through the last hour. She'd been led back by the driver through the vast open space of the large warehouse. She'd seen what looked like bags of fertilizer, stacked high, piled up next to a black van. There was a room next to hers, identical to hers, as far as she could tell, which she assumed was where they were holding the UPS driver. He'd been brought in first. Her wrists were secured behind her back, but she could tell her cell phone was no longer in her pocket. She figured one of the men had taken it at some point. Maybe right after she'd been knocked unconscious. Maybe as the driver sped away from her home, maybe after they'd cuffed her with what felt like a zip tie. Jami thought about how long it would take for Blake to find her. Then she wondered how he possibly could.

Then her thoughts drifted back to her kidnapper. Someone she knew. Or someone she thought she knew.

He kept the door to the room she was in open most of

the time. So he could keep an eye on her, she guessed. He no longer used the mask. Like he'd decided he no longer needed it. The man came in and out of view often. On the phone, pacing the floor, supervising the men on the opposite side of the warehouse. They had worked together once. A long time ago, during a very brief stint at the FBI. Before she had left the Bureau and took a job at DDC's first field office in Chicago, well before she'd transferred to Washington.

The man had been an interrogation expert for the Bureau, part of their HIG—the High-Value Detainee Interrogation Group. They had never spoken at length. Not that she could remember, at least. But she knew of him. And he, presumably, knew of her, too. They'd passed each other in the hallways. Given each other polite nods. Maybe said a few *good mornings*, but she couldn't be sure. But what Jami was sure of was that she had never worked with him directly. She didn't even know his name. But she'd heard him speak and was sure the man's accent was Russian. So she figured he had been hired for interrogations involving foreign agents picked up inside the United States, which happened more often than most people realized.

But now she was questioning everything having to do with the man.

Had he been interrogating all of those Russian agents? Asking them questions? Or giving them answers?

The man appeared, and she looked up at him. He took a cell phone out from a pocket. Not hers. A burner.

"What are you doing?" she asked.

"Proof of life," he said, snapping a picture of her and dropping the phone back into a pocket.

"I know you. We worked together. At the Bureau, years ago." She paused. "Why are you doing this?"

The man stared down at her. He said nothing.

"What are the chances?" She narrowed her eyes. "What are the odds that we'd know each other like that?"

"Close to zero," the man replied.

"Then tell me why I'm here," she asked, thinking: *means, motive, opportunity.* "Why me? And why now?"

But the man just shook his head. "Not yet," he replied. Then he glanced over his shoulder and barked a command, and another man appeared. The big guy from the truck. The one who had a weapon trained on her. The Russian grabbed his cell again and started recording as the big guy entered and grabbed her by her hair. He delivered a blow to her stomach, then to her face; then he dumped Jami back onto the floor.

14

THE PHONE CALL HAD BEEN FROM TOM PARKER. WHEN I SAW
it was him, I put the call on speakerphone so Lynne May
could listen in, but motioned for her to stay silent. She
crossed her arms disapprovingly and watched me as I
paced. I told Parker I had left something at the house.
Explained I had told Simon to let him know I'd be right
back. He said that was why he was calling. He didn't want
me to come back. Not yet. Instead Parker wanted me to meet
up with Mark Reynolds and decide how we should coordinate with Agent Rivera over at the White House. I said I'd
head to the Hoover Building shortly and I'd be in touch.

I clicked off and gripped my phone.

Lynne May moved her hands to her hips and tilted her
head again. She said, "You need to tell him."

"No."

"Why not?"

"Because if I tell anyone, including him, they said they'll
know, and then they'll kill her."

"You told me."

"No, you figured it out."

"How will they know? Have you thought about that part of it? Do they have some kind of informant?" She took a deep breath and let it out. "Think about it, Blake. They took her for a reason. First, I don't think they'd have a way of knowing if you told someone about this. Not unless they have someone working within one of our agencies, which would be highly unlikely. Second, they can't kill her even if they want to. Jami's the only leverage they have. If they kill her, then this whole thing's over. Am I missing something?"

I shook my head slowly. "I wish I knew, Lynne."

She looked me over for a spell. Thinking. Then she said, "Blake, this is going to be a very busy day. You of all people understand that. Keeping both presidents safe, dealing with any potential fallout is going to take a lot of effort. I'm down a person. So I need to call Base for help. They'll ask why I need additional staff. I can't just say one of my agents is missing. So I have to report her missing first, before I ask them for help."

"Please don't do that."

"I have no choice."

"We all have choices, Lynne. I will make up the difference. I'll pick up the slack. Besides, all you committed to with Parker and Mulvaney was to have your people analyze the recording of the phone call. You were never expected to have anyone out in the field. I can figure this out. I can find her. I know I can."

May said nothing.

"Her life is in danger. You've known me for a long time. Haven't I proven myself to you by now? Please..."

No reply. Just a faraway glance as she crossed her arms again and shook her head slowly but definitively.

But before I could say anything else, my cell phone buzzed again. Loud and urgent and unrelenting.

May glanced down at the phone in my hand. She flicked her eyes back up at me. "Answer it," she said.

The caller ID said it was an unknown number. It was a video call. And it wasn't coming from Jami's cell. I answered and held the phone out so I could watch. Lynne May stepped up beside me, positioning herself so she was out of the frame and could see the screen but so the person on the other end could only see me.

A person wearing a black ski mask appeared. Two holes punched out for eyes. No cutout for the mouth. He said, "I thought we had an agreement, Mr. Jordan." It was the same voice I'd spoken to earlier.

In my peripheral vision, I saw May turn her head and glance at me, trying to understand the context.

I said, "I haven't agreed to anything yet."

"You were given an order. A clear one. I told you to follow every command if you wanted your wife to live."

"I don't know what you're talking about."

"Her phone," he said. "You used the FBI's Stingray program to try to find her."

"No I didn't."

The man in the mask stared a moment longer, then he tapped his screen, and the view flipped. It was no longer showing his face behind a mask, but what was in front of him. There was a makeshift cell. Jami was on the floor, her wrists tied behind her back, beaten, a bruised face, matted-down hair, drenched in sweat, gagged. She looked out of it. Just stared blankly. The man in the mask grunted an order, and a large man appeared. He wore no mask. He walked past the camera and moved forward slowly, toward my wife.

He grabbed her by her hair and pulled upward, forcing Jami to her feet. He balled his free hand into a fist.

"Stop!" I yelled.

But nobody listened. Instead the big guy punched Jami hard in the stomach. She bent forward. He held her upright. A few seconds passed and she gasped for air. A muted sound because of the gag. Then he punched her again, then he punched her face, then her legs gave out, and the guy let her fall to the floor. The view flipped back again. The man in the mask said, "Apparently you're not convinced yet. Maybe that will help you decide. If you want to play along, she'll live. If not, she won't. Your choice. I will be in touch."

THE CALL ENDED. I LOWERED MY HAND AND GRIPPED MY phone again. My chest was heaving up and down. Lynne May stood to the left of me, closer than before. Watching me, studying my face, deciding something. She said, "They're serious, to escalate things so fast like this." She paused. "Who would've used Stingray?"

"I don't know."

There was another pause. Longer this time. She was thinking some more. She said, "What do you need?"

I took a breath and let it out. "I'll need help from Morgan Lennox out of Chicago. To find these people."

She nodded. "I'll call Roger Shapiro; I'll tell him I need Lennox for something I'm working on. What else?"

"Forget you were here. Don't talk to anyone about this." I paused a beat. "And stay the hell out of my way."

15

I watched as Lynne May drove away the same as before. Only she didn't come back this time. I closed and locked the front door and paced inside my house, thinking about Jami and the man in the black ski mask and the other man. The big guy. And there had been another man I'd seen on the video upstairs. The UPS driver. He was the only person I hadn't seen in the video call from a few minutes earlier. I went upstairs and sat back down at my computer. I rewound the video footage and stopped it at the spot right before the truck had pulled away. There was a number on the back of the vehicle. I rewound the tape some more and stopped it in the only spot where four people were visible: the UPS guy, the man in the ski mask, the big guy, and Jami. Only the side of the big guy's face was visible. I snapped a photo of it with my phone. I studied the image. Then I jogged down the stairs and went outside, and I climbed into my SUV.

Twenty minutes later the Hoover Building came into view up ahead as I made my way to FBI headquarters. I assumed Parker wanted me to find Mark Reynolds and coordinate with him on how we were going to assist Agent Rivera with building a perimeter for the peace treaty signing. But I had other plans. I thought through how I could work with the Bureau and the Secret Service to help keep both presidents safe while trying to find Jami. I pulled up to the guardhouse and showed a woman my Homeland credentials. She nodded and pushed a button and let me through. I found a space and parked. I didn't want to waste time with checking my weapon, so I left it under my seat and jogged to the lobby and stepped inside. I showed my credentials again. A man behind the desk looked them over for a moment and said Parker had called ahead and told him to expect me. He asked if I was there to see Mark Reynolds.

"Yes," I said.

Part truth. Part lie.

"Need me to take you upstairs?"

I shook my head. "I know where I'm going."

TWO MINUTES AFTER THAT, I ARRIVED AT THE FOURTH FLOOR. The lobby was dark. Not much lighting inside. There were very few people walking the halls. I moved down a long dark hallway, looking for Mark Reynolds's office. I found it empty. The light was on, and his laptop was docked, and the screen was lit up, but Reynolds wasn't there. I eventually found him inside a joint workroom, standing next to a whiteboard.

"Took you long enough to get here, man."

"Sorry," I said.

"Guess you're as busy nowadays as I am."

"You have no idea." I glanced up at the whiteboard. "So what do you have?"

Reynolds walked me through what he was planning. He shared all of the details about the Pullman House with me. He drew the streets surrounding it and explained why it was the safest bet. Rivera said the Secret Service had used it once before and were familiar with it, so everyone was on board.

I asked about schematics for the building. We needed them on hand, and I wanted to look them over. Reynolds thought that was overkill, but I reminded him about what had happened several years earlier with President Keller's kidnapping. Reynold thought it through, and then he said he'd try to get me a copy.

Reynolds walked me through the perimeter his Bureau guys would set up. They were going to block off two streets in every direction. I told him to double it and reminded him we would have not one but two presidents in the same building at the same time. I said Mulvaney would agree with me, and he nodded.

"What time does Keller want to do this?"

"Eight o'clock local time," he said. "Tonight. Primetime on the east coast. Five o'clock on the west coast."

"Maximum exposure," I said. "He wants the biggest viewership he can get."

Reynolds nodded.

"So when is the White House announcing the press conference?"

"At five. The press secretary's making the calls. The media will know something's up when we set up the perimeter, but they won't know what. Rivera had them put dinner with Stepanov on the official White House schedule. We'll try to keep this a secret as long as we can, but the press catches on fast, man."

I nodded vaguely and glanced back at the whiteboard. "How many men is Mulvaney giving you?"

"About twenty."

"Is that enough?"

"Agent Rivera has twice as many. They'll be inside and out. Every inch of that building will be covered. The Secret Service is already down there securing the building."

"Okay."

"Trust me, man. We won't have any issues tonight. Nobody will get in—or out—unless we want them to."

"Okay," I said again. "When do we need to be down there?"

Mark Reynolds pointed at the whiteboard. "As soon as I review the plan with Mulvaney, I'll head out. You can head over now if you want to. Rivera's expecting us. I'll meet you as soon as I can get over there."

I stared across the room, thinking about Jami, seeing her being beaten, replaying it in my mind.

The room fell silent. Nobody spoke. Then I became aware of it. Reynolds said, "You okay, man?"

I turned and looked at him. "Yeah," I said. "You have my number. Call me when you're on your way."

Reynolds made no reply. Just nodded and went back to the whiteboard and made some notes. I found my way back to the elevator and stepped inside. I stared at the numbers to the different floors of the building all lit up, waiting on me to make a decision. I heard the warning from Jami's kidnapper in my head again. His voice loud, his words precise. I moved my hand over to the buttons. I hesitated. Then I pressed three.

THE ELEVATOR DOORS OPENED UP TO THE THIRD-FLOOR LOBBY. It was dark. Identical to the fourth floor in every way. Only there were a lot more people buzzing back and forth in and

out of offices than there was one floor up. I passed by
Mulvaney's office. His door was closed. I heard him on the
phone. Calling his guys in, I guessed. I kept moving and
found the small office I was looking for and knocked twice.
A familiar voice inside said to come in, and I stepped
through. Chris Reed glanced up at me and stood. He
motioned for me to enter and stretched out his hand, and I
shook it. He asked, "What are you doing here?" and sat back
down and gestured at the two chairs on the other side of his
desk, inviting me to take a seat. I closed the door behind me
and sat down on one of the chairs across from him as my
friend leaned forward.

I took in a deep breath and let it out as I glanced around
his office. "Do you know about the peace treaty?"

Chris nodded. "Mulvaney stopped by earlier and told
me about it."

"We had a meeting about it this morning. Parker wants
me to work with Reynolds and Agent Rivera."

"Mark's office is one floor up."

"I know where it is, Chris."

My friend said nothing for a long moment. Just sat there,
studying me. Silence filled the room. He narrowed his eyes.
He knew something was off. "What's wrong?" he finally
asked me. "Why are you here?"

The minute you talk to someone, I'll find out about it.

I glanced away again, thinking.

And a minute after that, she dies.

Chris was staring at me. He leaned forward some more
and said, "Talk to me."

I turned back and said, "Can I trust you?"

He furrowed his brow. "Of course."

I reached into my pocket. I pulled out my phone and
thumbed the screen and found the picture I'd taken. I

leaned across and set my phone down on the desk directly in front of Chris and leaned back in my chair.

"What's this?"

"Approximately two hours ago, Jami was kidnapped by the people in that image. The big guy is second-in-command, I think, to the one in the ski mask. He's in charge. I think that's why his face is hidden." I paused. "Based on his body language and how he's standing, I don't think the delivery driver is part of it."

Chris glanced up briefly. "You got all that from a picture?"

I said nothing.

His gaze lowered, and he stared at the image on the phone. "Who are they?"

"That's what I need to find out."

"Who else knows?"

I explained how Lynne May was involved. How she had been at the meeting earlier that morning with Mulvaney and Reynolds and Parker. How Jami had never showed up. How I'd called Jami after the meeting to check on her. How the kidnapper answered instead. I told Chris how I'd headed home only to find Lynne May there already. I walked him through the footage I'd captured, how May had entered my home, the video call I received. How they were beating Jami and how bad she looked, like she'd been drugged maybe. How I snapped a photo from the security footage. I left out the part about having to work a list.

Chris stared at the image, thinking. Then he looked up at me and said, "We'll get her back." Then he studied the image again on the screen. "There's a number on the back of the truck."

"I know."

"I can probably trace it. I can find out who was driving it."

"Don't."

"I have a buddy who delivers for UPS. There's a hand-held device they carry with them. They use it to scan their packages as they deliver them. But it also acts as a GPS unit. I can work on trying to locate the truck."

"No," I said. "How it happened doesn't matter. And I don't want to tip anyone off that there's a problem."

"They're probably aware already. They have to keep a very tight schedule. Any delay sends up a red flag."

I said nothing.

"What else can I do?"

"You and Lynne May aren't the only ones who know," I said. "There's a third person. Somebody used your Stingray program on Jami's cell an hour ago. The guy called me out on it. He thinks it was me. He had warned me about it already. He told me if I tried to track her down, he'd know about it. And he did."

"Who would've done that?"

"I need you to tell me."

"Okay."

"And I need to know how the kidnapper found out."

Chris nodded as he held onto my phone. "Anything else?"

I shook my head.

"You sure?"

I stood. Said, "Keep your cell on. I'll be tied up with Reynolds. I may need your help if I can't break away."

He looked up at me. "Sit down, Blake."

I just stared down at him.

"Tell me the rest."

"I don't know what you're talking about."

Chris stood and maintained his stare. "Blake, you're here asking if you can trust me. But can I trust you?"

I said nothing.

"They always want something. So what is it? What are they asking you for? Money? Information? Access?"

"They're not asking me for anything."

Chris held my phone out in front of him. I saw the image of Jami and the men. "We go way back," he said. "You've always had my back. And I've always had yours. I think that's why you're here, isn't it? Because you know I'd do anything for you. Same with Jami. But I need to know what I'm getting myself into first."

I reached across and took my phone. I hesitated. Then I said, "They want me to complete a set of tasks."

"What kind of tasks?"

"I don't know yet. They're making me wait before they tell me. They said they wanted to convince me."

Chris thought about that for a spell. Then he asked, "Are you going to do the tasks?"

I said nothing. Just sat back down. Chris did the same. The office grew quiet as we both sat in silence. I dropped my cell phone on his desk in front of me. I took a breath and closed my eyes. I replayed images of Jami being punched by the big guy. I saw the man in the black ski mask. Cutouts for eyes. Russian accent.

"You should tell someone."

"I just did."

"What about Parker?"

I shook my head and opened my eyes and looked away. "I can't. I shouldn't even have told you."

Then my phone buzzed on the table. Chris and I both glanced down at it. Then we looked up at each other. We both leaned forward. The screen displayed the words

UNKNOWN CALLER, upside down for him, right side up for me. No videocall this time. Just a regular phone call. Chris said to answer it and put the call on speakerphone as he dug his own phone out of a pocket and thumbed the screen to unlock it. I reached across and answered it. Silence on the line. "This is Jordan," I finally said.

"You've had plenty of time to decide," the voice said. "I need your decision. Will you complete the list?"

I looked at Chris. He stared back at me and nodded, saying: *I'll help you.*

"Yes," I said.

"Good," the voice said. "The first task is simple. There's a record for a man named Viktor Babushkin. I want you to delete it. But there's a slight problem, Mr. Jordan. It's not on file at DHS. It's with the FBI."

Chris nodded again. Less decisively this time, saying: *I'll do my best.*

I thought about how it worked. The red flags it would raise if I did what I was being asked. "Okay," I said.

"You have twenty minutes."

"That's not enough time," I said, but there was no response. The line went dead. The screen faded to black.

16

I GLANCED DOWN AT MY WATCH AND MADE A MENTAL NOTE OF the time. Chris Reed picked up his cell and thumbed it again, then set it back down on his desk. He ran his hands through his hair and slid them down his neck and stared across at nothing, thinking, playing the different scenarios across his mind on what could happen the moment he tried to delete a file. His eyes flicked over to me. Then he swiveled in his chair and tapped his keyboard, and his laptop came to life. I stood and walked up behind him and watched over his shoulder as he entered his credentials to get past the lock screen, and he shook his head.

"I've never purged a record before," he said.

"But it's possible?" I asked.

"I don't see how."

Chris double-clicked on an icon, and a splash screen with the FBI logo displayed for a brief moment. Then a program appeared on his screen. It was the same program all intelligence agencies used. Only this instance of the application was customized for the Bureau. Chris typed in the name Viktor Babushkin and hit enter. An hourglass appeared. We waited as the database combed through hundreds of thousands of records and eventually found a match. The file displayed on the screen like a briefing report, or a jacket, as we called them, with a name at the top and a picture to left of it with little arrows superimposed over it, indicating if there was more than one image to view. But there was no image, and there were no arrows.

Underneath the name and the missing profile picture was a general overview section. I leaned in closer. Chris scrolled down to see how much there was on the man. The information the Bureau had was limited to a single screen of details. Chris scrolled back up and started reading from the top as I checked the time.

"Who is he?" I asked, glancing back up.

Chris lifted a finger and brought it to the screen. He followed the text as he read like someone would do while studying something they had limited time to comprehend and if they didn't want to lose their place. "There's not much on the guy," he said as I read along with him, digesting as much as I could as quickly as I could. "Looks like he was busted by our guys for suspected espionage last year, but then we let him go."

I read on. The Bureau had been involved in a joint operation with the Central Intelligence Agency involving a foreign national here on a student VISA attending Georgetown for a study abroad program. The university had opened a campus in Qatar five years earlier, which the file noted was highly criticized by government officials over its appropriateness given Qatar's alleged links to state-sponsored terrorism. Once the campus was opened, Americans were offered the ability to study overseas, and the same opportunity was given to students in Qatar, so Viktor Babushkin spent a semester in America. Through a series of investigations, the CIA discovered that someone in a dorm room had obtained unauthorized access into various government computer systems. They were siphoning information and uploading the documents to a website using what they thought was a private VPN but was actually hosted by the Bureau.

"So they picked the guy up; but in the end, they couldn't prove it was him?" I said as I read ahead.

"Looks like it," Chris said.

He got to the bottom of the document as we finished reading; then he scrolled back up to the top of it. Chris turned in his chair and looked up at me. I nodded once at my friend and told him to purge the file.

But he was unable to. "The option is grayed out," he said, pointing at the screen. "I can't delete the file."

TEN MINUTES HAD PASSED SINCE THE CALL HAD BEEN disconnected. We took another five to think through our options. Chris suggested we call Lynne May since she was the only other person who knew my situation. But I said that was a waste of time. She was management, like Mulvaney or Parker. She'd need an analyst who might be able to give us ideas.

And that gave us only one true option.

Chris reached across his desk. He opened a line on his phone and dialed a Chicago number and put the call on speakerphone. The line rang once. I was pacing around the small office as the line rang a second time. Then a man I knew well, someone who'd worked for me at the Chicago DDC field office, answered.

"Morgan Lennox," he said with his characteristic Australian accent.

"Morgan, it's Chris Reed."

"Chris, how are you?"

"Not good, I'm under a time crunch, and I need your help."

There was a pause on the line. I could almost see the puzzled look. "What seems to be the problem?"

Chris explained the issue as quickly and as concisely but as vaguely as possible. There was a record in the interagency program that he needed to purge ASAP. But the option was grayed out. Chris couldn't do it.

"They removed that ability a while back," said Morgan. "Only a few people have that level of access now. Plus it doesn't really remove the record permanently, mate. It archives it instead. The delete option was only there in case someone had inadvertently entered a duplicate record. Easy to do with aliases and multiple agencies all using the same interconnected system. It was a cleanup effort someone started. They thought it would help make the database faster to search. If you get rid of the dupes, it speeds things up."

Chris looked at his watch. I did the same from behind him. Four minutes until I'd get another call.

"Morgan, we need your help," Chris said, growing more concerned. "We're running out of time."

There was another pause on the line. "We?" Morgan asked.

Chris glanced over his shoulder at me. A mistake. He corrected it by saying, "The Bureau. I've been asked to have this record purged from the system right away. If it's not done within the next three and a half minutes, something bad could happen. Someone's life is in danger. Please, is there anything you can do?"

Morgan thought about it through thirty excruciatingly

long seconds. Then he said, "Possibly. Chris, if your goal is simply to remove the file from the FBI's instance of the system, you could just transfer it to DDC."

I furrowed my brow. Chris glanced back at me, and we shared a look. He asked, "What do you mean?"

"Well, if you transfer the record to me, then your local copy will be gone."

"It'll look like the record was completely purged? To someone who might not know how it all works?"

Another pause. "From an FBI perspective, I believe so. It just simply won't exist unless I transfer it back."

I nodded. We had a minute left. Morgan walked Chris through it. Then Morgan said, "There's a problem."

17

CHRIS AND I SHARED ANOTHER LOOK. "WHAT'S THE problem?" he asked.

We heard frantic typing from the speakerphone. Morgan said, "It seems as if the file has queued."

"What do you mean it queued?"

"I mean I wasn't able to take possession of it. The thing is sitting in a queue, waiting to be reviewed by DDC management. Which means it'll sit there indefinitely until Roger Shapiro gets around to looking at it."

Shapiro was Morgan's boss at DDC's Chicago field office, the person I ultimately reported to when I ran the place years ago. This would be trouble. Chris looked at me. "Don't do anything with that file," he said.

Morgan paused, then asked, "Why not? All I have to do is walk down to Shapiro's office and ask him to—"

"No, don't tell him anything."

Silence on the line. Morgan said, "Okay, mate, do you want to tell me what the bloody hell is going on?"

Chris looked at me again. I shook my head. Chris said, "Not right now, Morgan. Just don't say anything to Shapiro.

I'll call Lynne May. I'll have her do it. She can accept a file from another DDC field office, right?"

Another pause. "I suppose so."

"Thanks for your help. I'll be in touch."

With that, Chris pressed a button on his phone to disconnect the call. He pressed it again and waited to hear a dial tone; then he punched in the numbers for the DDC field office located across the street from the Hoover Building. There were four long rings, then a brief pause where it wasn't clear if Lynne May had picked up or not. Then we heard a recording of her voice stating her name and asking us to leave a message or to call on her cell. Chris grabbed a pen and wrote down the number May's recorded voice recited. Then he pressed the button twice again to start over fresh with a new dial tone and began dialing.

But before he could enter all ten digits and place the call, there was a knock at the door, loud and rushed and urgent. The door swung open, and Peter Mulvaney stood in the doorway and stared at me. He furrowed his brow, and then he looked at Chris and said, "Reed, did you just send a file over to DDC?"

Chris hesitated for a fraction of a second. Undetectable to most people, but completely obvious to me. In the SEALs, I'd studied microexpressions and was trained to look for tells from people when they were lying. A lot of it was in the eyes, if the person looked away when answering a question. Some of it was in the face and the way a person would bite their lip or make some other kind of facial expression. But often the only tell, especially for someone like an agent with one of our government agencies, was hesitation. But Mulvaney either didn't notice it or wasn't aware of it because he just listened closely as Chris replied.

Chris said, "I got a call from Lynne May a few minutes ago. She asked us to send a file over to DDC."

Mulvaney thought about that. "Person of interest?"

Chris nodded and answered, "Possibly," realizing immediately that the Bureau director believed whatever was in that record might be related to the intercepted Russian phone call he'd been briefed on earlier.

"I certainly hope so; otherwise why is she focused on this with everything else we have going on today?"

Chris said nothing. Just nodded his agreement.

I glanced down at my watch. One minute until the next call would be coming in to check on my progress.

Mulvaney said, "Next time, talk to me first. I might want to take a look at a file before you send it out." Chris made no reply. Mulvaney eyed me briefly. "I'm glad you're still here. There's a change of plans." Then while keeping his eyes on me, he said to his agent, "Reed, I want you to go with Jordan and work with him and Reynolds. I just got off the phone with Tom Parker. We both agree it's all hands on deck."

"Yes, sir," said Chris as Mulvaney shifted his eyes away from me and back to my friend.

"Reynolds just left. Get over there and help him set up the perimeter. Agent Rivera is already down there."

My phone started buzzing in my hand. I glanced down. *UNKNOWN CALLER*. "I need to take this," I said.

Mulvaney nodded and pointed at Chris. "Keep me updated."

Chris said that he would, and Mulvaney pulled the door closed behind him. I remained standing and glanced down at my phone. I answered on the third ring and put it on speakerphone as I said my name.

"Have you completed your assignment?"

"Yes," I said.

"The file is completely deleted?"

Chris nodded for me to say yes. And I started to. But I could tell there was something in the caller's voice. Something in the question. The way he asked it. Chris stared up at me, urging me to answer affirmatively. Instead I said, "I wasn't able to delete the file. I found it in the FBI's instance of the database, but the option to delete the record was grayed out." I paused. Chris's eyes grew wide. "So no, I couldn't delete it."

Silence on the line. Nobody spoke. Then the man finally asked, "So what did you do?"

"I had it transferred to DDC. It's in a temporary inbound queue, waiting to be accepted. I'll take care of it."

There was a pause. He asked, "How did you access the FBI's instance if you're with Homeland Security?"

Chris raised his eyebrows and sat back in his chair. I said, "I have different security clearance from my counterparts in the government. Along with that comes authority bestowed to me by the President of the United States himself. I make a phone call, and people do what I say. No questions asked. They couldn't delete the file, so I had it transferred. Now I'll make another call. I'll have someone move the file out of the queue. It won't be deleted, but it'll be buried. It won't be seen. Not by the FBI. Not today. Maybe not ever."

There was another pause. Then the man said, "Very well. I have your next assignment. Head downtown. There's someone being detained at a CIA safe house on P Street. I want you to release them immediately."

I thought about the request. "I can't do that. Not if they're being held by the CIA. They won't listen to me."

"Mr. Jordan, you just told me you have authority bestowed to you by the president himself. You give an order and people do what you say. So find a way to release them. You have one hour." The line went dead.

18

Jami Jordan blinked hard and stared straight down at her stomach. She wasn't sure how long her head had been hanging low, but when she raised it, she felt a lot of pain. The kind of pain one feels when they've been in the same position for a very long time. Jami blinked some more. Her vision was blurry but became clearer with every passing second. She tried to lift her arms to rub her eyes and realized she couldn't. They were strapped to the armrests. Two thick leather straps secured them firmly in place. There was very little give in them, but she tried to move them anyway. They wouldn't budge. Not even a little. The room was dark, but faint orange light from a portable lantern in an adjacent room let her see that there was a table directly in front of her. It was wooden and damaged from the humidity during several months or maybe several years of hot stagnant air and poor circulation in the abandoned warehouse. She blew air up with her mouth to try to get a few stray hairs out of her face as her eyes continued to adjust. Then she heard the sound of movement. Footsteps. Someone approaching. The light grew brighter. The Russian appeared in the doorway, holding the lantern with one hand and a small metallic briefcase in the other. He eyed her momentarily, then stepped the whole way through and set the lantern on one side of the table and the small briefcase on the other side, closest to where he stood.

Jami looked up and said, "I know you."

The man said nothing in return. Just popped open the two latches on both sides of the suitcase and lifted the lid, then turned it on the table slightly for the lantern to illuminate the contents so he could see inside.

"Hey," she said, louder, more commanding, demanding his attention.

The man glanced at her. His face half-lit by the lantern's glow.

"I don't know your name, but I know who you are. We worked together once. Not far from here." Jami paused for a moment, thinking. The man made no reply and lowered his gaze and reached into the suitcase. "We passed each other in the hallways. Our paths never truly crossed. But I know what you did over there." She glanced at the suitcase and stared at it, thinking. "You were good at your job."

"Then you know what I'm capable of," he said.

Jami didn't speak for a long moment. She just watched in silence as the man pulled out several instruments from the suitcase, some visible to her, others hidden. She said, "What do you want from me?"

She watched as a smile grew on the man's face as he brought a small vial from the suitcase and turned and held it so the warm glow from the lantern was directly behind it and he could verify what he was looking at. He turned back to retrieve something else. A needle. He stuck it into the vial and filled it completely.

"Your cooperation," he answered. The Russian smiled as

he lowered the vial and set it on the table and raised the needle and got the air out. Two drops of liquid escaped and ran down the needle, ran down the base, then ran down his fingers. The man held onto it and closed the suitcase with his free hand and set the needle on the table, in front of the lantern, so she could see it. Then he left the room and disappeared for a whole minute. When he returned, he was carrying something under his right arm. He used his left hand to push his suitcase with the instruments away, and he set the laptop down in front of her. But it wasn't his laptop, it was her laptop. Her DDC laptop. She recognized it immediately. It had her maiden name on it. A white sticker affixed to the lid. It read J. DAVIS. He stood over her and stared down at her.

"What do you want from me?" she said again, drawing out each word, punctuating each one as she spoke.

He held the needle to her arm and said, "I want you to log in. And I want you to do exactly as I say."

19

CHRIS TOUCHED THE SPEAKERPHONE BUTTON ON HIS LANDLINE to disconnect the call and stared up at me. "Why'd you tell him you couldn't delete that file?" he asked. "That was an unnecessary risk, Blake."

"He knew," I said as I looked around the small office, thinking about it. "I wasn't going to. I was going to lie and tell him that I did it. But there was something about the way he asked the question. I could tell. Like he knew it couldn't be done. Like when you ask someone a question you already know the answer to."

"How'd he even know there was a file? Do you think he's FBI? Or knows someone inside the FBI?"

I looked away, thinking about it. "I don't think so. Otherwise he would've asked them to do it. Not me."

"But you're not FBI, either, Blake. You're Homeland Security. Why would he think *you* could do it?"

I glanced at my watch. "I don't know, but now we have to worry about the safe house; we have an hour."

Chris told me he knew where the safe house was. He reminded me we'd been there together once. It was a place on P Street in Georgetown that the Bureau also used. Chris grabbed his keys, and we stepped out of his office. We ran into Mulvaney again. This time by the elevator. He told us Reynolds had just arrived and was at the building, waiting on us. We needed to get down there ASAP to help Metro PD set up the perimeter. Mulvaney went back to his office, and we took the elevator down to the first floor.

WE ENTERED THE PARKING GARAGE. I WAS THINKING CHRIS was going to go with me to the safe house. But instead he stopped moving and stared across at me as random vehicles drove past us, entering and exiting. "I can't go with you," he said. "I know Mulvaney. He's going to call Reynolds and say we're on our way. He'll call him again in twenty minutes to see how things are going. If I'm not there, I'm in trouble."

"Chris, I really need your help," I said.

"I know," he said as he reached for his cell phone and began typing a text message and then looked up as he continued to type. "Do you still remember the layout of the place? From the last time you were there?"

I nodded vaguely. Said nothing.

He looked back down at his phone. "Not much has changed. I was just there a week ago. The CIA and the Bureau were questioning someone. An informant, I think. I was the one who moved them there."

"Do you think it's the same person? Whoever's there right now?"

Chris shrugged. "I doubt it. They tend to move people around every few days. As a matter of safety."

"The man you took into custody, could he be involved in all of this?"

"I don't see how. And it wasn't a man. It was a woman. Emma Ross needed a safe place for her to stay."

I thought about Emma Ross. A woman who had previously served as chief of staff to President Keller. She'd lost her job, then worked for the mayor of New York. When the man had abruptly left office, she moved back to DC after taking a job with the Central Intelligence Agency's domestic counterterrorism operations.

Also known as Base, DDC's parent organization.

Another vehicle passed by us, and I became fully present. I said, "I want to know who's there now. The person this guy wants me to release. Do you think Emma knows?"

"Maybe, but I wouldn't ask her about it directly. Not on the phone. You'll need to meet up with her."

"I don't have time for that."

Chris checked his watch. "Then you'll need to find out after you release the protectee. If you release them."

"You don't think they'll let me?"

"You're not walking out of there with anyone. You'll need paperwork. And they'll make a phone call to their boss. He isn't going to listen to anything you say, even with your level of authority. You could get the president himself on the line and they're not going to release anyone. They're cautious." Chris glanced away and thought about it some more. His eyes flicked back. "They may not even answer the door."

Chris stared at me and gave me a knowing look. Then he told me that he'd texted me the code for the door. He reminded me that the safe house used a keypad entry system. I closed my eyes, trying to remember, and I could see the front door from the last time I'd been there. I opened my eyes and nodded once.

"Thanks, man," I said. "Tell Reynolds I'm on my way and I just needed to take care of something."

Chris nodded back. He held an open palm out, and I grabbed it and pulled him in. "Good luck," he said.

I said nothing.

I USED THE DRIVE TO GET MY THOUGHTS TOGETHER. I thought about a lot of things along the way. I thought about the caller and his faint accent. He wasn't American, but spoke perfect English. It wasn't his first language. If I had to guess, I'd pin the accent as Russian. I thought about the file he needed out of the FBI's system and wondered what good it would do just being transferred to another agency. I thought about the person I was going to meet at the safe house, and I wondered if it was the same person Chris had handled. If it was, then the agency feared for her life in some way. She was being given room and board and a safe place to stay like a battered woman seeking refuge with a friend would. Either she had given the CIA useful information and the agency needed time to work out what to do with her, or maybe she needed a new identity and safe passage out of DC. Or maybe she had information not yet revealed. Maybe the CIA wasn't protecting her but keeping her from leaving. Maybe she was being detained. I wondered who she was and why the caller wanted them released. Then I thought about Jami.

Her screams still echoed through my mind. They had been faint, but her voice was piercing. I pictured her far away from the phone. I thought back to the video call from her kidnapper. I could see Jami being held in a makeshift cell, being beaten by a man with his face turned from me. A big guy. And I could see her kidnapper, his face hidden with a black mask, unidentifiable in every way. Except for one. His voice.

I made a left turn and arrived at the east end of P Street. I pulled to the side of the road and brought my SUV to a stop. I put the vehicle in park; then I pulled my phone out from a pocket and dialed Lynne May. She didn't answer. After checking the time and seeing I was running out of it, I dialed a Chicago number and waited through two long rings.

"Morgan Lennox," my friend said, answering the call.

"It's me," I said.

"Blake, what can I do for you, mate?"

I stared out the windshield, praying I was making the right decision bringing another person into this.

"Are you still there?" he called.

I took in a deep breath and let it out. "Morgan, I need your help," I finally said. Then I proceeded to tell him everything that had happened. I told him about Jami and the surveillance footage I'd seen at my home. About Lynne May and about Chris Reed's involvement. About the kidnapper and the video call he'd made. About Jami being held against her will, being beaten by one of the men. Morgan asked if anyone else knew, and I said no. Then he asked me if this had anything to do with the file Chris wanted transferred out of the FBI's instance of the database. I told him it did, but I didn't know why the kidnapper wanted it removed.

"Well, I do," he said.

"What are you talking about, Morgan?"

"The file's gone now. It's no longer in the queue. I was waiting to talk to Roger Shapiro about it, but before I could, it just straight up disappeared from the queue. I searched everywhere for it, and I'm not seeing it."

"Someone deleted it?"

"No, but they pulled it out of the queue and then moved it. No way for me to see where it went."

"It was Lynne May," I said. "Chris was going to call her to see if she could get to it before Shapiro sees it."

"It wasn't May." Silence. "I don't know where it went, but I can see who accessed the queue—it was Jami. I was wrong before. Apparently it's not just management who can take files from the queue. They must've changed the process."

My thoughts drifted back to a few hours earlier. I had stepped into my house and cleared it, looking for Jami. I hadn't even thought about her DDC laptop. I remembered her working on something as I was leaving for work. She'd had her laptop on the kitchen counter. I closed my eyes and saw the counter empty. It wasn't there when I had reentered the house. I opened my eyes and stared ahead. "Can you trace it?"

"I beg your pardon?"

"The location," I said. "Where Jami used her laptop to access DDC's system."

"No," he replied. "It's a security thing. We use VPN to connect remotely. Everyone does outside of a field office. No way to track it back to where any of our agents or analysts log in from. It's a safety precaution."

I nodded to myself and stared ahead. "Morgan, I've been given the next task, and I only have—" I checked my watch "—thirty minutes to do it. He wants me to release someone from a CIA safe house on P Street."

"No," he said. "I know what you're going to ask me. There's no way of knowing who protectees are."

"Then you know the next thing I'm going to ask you."

"Yes," he said, typing. "That I can tell you. I can confirm that it was arranged by the CIA. By Emma Ross."

20

EMMA ROSS GLANCED AT HER WRIST TO CHECK THE TIME AS she moved slowly along the wide sidewalk of the Ellipse, the fifty-two-acre park located south of the White House fence and north of Constitution Avenue. Tired parents with the day off or maybe spouses of government officials sat on old wooden benches, watching their children play. Emma scanned the faces, looking for someone. But he wasn't there. Not yet. She glanced over her shoulder as she moved and saw the White House in the distance. Her thoughts drifted back to her old life. A life where she had served as President Keller's chief of staff. A life where she had had a seat at the table, coordinating her boss's busy schedule, involved in every aspect of his administration, in one form or another. It had been the honor of her life serving in that role. A job she loved. A job she was good at. She found an empty bench and took a seat and looked again. Then out of nowhere, Ethan Meyer appeared from behind her, glanced at her as he approached, and sat down next to her.

He crossed his legs and kept his eyes forward and said, "Make this quick, Emma. I'm very busy today."

"If you allowed me to talk to the president directly, you wouldn't have to deal with me."

Meyer glanced at her sideways; then he faced forward again and looked away.

"Ethan, I know about the peace treaty."

"Then you know I don't have much time." Meyer glanced at his watch. "I have a lot I need to do still."

She paused. Then she decided to ditch the speech and cut to the chase. "You need to change the venue."

Meyer turned again, and this time he fixed his eyes on her. "We will do no such thing. There's a reason why we're having the signing in a more public forum. The president wants his supporters there in person. You of all people know how important optics are. He's up for reelection. This is a big win for us, Emma."

Meyer looked away as she turned her head and watched him; then she glanced around to take in the crowd and make sure nobody was watching them. She said, "Ethan, I'm fully aware of what this peace treaty means. And how hard Keller's worked for this. We've been at war with them for many, many years."

"Our war was with the Taliban and with Al Qaeda, not Afghanistan. And certainly not with Russia."

"You're twisting my words, Ethan. They've been aligned for a while, whether you want to admit it or not."

"We're not changing the venue."

"There was a phone call originating from outside the United States. It was intercepted a few hours ago."

"Your point?"

"Someone was given an order to take out the president."

Meyer glanced at her again. His expression asked: *Which one?* Her expression answered: *Does it matter?* "Emma, I have the highest regard for the Secret Service," he said as he stood. "If there was a credible threat, we'd know. You don't call the shots. Not anymore." He paused. "It was good seeing you, as always."

As he turned, Ross stood and said, "Ethan, you're going to change the venue. And you're going to do it as soon as you get back to your office. Because if you don't, I'll make sure the *Times* finds out what you were *really* doing before the president picked you to replace me—and I don't think you want me to do that."

Meyer kept his back to her, thinking, a realization, a debate. He said nothing back. Then he walked away.

21

I TOLD MORGAN THAT CHRIS REED HAD TAKEN A WOMAN TO the safe house a week earlier. He couldn't confirm if it was the same person being kept there. But since the CIA was DDC's parent organization, he had access to see who had requested the protectee to be moved there, and he was positive it was Emma Ross and she'd know more.

"You need to call her," he said.

"I can't bring another person into this. I wasn't supposed to say anything to anyone. Now three people know. Morgan, the guy said he'd kill Jami if he finds out I talked to anyone. I just can't take the chance."

"You don't trust Emma?"

"No," I said as I reached for my weapon from under my seat.

"Well then, I guess you're going to have to find out who the protectee is all on your own."

I glanced ahead and thought about that. I thanked Morgan for his help. Then I clicked off and stepped out.

. . .

SIMON HARRIS RETURNED FROM THE VENDING MACHINE AND cracked open a can of Mountain Dew as he sat back down at his desk. His cubicle was smack-dab in the middle of the large floor. Empty desks surrounded him. He heard the rain pick up outside and looked out through the tall glass windows that lined one side of the floor. The storm was getting worse. Simon took a sip of his drink and set it down. Then he turned back and thought some more about Blake and the way he had left earlier.

He didn't like it.

Then he thought about Jami and how he'd used Stingray earlier to try to locate her and how confused he'd been when the program's response was that her phone was turned off. Parker had given him another assignment. He set his questions aside so he could focus on the task and knock it out. He'd become better than he'd been when he first transferred from Lynne May's DDC team to Parker's at Homeland. Morgan had taught him a lot of things along the way. Simon still had plenty to learn, but he'd learned a lot already. But the biggest thing Simon had learned from the senior DDC analyst out of Chicago was to trust your gut.

Simon wrapped up the task he'd been asked to do and sent Parker an instant message letting him know he was done. Parker's door was closed, and he didn't want to bother him. He sat up tall and looked out over the short cubicle wall and saw his boss inside his office, reading the message. Parker glanced his way, through the blinds of his office window, and nodded his appreciation. Simon sank back down into his chair as his thoughts returned back to the nagging open loop he hadn't closed yet. He decided to trust his gut.

He went back to the Stingray program and entered Jami's cell phone number and searched again. There were no results, just like before. Just an OFFLINE message indicating her phone was not only off, but the battery was likely removed. He grabbed his soda and took a long drink. Then he had another thought. He pinged Lynne May's phone again, knowing if anyone reviewed the logs and saw he was looking up the special agent in charge, he'd have some explaining to do. A second later, the app pinpointed her location. May was at the DDC field office across the street from the Hoover Building, where he expected her to be.

Then he typed Blake Jordan's number again and hit enter and took another sip of his soda as he waited.

I LEFT MY SUV AT THE OPPOSITE END OF THE STREET AND made my way toward the safe house. I looked all around as I moved, casually checking inside parked cars as I moved past them, looking up at dark windows with drawn curtains, scanning rooftops, eyeing vehicles as they drove past. I saw nothing to be worried about. But someone had to be here somewhere, watching, waiting for me to release the protectee.

Thunder rumbled in the distance. Closer than it had been before. The sky was getting darker. Then it opened up, and rain started falling. I looked forward and saw the safe house thirty yards ahead of me. I thought about the last time I'd been here. I vaguely remembered the layout and refamiliarized myself with it as I approached. I remembered what the downstairs looked like, the foyer, the kitchen, a side room. Bedrooms upstairs. I remembered how I'd entered it before. There was no way to get inside from the back. I turned and walked up to the door and stood underneath an awning, shielded temporarily from the rain.

There was a camera mounted in the corner, up and to

the left, watching me. I ignored it and used my knuckle to ring the doorbell, and I waited. Nothing happened for a minute. I rang the bell again and waited and felt someone watching me from the camera. So I glanced up at it and reached into my back pocket for my credentials and held them up to the lens and said, "My name is Blake Jordan. Homeland Security." I held my credentials there a moment longer; then I lowered my hand and stood patiently and kept waiting.

Then I sensed someone coming to the door, and a few seconds later, it was pulled open. A young guy somewhere in his early- to mid-twenties stared back at me. *A rookie.* "Can I help you?" the guy asked.

"My name is Blake Jordan," I said again and handed him my credentials. "I need to see the protectee."

"I don't know what you're talking about," he said, glancing down at my DHS badge, refusing to take it.

I stuffed my credentials back into my pocket and looked past the young man, into the house. "This is a safe house run by the FBI and used by all government agencies. Most recently by the CIA. Emma Ross, to be specific." My eyes moved back to the rookie. "She asked me to stop by to check on them. So let me in."

The guy thought about that for a moment; then he must've decided if it was true, he would've heard from her himself. "Sir, I told you, I don't know what you're talking about. I think you have the wrong address."

The guy had been given orders. That much was clear. I glanced down briefly and saw a firearm on his hip.

"Okay," I said, glancing up, deciding I'd have to play this differently. "My mistake. Sorry for the trouble."

The young man nodded and closed the door fast. I noticed there was no spy hole in it. Too risky for a safe house. A tool could be used against it to look inside the home. Or a bullet could be sent through it when light from inside disappeared and it was clear someone was looking outside. I waited there and counted to ten and punched in the code that Chris Reed had texted me. Six digits, six short beeps as I entered the numbers in. Then I heard the door unlock, and I grabbed my Glock and pushed the door open.

"Put your hands on your head!" I yelled as I stepped through.

The young man was at the end of the foyer, his back to me, on his way to the monitors to look outside at me. He hadn't made it. Instead he just froze in place and glanced over his shoulder and stared back at me.

I kept my right hand gripped on my weapon and used my left to close the door behind me. I looked all around the home, looking for who else was inside. But I saw no one else there. "Where are they?" I asked.

The rookie said nothing.

I took a step forward and rested the muzzle of my weapon against the side of his head. "Start talking."

"Upstairs," he finally answered.

I glanced across the room and saw the stairs along the left side of the wall. "What's your name?" I asked.

"Agent Matt Ryan," he said as he faced forward.

"Agent Ryan, I want you to slowly reach for your sidearm, and then I want you to set it down on the floor."

Ryan glanced back over his shoulder again, taking another look at me.

"Feeling brave?" I asked. "Are you thinking about making a move against me?"

"Who are you?"

"I told you already."

"If you're who you say you are, do this the right way. Call Emma Ross. Have her call me. Do this properly."

I glanced at my watch and said, "I don't have time for that. And neither do you. Now do what I asked."

He thought about it for a moment. Then he slowly reached for his sidearm and set it down on the floor. Ryan turned to face me as I kept my weapon trained on him, and he stared at me. "Don't do it," I said. "I know what you're thinking. You're planning your next move. You're deciding what you're going to do. You're thinking if you can catch me off guard, you can do something. Something heroic. That's a bad idea."

"Who are you?" he asked again. "And I don't mean your name."

"I'm a guy on a deadline." I glanced past him and looked at the stairs again. "Who is the protectee?"

The man named Ryan shrugged. "A whistleblower. That's all I know. And the less I know, the better."

"Take me upstairs," I said.

Ryan eyed me a moment longer. He was thinking hard about something. Deciding. Debating. Planning his next move. Maybe waiting for something. Maybe he was stalling for some reason. I told him again to let it go. I warned him against it. I told him I'd been at this a lot longer than he had. Then I thought about Jami. I told him I had nothing to lose. He nodded his consent and turned and walked toward the staircase.

I scanned left and right as we moved. We got to the stairs. The guy was moving slowly. He was taking longer than he needed to. "Keep moving," I said in a low, quiet voice, trying not to startle the protectee.

"What are you going to do to them?" he asked.

"Nothing."

"Then why are you here?"

"I just want to ask some questions."

Ryan said nothing.

"Keep moving," I said again, firmer this time. An order. Not a request. The guy was intentionally moving slowly. Taking his time. He nodded vaguely. Then an arm reached around my neck from behind. Ryan turned back and grabbed my gun.

I struggled to breathe.

Then the world faded away.

22

I BLINKED HARD AND LIFTED MY HEAD AND FOUND MYSELF IN A chair with two men sitting across from me. Same intense look to both of them. Agent Ryan and another man, same general age, maybe slightly older. A rookie and a guy who'd been around for a few years. Maybe showing the rookie the ropes. Maybe teaching the younger guy what to do. Maybe this was on-the-job training. Both of them were staring at me.

"Blake Jordan," said the man named Ryan. I glanced down and saw him holding my credentials. "That's what this says your name is. But who are you really?" He passed them to the other guy sitting to his left. He looked them over for a moment, then tossed them onto a coffee table next to my Glock and my phone.

"They're real," I said.

The guy next to Ryan shook his head. "Can't be," he said. "Someone who works for DHS wouldn't break into a CIA safe house and hold a federal agent at gunpoint. It just doesn't happen. It's uncalled for, really."

"I needed to talk to the person you have upstairs. The protectee. Your friend here wouldn't listen to me."

"He listened to you. He just didn't think he should let you. Neither do I. We don't take orders from you. That is, if you are who you say you are. But I have a feeling you're not. I have a feeling you're lying to us."

"I'm not."

"Really?" asked the older guy. "Why didn't you go through the proper channels, then?"

I said nothing.

"Why didn't you make a phone call like my partner suggested? These things have to come from the top down. That's how it works. If you were DHS, you'd know that. But like I said—" he paused "—you're not."

My heart was pounding in my chest. I looked around the room, trying to find a clock, but there was none. I wondered how long I had blacked out for. It couldn't have been more than a few minutes. I thought about my options. I weighed the pros and cons in my mind. Then I said, "Fine, call it in, then. Call DHS."

Agent Ryan stared at me briefly. Then he glanced to his left. He wanted his partner to do all of the talking. The older man stared a moment longer; then he smiled. "I don't have to call it in. Instead, I want you to tell me why you're here. In fact, I'm going to make you talk." He glanced at the rookie. There was something in the older guy's eyes. Something I didn't like. He faced me again and said, "I'll be right back."

The guy stood and disappeared, past my chair, into the kitchen. I heard him rummaging around in some of the drawers, looking for something. I tried to look over my shoulder, but I couldn't see what he was doing. So I turned back and stared straight ahead and said, "Agent Ryan, please. You have to believe me. Call Homeland Security. Ask for a man named Tom Parker. He'll vouch for me." I paused a moment, thinking. "Better yet, call Emma Ross. You say you only take orders from the top down. She'll confirm who I am."

Ryan said nothing.

I heard the guy finish up and start heading back. "Please, just make one phone call. Please call her now."

The other guy reappeared. He dismissed Ryan and told him to head upstairs and look after the protectee. He waited until the young guy disappeared; then he stared at me again. There was a knife in his hand.

"What's your name?" I asked.

"You first."

"You already know."

He smiled and moved his chair closer and placed it so it was only a few feet in front of me. Then he sat down. He looked at the knife and turned it from one side to the other. Then he glanced up and stared.

I said, "You want me to follow protocol, but look at what you're doing. You want me to think you're going to use that knife on me. Is that protocol? Is that what they teach you? Is that how you're supposed to handle a situation like this?"

No response.

"I know what you're doing. You think you're going to get information out of me. Before you call this in." I narrowed my eyes and stared back. "This was a first assignment for you, wasn't it? Years ago. And now you're tired of it. You're ready for a promotion, but you know you're a year or two out from one. So you're hoping to speed things up a bit." I paused. "You're making a mistake."

The guy laughed to himself. Then he stood and took two steps closer to me and punched me in the gut. The wind was knocked out of me, and there was a moment where I couldn't take a breath, then it passed, and I sucked air and looked up at him. He crouched and whispered in my ear, "Tell me why you're here."

"You're keeping someone upstairs," I said. "A protectee. Placed here by Emma Ross. I need to see them."

"Why?"

I sucked in air and struggled to breathe some more. Then I said, "I just need to ask them some questions."

"What questions?"

I said nothing.

"It's not a promotion I'm worried about," he said. "It's being demoted, or possibly even fired, for letting someone break into one of our safe houses. How do you think that would go over with my superiors?"

The guy balled his fist and pulled it back and punched me in the gut again; then he punched my face hard. I could taste blood in my mouth. The guy took a step back and sat down again. He stared across at me and pulled the knife out from a pocket and looked down at it again, admiring it. I said, "I can't tell you why I need to talk to them. For the same reason your friend upstairs wouldn't admit that this was a safe house when I came to the door. You have to believe me. My credentials are real. I work for Homeland Security."

The guy made no reply.

"How do you think I got inside? How do you think I knew the code to the door? I entered the way I did because your partner wouldn't cooperate. I need to talk to your protectee, and I'm running out of time. Please..."

"Here's the thing," he said as he moved his chair closer and placed the blade on my thigh, "even if you're who you say you are, I have a responsibility to question it. And like you said, you're my ticket out of here." He held onto the blade with a tight grip, and I felt the sharp tip tight against my jeans. He pressed harder. "What questions are you going to ask my protectee?"

I said nothing.

He pressed harder. "Start talking."

The tip of the blade punctured my jeans, and I felt a sharp pain in my thigh. I watched as a ring of crimson formed around the tip of the blade, and I winced in pain as I watched it grow wider by the second.

"Stop," called the rookie as he jogged down the stairs, holding a phone. "I have Emma Ross on the line."

23

THE OLDER GUY TURNED AND WATCHED OVER HIS SHOULDER AS the rookie approached with his arm extended. He had the phone call with Emma Ross still in progress. The rookie slowed as he got to us and held his hand out, waiting for the older guy to take it from him, which he did a few seconds later. "This is Mason," the older guy said. He stood and cradled the phone against his ear as he wiped his blade and put it away. "How long?" He listened another long moment. "Alright." The guy named Mason disconnected the call. He turned and looked at the guy named Ryan and ordered him back upstairs and waited for him to leave. Then he set the phone down on the table and came back over to where I was sitting and sat down again.

"What'd she say?" I asked.

He turned his head to one side and narrowed his eyes. "She gave me a description. Five eleven, short brown hair, hazel eyes. She said she was on her way. She wanted me to make sure we keep you here."

"How far out is she?"

"Why does it matter?"

"I need you to let me go."

"She'll be here in twenty minutes. We can talk about it then."

"I don't have twenty minutes."

Mason forced a smile. "Then I can't help you, can I?"

The guy named Mason nodded to himself. Then he stood up tall in front of me. My cell phone rang on the coffee table that was behind him, five feet away from where he stood. He turned and glanced at it briefly. Then he turned back to look at me. But before he did, I leaned forward and hooked my right foot behind his legs. I caught the back of his kneecap and pulled hard just as the guy was turning back to face me. He lifted his arms and stretched them out, trying to grab onto something that wasn't there, and fell back hard.

Mason hit the back of his head against one of the sharp corners of the coffee table. It caused a loud thud that I was sure could be heard throughout the rest of the quiet house and all the way upstairs. But nobody came down to investigate. Mason just collapsed onto the carpet and remained there, his chest rising and falling every couple of seconds as the man breathed hard. He was completely out. I didn't know how long I'd have until he'd come to, so I stood and walked to the kitchen and found the drawers he'd rummaged through. I turned backwards and opened them with my hands that were still zip-tied together behind my back. I pulled each drawer out until I found the knives. I took a paring knife and gripped it in my hand and sliced through the tie. I freed my hands and set the knife down. There was a collection of unused zip ties in one of the drawers I had gone through. There was a map on the counter. I massaged my wrists as I looked it over. I moved to the front, and I found a closet with coats and a single bulletproof Kevlar vest. No government identification on the coats.

I went back to the kitchen and saw Mason in the main room, still on the floor, still out of it. I thought some more. Then I grabbed a few of the zip ties, and I walked back to Mason. I turned him over on his stomach and tied his wrists behind his back the same way he'd tied mine. Then I reached for my credentials, phone, and gun, and stuffed them into my pockets. Then I took Mason's knife. I took the extra zip ties and looped them together and tied him to the coffee table. I kept a few more in my pocket. Then I reached for my Glock and aimed it up the stairs as I moved. I listened hard, but I heard nothing and saw nothing. Ryan wasn't there. I figured he was in one of the rooms with the protectee. I climbed the stairs and found a closed door. I gripped my weapon tight and used my free hand to try the doorknob. It was unlocked. I raised my Glock and kept it level and pushed the door open, and I stepped inside fast. Ryan was at a window, looking outside. And to his right was a woman staring at me.

Agent Ryan reached for his weapon. "Don't even think about it," I said, leveling my Glock at the man. But Ryan did think about it. Only for a moment. Then he changed his mind and raised his hands. "Turn around," I said, and Ryan did as I asked. The woman watched me from across the room. Her body was trembling. I moved closer and took the sidearm from the agent and carefully set it on the floor. Then I grabbed a zip tie and tossed it to the woman. "Tie his wrists together," I said. "Behind his back."

She stared at me for a moment. Then her eyes shifted to the agent; then they moved back over to me. She looked at the zip tie and did as I asked and stood back and stared at me some more. She was around my age. Mid-thirties, maybe. Dark features. Not American. I checked my watch: five minutes left.

I ordered Agent Ryan to move toward the bed, and I used another zip tie from my pocket to secure him to the bedpost. Then I took the woman by the arm and ushered her out of the room and to the stairs. But before we got to them, she pulled away from me and asked, "Who are you? Where are you taking me?"

"My name is Blake Jordan," I said as I reached into my back pocket and pulled out my credentials. "Department of Homeland Security."

She looked them over, then shifted her eyes back to mine. Then she turned and looked downstairs and saw the other agent on the floor, tied up, coming to. She turned back and asked, "Are you going to kill me?"

I narrowed my eyes. "No. Of course not."

"That man was protecting me; why did you use a zip tie on him?" She paused. "Why are you here?"

I stared back at her. "You tell me."

The woman said nothing.

I stared at her a moment longer. I stepped forward, and she stepped backward until she was up against a hallway wall. In a low voice I said, "My wife was kidnapped this morning. He's forcing me to do things for him. First he wanted me to hide a file from the FBI. Then he told me to come to this safe house and release you from it."

Her eyes grew wide. "You cannot release me," she said. "I am not a prisoner here. I'm being protected."

"I understand that."

"If they told you where to find me, then they know where I am. They're waiting out there. They'll kill me."

"They're not going to kill you. They're going to pick you up and take you away."

"They *are* going to kill me. Please, you have to believe me. He's lying."

"Maybe he is. But right now he has my wife, and I would do anything to keep her safe." I checked the time. Three minutes until the deadline. I looked at her and said, "I don't have much time. I need you to tell me who you are and why you're here."

She shook her head defiantly.

"Then tell me who the man blackmailing me is. So I can find him before he kills her."

She thought about it; then she shook her head again. I took her downstairs, past Mason, through the kitchen. Then I stopped and looked at the closet and checked the time again. Two minutes after that, we stepped outside. I told her to wait where she was. She was shaking uncontrollably. I promised her she'd be okay as I walked to my car.

Thirty seconds after that, I heard a gunshot.

24

I TURNED BACK FAST AND SAW THE WOMAN ON THE CONCRETE, in front of the safe house, thirty yards ahead of me. I looked up and saw a man on a rooftop across the street from the safe house. He had a rifle in his hand. That much was clear. He stood there for a brief moment, watching, making sure the woman wasn't moving. Then he glanced in my direction and saw me looking up at him, and then he disappeared. I hesitated for a moment, torn between running into the building to try to find the guy and going back to my vehicle. Thinking it through, I realized the man with the rifle had the upper hand. I'd learned as a SEAL years before to always take the high ground. The guy would most likely be taking the stairs. At some point he might change to the elevator or vice versa. Either way, there'd be a car waiting for him. I could follow them. But then I thought about the woman. She wasn't moving. She was still crumpled up in a heap on the doorstep of the safe house, perfectly still. The car would most certainly drive by to check on her. Maybe they'd even send another bullet into her before speeding off. Close range. As insurance.

Not much time had passed. Twenty seconds. Maybe thirty. Pedestrians were confused, still trying to understand what had happened, just standing around holding umbrellas and noticing the lifeless body in front of the building. I made my decision, and I ran, not toward the safe house but toward my parked SUV. I climbed in fast and started the motor and stomped hard on the accelerator. I didn't even bother with the door. It closed on its own as the vehicle lurched forward, and I drove toward the woman. She still wasn't moving. People were running toward her, finally realizing what had happened. I stopped in front of the safe house and unlocked the doors and climbed out. I jogged around the hood and checked her for a pulse.

"Is she okay?" an older gentleman asked, and I shook my head.

"No," I said as I knelt underneath the awning. "I need to get her to the hospital. Open the door for me."

He moved over to my parked vehicle and opened the passenger-side door. I crouched and placed my hand on my thigh and the blood that had pooled around it. I smeared it on the concrete. Then I grabbed the woman with two hands and picked her up. The jacket covered her body. It was soft to the touch. Her head hung lifelessly as I stood and moved over to my SUV and set her inside and told the guy thanks. I closed the door and ran to the driver's door and climbed back inside. I rammed the gear shift into drive and stomped on the accelerator again. There was a narrow opening between two idling cars. Their drivers had alarmed expressions on their faces. My tires spun, and I accelerated hard and drove fast in between them. My cell phone started ringing. I glanced to my right. The woman's eyes were closed. I said, "This is Jordan."

"Where are you taking her?" a voice asked. The voice of Jami's kidnapper.

"You didn't tell me you were going to kill her." I paused. "She's bleeding out. She's not going to make it."

The man said nothing.

"You told me to release her and your people would pick her up. That was the deal. You lied to me."

"Mr. Jordan, had I told you my intentions from the start, would you have followed through?"

"You know I would've," I said, thinking about Jami. I drove on a moment longer and said, "Who is she?"

"That is not something you need to be concerned with." He paused a moment. I heard another cell phone ring on his end. He said, "Mr. Jordan, I will call you back soon with your next assignment. Be ready for it."

I pulled my phone away and saw the call had ended. I set it down and checked the rearview, then the side mirrors. Nobody was following. I turned to my right to look at the woman, and I said, "I think it worked."

THE WOMAN STAYED PERFECTLY STILL BUT OPENED HER EYES and looked at me. "Are you sure?" she asked.

I checked the mirrors again and made a sharp turn and accelerated. "I don't see anyone following us."

"Where are you taking me?"

"They probably think I'm driving you to the hospital," I said. "There's one less than a mile away from us."

She felt around her stomach and winced in pain. She said, "I don't think I need a hospital."

"I know that, but they don't. So I'm just going to drive around so they lose the trail. They're going to drive to the hospital. They'll circle the lot for a while, looking for my vehicle. The next time I talk to the guy, I'll make it sound like I didn't stay long. I'll make it sound like I ran into the ER, like I carried you inside and left you there, and then I got out quick. They won't know for sure."

"You think they'll look for me? Inside the hospital?"

"They will, but they won't find you. I'll take care of it. Unless they have access to the morgue, it'll be fine."

She thought about that and asked, "Is it okay to move yet?"

I checked the mirrors one more time. "Yes, just stay low."

She grew quiet and stared at me some more. Then she straightened up and unzipped her coat. Underneath it was the Kevlar vest I'd seen inside the closet in the safe house. She removed it and threw the vest along with the coat into the back seat and ran her fingers through her hair, then sat back. Then she stared at me again. She didn't speak for a long moment; then she said, "They could've killed me."

"They did kill you. That's what we need to make them think."

"I mean, they could've shot me. In the face."

"They wouldn't have."

"How do you know?"

I turned to look at her for a moment before I moved my gaze back to the road. "Because I was a sniper. When I was in the Navy. I was in one of the SEAL teams. I didn't go for a headshot if we needed an ID."

She said nothing. I noticed her fingers trembling. She balled her hands into fists and crossed her arms. "You should have left me in the safe house. That's why they put me there, to keep me safe from them."

"They were coming for you one way or another. If I hadn't gotten you out, they would've gone in for you."

She thought about that a long moment. Then she said, "Who are you?"

"My name is Blake Jordan. I'm a federal agent. What I told you inside the safe house is true. The people who want you dead took my wife. The man who just called me has her." I glanced right. "Who are *you?*"

She took a deep breath and let it out. "My name is Miriam Hassan. I'm a CIA informant. A whistleblower."

25

I KEPT DRIVING, TAKING MORE TURNS EVERY COUPLE OF BLOCKS down busy streets. I reached for my cell and called Morgan Lennox. He answered immediately, and I said, "Morgan, I need you to do me a huge favor."

"What is it, mate?"

"Do you think you could access records from one of the local hospitals?"

"With one arm tied behind my back. Which one?"

"George Washington University. I need you to fake a record for me. The name is Miriam Hassan."

Morgan said nothing.

"Make it look like she was admitted ten minutes ago for a gunshot wound to the chest. Have it say a man fitting my description brought her in and left her there. Make it so she was pronounced dead on arrival. Morgan, it needs to look like she's in the morgue, waiting on someone to claim her body, okay?"

"Doing it now."

"Thanks," I said.

"Blake, I just received word that something may be

changing with where the two presidents are going to sign the peace treaty. I'm hearing the location may be in question. Have you talked to Tom Parker lately?"

"No."

"Well, just a heads-up that the FBI and Metro PD have stopped building a perimeter around the building."

"Thanks," I said again and disconnected the line.

I checked the mirrors and saw nothing concerning, so I pulled to the side of the road and put the gear shift into park. I turned and stared at the woman sitting next to me. I said, "How do you know Emma Ross?"

Hassan said nothing.

"You said you were a CIA informant. A whistleblower. So what's the connection?"

"I'm not supposed to talk about it."

"Yeah, well, I'm not supposed to talk about my situation either. But I've had to take a risk here and there."

"It's different for me. If I talk, I'm dead."

"You're dead already, as far as they know." I sat there for a spell, waiting. But it was clear she wasn't going to talk. So I faced forward and stared out the windshield. "You gave the CIA information. You feared for your life. In exchange for the information, Emma Ross said they'd keep you safe while she tried to figure out what she was going to do with you."

Hassan said nothing.

"She gave you options. She could relocate you within the United States. Send you to a place like Nebraska or Utah. Give you a new name and a new backstory. But in the end, you were against it. You'd stick out like a sore thumb. You knew it, and she agreed with you. Therefore she's coordinating safe passage to your home country, which I'm guessing is Qatar. Or maybe Afghanistan." I turned and saw her eyeing me. Then she looked away, deciding what to share. My phone buzzed. It was Emma Ross. I declined the call. Then Parker called me. I didn't answer.

Then after a long moment she said, "My husband and I came to the US a few years ago. He worked at the university. I overheard a conversation a week ago. I decided to come forward."

"What did your husband say that concerned you?"

"It wasn't him who said it. It was the people on the other end of the line. There were late night phone calls. Which made me suspicious. One night I heard his phone ring, so I snuck out of the bedroom and listened. I expected to hear a woman, but it was a man's voice. It was tinny, but I could hear it clearly. He wanted my husband to drive a truck full of explosives and leave it parked somewhere." Miriam Hassan looked at me for a brief moment to judge my reaction. I nodded for her to go on. "He told him no."

"Then what happened?"

"I went back to bed. I waited for a long time with my eyes closed and faced away, just listening, waiting. But he never came to bed. I figured he was downstairs thinking about it. Maybe even considering it. Eventually, I fell asleep. But when I woke up the next morning, he was gone. I tried calling him on his phone, but he didn't answer. After a few hours, I got worried, and I called the police. Metro PD said I had to wait twenty-four hours. So at midnight I was about to call them again, but they knocked on my front door. They knew about the phone call. They questioned me. I didn't know what to do, so I told them everything."

"So they called the CIA?"

"No, they called DDC first. They came out and interviewed me a few hours later. I told them what I knew. They went and traced the call and were able to confirm it originated overseas. So they brought in the CIA."

"Emma Ross," I said.

Hassan nodded. "She said she was with the team that oversaw the various DDC field offices. She said they were like a liaison between domestic terrorism threats and the kind of threats the CIA deals with overseas. She said she reported to the deputy director of operations himself. She had some people talk to me, and I told them what I had overheard. She promised to keep me safe."

"Did they figure out who your husband had been talking to?"

She shook her head. "Not yet. They're looking into it. But I heard the voice again. On the phone."

"When?"

She stared at me. "Two minutes ago. The man you received a phone call from. I think it's the same voice."

My cell phone rang again. "This is Jordan," I said, answering it.

"Mr. Jordan, you did well, although attempting to save the woman's life was not helpful to our cause." Hassan was listening to the voice and nodded at me slowly. *It's the same voice*, her nod was telling me.

"She didn't make it, you son of a bitch. She was bleeding out." I paused. "Why'd you have to kill her?"

"Mr. Jordan, I suggest you focus. There are more tasks I need you to do for me."

"Let me talk to her," I said, thinking about Jami. "Before I do anything else."

"Later," the voice said; then the call was disconnected. I held onto my cell phone and looked to my right.

Hassan stared at me as I sat in silence, deciding what I should do next. I checked for traffic and pulled out and gunned it hard as I headed back to the NAC.

No more games. No more lies. It was time to come clean.

26

I PULLED INTO THE NEBRASKA AVENUE COMPLEX TWENTY
minutes later. Miriam Hassan stayed low in her seat the
whole time. She didn't need to. I told her nobody was
following us, but she insisted and said she felt safer that
way. We got to the guardhouse, and the guy looked inside
my SUV, then looked back at me. Hassan had no identification on her. I explained to the guy that she was with me, and
he could call upstairs later and talk to Parker, after I met
with him, and he would vouch for her. I explained how the
woman had been in hiding with the help of Emma Ross. He
nodded toward the parking lot and said that Ross was here. I
turned to Hassan. We shared a look. Then he let me inside
and said he'd call Parker now, not later.

As I pulled into the lot and parked my SUV, the sky
opened up. It was a light sprinkle at first; then after thirty
seconds, it turned into a full-on downpour. I reached back
and grabbed the coat and gave it to her. I said we needed to
head to the main building. Hassan wasn't convinced that we
were safe. There wasn't anything shielding us from someone
out on the street taking a shot at us. And she was right. The

NAC was a different kind of government building. Instead of being in the heart of DC's concrete jungle, its sprawling campus was scattered across thirty-eight acres of lush green grass. I promised her we'd be okay and said again that we needed to move, so she put the coat on, opened her door, sat up, and climbed out. Then we hustled toward the main door and headed up to the second floor, where Parker was waiting.

"What the hell's going on?" he asked as soon as the elevator doors opened. Behind him, Simon Harris stood with his arms crossed, head tilted, eyeing me closely. The same look he'd given me earlier as I left.

"We need to talk," I said.

"Damn right we need to talk." Parker shifted his gaze to his left. To Miriam Hassan. "Who the hell is she?"

"Parker, let's go to a conference room. Please."

He furrowed his brow and paused a moment longer; then he turned and nodded at Simon Harris. Simon swiped his badge to unlock the door and pulled it open. Then he motioned for us to step inside.

"Come on," I said, grabbing Hassan's arm and pointing inside. We walked through, and Parker followed us in, and Simon followed Parker. I stepped back into the conference room we'd met in earlier that morning. Inside, at the far end of the table in the dimly lit room, sat Emma Ross herself, alone, leaning back in her chair, watching us, biting her fingernails. I figured after she'd arrived at the safe house and Hassan and I weren't there, she had decided to come back to the NAC to talk to Parker. Ross stared at me; then she shifted her eyes to Miriam Hassan and left them on her, watching as she sat down next to me. Parker waited for Simon to step inside; then he closed the door hard. The entire glass perimeter of the room shook as a result, swaying back and forth for ten long seconds until it stopped. Parker took a seat at the head of the table. Simon remained standing along the far wall by the door and crossed his arms again.

"You have some explaining to do," Parker said as he glanced at Emma, then shifted his eyes back to me. "You abandon your assignment; you take out two CIA agents; you ignore my phone calls—start talking."

I looked at each of them in turn. Then I said, "What I'm about to tell you must stay in this room."

Parker said nothing. Just continued to stare along with Simon, his daughter, and Miriam Hassan.

I went on to explain everything that had happened over the last several hours. Why Jami wasn't at the meeting that morning, the phone call I received, Lynne May showing up at my home, and the video of Jami's kidnapping I had found. I told them all about the phone calls from her kidnapper, how he'd given me proof of life but had made it perfectly clear that if I didn't follow his every command, he would kill her.

When I was through, my cell phone rang again in my pocket. "It's him," I said as I looked at the screen. After a brief moment of silence, Parker pointed at my phone and told me to answer it on speakerphone.

"Yes," I said.

The voice said, "I've confirmed the woman is dead. You should've left her body in front of the safe house. We had planned on picking it up. Now there will be questions. You've complicated things, Mr. Jordan."

"And now you've complicated things for me," I replied. "Those two agents are going to come forward. I'm sure they have me on video surveillance. They'll call their superiors. I won't be able to do any more tasks for you once they pick me up. Did you even consider that?"

No reply.

"I want to talk to my wife."

"You will have your chance."

"No," I said. "I want to talk to her now."

"I have another task for you, Mr. Jordan."

"I'm not doing another damn thing for you unless you put her on the phone right now."

Parker raised an eyebrow. Emma Ross stared. Miriam Hassan furrowed her brow and looked away.

We heard muffled sounds, like the man had pulled the phone away from his face and pressed it to his chest. We heard him order a muted command. Then thirty seconds later she was on. "Blake?" she called.

"Are you okay?"

"Two hostiles, large warehouse," she managed to get out before the kidnapper pulled the phone away.

There were more sounds, grunts, a muted scream from Jami. Her kidnapper said, "She'll pay for that."

"If you touch her, I'll kill you."

"And if you don't want me to kill her, you will find a way to stay active, out in the field. Take care of the surveillance footage if there is some. Buy yourself some time. Your biggest assignment is coming up."

With that, the call was disconnected. Miriam Hassan turned back. Her mind was racing. I imagined her hearing the man's voice and memories of her husband rushing back to her. Emma looked at Parker; then she turned to face me. "You helped me with Elizabeth," she said. "Back in Chicago. The least I can do is help you." She paused. "I'll take care of the surveillance footage. And I'll tell the CIA guys to keep quiet."

"Thank you," I said.

She told Hassan to go with her, and they left the room. Simon followed and left in a hurry, like he'd just thought of something. When the door closed, Parker said, "Jordan, when the hell are you going to start trusting people? We spend more time together than we do with others, more than with our own families. The president is trusting us to build this team, and before we can do that, we need to be a cohesive unit. Didn't they teach you that in the Navy? We sure as hell learned it in the Army. We had to become a family. We don't need to know everything about each other, but if you can't trust me, who the hell can you trust?"

I said nothing.

Then the door to the conference room opened fast. Simon entered, carrying his laptop with him. The door closed slowly on its hinges as he walked around the table and sat down. "I tracked you down," he said. "Using Stingray. And I retasked a satellite over to the safe house. Maybe we can use it to find the sniper."

27

JAMI JORDAN WAS BEING HELD TIGHT BY ONE OF THE MEN. HE had one arm wrapped around her body and a hand covering her mouth. When her kidnapper disconnected the call, he walked over to them and stared for a moment, then nodded to the door, signaling for his man to let her go and give them the room. His man obeyed and left them alone. Jami turned and eyed him for a long moment and clenched her fists as he moved to the door. She watched him disappear as her kidnapper took two steps closer to her. "Your husband asked for proof of life; otherwise he wouldn't do any more tasks. You made a mistake in telling him how many of us there are and where you're being held. Tell me, how many warehouses do you think there are in DC?" He shook his head. "He won't find you in time. We only have a few hours to go, anyway."

"He'll find me," she said. "And then he'll kill you. He'll kill all of you. And if he doesn't do it, I will."

He smiled. "He won't kill me. I will kill him after I take out the two most powerful men in the world."

Jami narrowed her eyes. "What are you talking about?"

"What are we doing here? What do you think this is all about? What do you think the end game is?"

Jami said nothing. Just kept her eyes fixed on the man, watching him closely, thinking about it.

"What is happening today?" he pressed.

She made no reply and slowly shook her head, trying to understand the question. Jami watched as the man's expression shifted from anger and rage to an expression of disbelief.

"You don't know, do you? Today your president and my president are signing a treaty. It's supposed to be a secret. It's the reason why Stepanov traveled all this way to America. That's not what the news is reporting, though. They don't know. Not yet, anyway. But they will soon. And once that treaty is signed, my home country will start the process of getting rid of its weapons of mass destruction. We will be completely defenseless and relying on a piece of paper signed by one American that could simply be ripped up by another man four years later."

"That wouldn't happen."

"It's happened before. Every four to eight years, does it not? One party comes into power and promises an end to wars happening in foreign lands. They pull out troops; they sign treaties; they make deals. Then within a year or two, Americans feel their country has swung too far and must go in a new direction. Two years after that, the other party comes into power, and everything swings back. Round and round we go."

"You think you can stop the treaty from being signed?" she asked. "How?"

"Simple. You kill both presidents. Before it's signed. You send a direct message. A message that says don't try this again. A message to both countries and their citizens. A message that makes both parties question their own misguided beliefs. Weapons of mass destruction are necessary. They keep adversaries in check."

"You're insane."

"Am I?"

"Killing a president isn't easy, let alone two of them."

He smiled again. "I have a man on the inside. And your husband is going to make sure they carry out the task."

28

I STOOD FROM MY CHAIR AND WALKED OVER TO WHERE SIMON was sitting. Parker did the same. Both of us stood behind the analyst as he navigated a series of programs on his laptop screen. "Explain," said Parker.

"Mr. Parker, before Emma arrived, I used some of my downtime in between assignments to figure out what was going on. I used the Bureau's Stingray program to track down both cell phones, Jami's and Blake's. Jami's was offline. Blake's wasn't. I used the program a second time and found him at an address I recognized from somewhere. I looked it up in our internal directory and confirmed the address was a safe house used by the FBI and the CIA. You were on the phone, talking to Peter Mulvaney, and I didn't want to interrupt you. So I took it upon myself to retask one of our satellites."

"And you left it there?" asked Parker.

Simon nodded.

"What are you saying?" I asked, realizing Simon was the one Jami's kidnapper had seen tracking her.

"I may be able to rewind the video feed from the satellite and find out where the sniper went."

We watched as Simon gained access to the satellite he had repositioned. The screen changed, and an aerial view of the downtown Washington streets came into view. Simon took a sip of his Mountain Dew and set the can down on the table. Then he reached for a composition notebook he'd brought from his cubicle and thumbed through it as he mentioned how Morgan Lennox had taught him what he was trying to do.

After another minute of flipping through the pages, Simon said he'd found what he was looking for and set the notebook down on his desk to the left of him and kept the pages open so he could reference them. Then he navigated various settings on the virtual control panel that handled the live feed coming from the satellite. The front of the safe house was clearly in view. Metro PD officers had patrol cars parked out front. Black government SUVs were blocking the street, and I saw officers entering and exiting the safe house and a few crouched down in front, studying the blood I'd left smeared on the sidewalk. Onlookers holding umbrellas were pointing up, toward the tall buildings across the street. Simon zoomed out more, and a broader view of the landscape appeared. Cars were running north and south and east and west. Simon referenced his notebook, then he turned back and clicked on something, and the live video feed paused. The vehicles stopped moving. The law enforcement officers and onlookers, who had been large enough on the screen to make out, now looked like tiny ants on sidewalks. Now they were frozen in time, midstride.

"Got it," said Simon as he clicked an icon on the navigation pane, and the video rewound slowly, and then he panned out a little bit more to broaden the view as the clock ran backwards, slowly, a minute at a time.

"Slow down," I said as I checked the timestamp on the screen. "You're almost there."

"I know what I'm doing," he replied as he zoomed in a little more.

The three of us watched as cars moved in reverse and people walked backwards on the street. I saw myself come into view. I drove backwards and stopped in front of the safe house. I climbed out and jogged around the hood and went to the passenger door. An older man opened it for me. I then pulled Miriam Hassan out and laid her on the concrete in front of the building she'd been hiding in. A second later, I stood and ran backwards to my car. I got inside and reversed it to its previous position down the street. Simon slowed the video some. I walked backwards to the entrance, and Hassan and I disappeared inside.

"Okay," I said as Simon paused the video. "Play it and be ready to stop the tape when I tell you to."

Simon nodded his understanding. He found the play button and clicked on it. There was a brief moment where nothing happened. Then Miriam Hassan exited the building, wearing a thick coat, with me directly behind her. We spoke for a moment. I was giving her instructions. I was telling her to stand there and wait. I told her I'd keep an eye on her. And I promised I'd come back for her if something did happen. Then I left her on the steps of the safe house, and I turned left and headed back toward my parked vehicle.

I leaned in and looked to the left of the screen. Rooftops from the buildings across the street were in view. On a sunny day they'd be white and shining and easy to see a man on top of them. But it was an overcast day. Drizzling rain continually falling all around. The rooftops were gray and hard to make anything out aside from large square air conditioners. I was still able to make out a dark figure crouched down small alongside the edge closest to the safe house, tracking me as I moved, watching, waiting to take the shot.

"There he is," I said, pointing at what I was looking at.

Parker leaned in closer to the screen and squinted. Simon nodded as he saw the figure and kept the video playing. I watched as Hassan stayed still, arms to her sides, looking left and right down the street, waiting for someone to stop by and pick her up as I'd promised would happen. Inside the house, she had insisted that someone was going to kill her. I brushed it off, but she grabbed my arms and held on tight. She was shaking uncontrollably. So I put the Kevlar vest I'd seen earlier on her and then the raincoat on top of that, and I told her I'd be down the street watching if anything happened. That didn't make her feel better. She tried to pull away from me. But I thought about Jami and what would happen if I didn't go through with completing the task. So I grabbed her and brought her outside and pulled the door shut, locking her out before I left her there. I watched myself move away from Hassan. When I was halfway between where she stood and where I parked, I saw her get hit and fall to the ground. People walking the streets stood in shock, as did I. Then I ran for my SUV.

"Lock it in," said Parker as he pointed at the dark figure on the rooftop.

"Done," said Simon, pausing the video and clicking on an icon in the menu that looked like a target, then clicking on the image of the man. He clicked on the play button again, and it took a second for the algorithm to kick in, then the video started again, and an icon that looked similar to the concentric rings inside a target appeared. It moved along with the sniper as he stayed crouched where he was for a few seconds, watching intently, making sure Hassan wasn't moving, maybe watching me to see what I'd do. Then he got up and slung his rifle over his shoulder and hustled to an access door, and he disappeared.

"What now?" asked Parker.

Simon told him to wait. We waited thirty seconds, then a full minute. I imagined the sniper going down the stairs, avoiding elevators. Then he emerged behind the building. The target overlay reappeared and tracked the man as he walked to a parked car. Simon paused the video again and zoomed out on the feed and pressed play and reapplied the target to the vehicle. "Got him," he said, looking up at me with a smile.

PARKER AND I CONTINUED TO WATCH OVER SIMON'S shoulder, but we no longer stared in silence. Instead we discussed what was happening and what our next move should be, should Simon be able to track this guy all the way back to wherever he had driven to. Simon insisted he was more than capable of doing that. For years he'd relied on Morgan Lennox's help, first at DDC, then here at DHS. Now he was trying to prove himself, I figured. Simon's cell phone rang, and he answered it as he sat in front of his laptop, which was still playing the feed. It was Morgan. I recognized the voice and the accent as he spoke urgently to Simon, communicating something he needed to know right away. Simon said he understood and hung up.

"Mr. Parker, DDC has just been advised the location of the peace treaty signing is likely going to change."

"About damn time," he said. "That's what Mulvaney and

I were discussing. We've been trying to convince them to change the venue for hours." He paused for a moment. "They need to have it at the White House."

"Is there a concern with the Pullman House?" I asked.

Simon shook his head slowly. "I'm not sure what happened. I guess we'll know more soon."

Nobody spoke for a long moment as we continued to watch the screen. Simon clicked on something, and he pinned the target to the center of the screen, and the landscape started to pan along with it as it moved. Parker glanced over to me and eyed me for a brief moment. He said, "What are you going to do, Jordan?"

I said nothing. I didn't need to. He knew what I was going to do. *I'm going to get her back*, I thought.

"What about the peace treaty? What about the active threat we have going on? I need you there on-site."

I looked at him for a moment before lowering my gaze back down to the laptop. "I agree with you," I said. "They need to hold the ceremony in a secure location. And you're right, the White House is the best option. I trust Agent Rivera. And I trust Chris Reed and Mark Reynolds. They can watch the perimeter for any issues and be on-site should anything happen. Rivera and his Secret Service team will man the inside. With Metro PD helping the FBI, you can't ask for more than that if you want things to be safe and secure."

"I'm going to need you with the president," he said. "That's nonnegotiable. I don't care how good Rivera's team is, I want you there. Keller is always our first priority." Parker checked his watch and shook his head. "Depending on when they want to do the signing, you might not have enough time to go after this guy."

"I can do both," I said as I kept my eyes fixed to the screen and Simon fast-forwarded the tape.

Parker rubbed his hand along his face and looked away, thinking hard, trying to understand something. He said, "Why do you think she was taken, Jordan? Why her? And why today of all days? The same damn day we have an active threat against one, maybe even two presidents? Have you thought about that at all?"

"Yes," I said as we watched the vehicle Simon was tracking exit the highway in Bethesda and turn south.

Parker didn't ask any more questions. Nobody spoke, and silence filled the large expanse of the conference room as I crossed my arms and stared at the screen, watching the sniper slow as he took surface roads. Then a large complex came into view. A warehouse. Simon clicked on something in the navigation pane, and the view zoomed in. Then several more small buildings appeared scattered behind it. I figured either it was abandoned or employees had left for the day. The man parked as Simon zoomed in even further, and we watched him step out, look all around, then move towards the building. Simon turned in his chair and looked up at Parker. Parker turned to look at me. "I'm going to get her back," I said. "You have a lot going on here. I know that. It's hard for me to ask, but I need your support."

Parker nodded. "We have some time until we find out what's happening with the signing. Simon, I want you to keep watch for us with the satellite." Parker offered his hand, and I shook it. "Go get her, Jordan."

29

I GOT ON THE HIGHWAY AND HEADED NORTH AND WEST, towards Bethesda. Simon checked in with me as I drove to let me know that something had changed. The vehicle the sniper had taken was still parked where the guy had left it. Nobody else had arrived, and nobody had left. But there was another vehicle on the north side of the building he hadn't noticed before. That meant there were two entrances, one from the north and one from the south. I told him I was halfway there and to keep his eyes on the screen. He said the satellite he was using had infrared capabilities. He just needed a few minutes to figure out how to apply the filter. I told him to check with Morgan if he felt he couldn't do it in time. I didn't want to take any chances. Simon told me I needed to trust him. He'd figure it out and would let me know if anything changed. I saw another call was coming through from Chris Reed, so I thanked him and answered the call.

"Hey, man, you okay?" asked Chris.

"Yeah," I said. "We think we found her."

"Where?"

"A warehouse in Bethesda. I'm headed there now."

"You're going alone?"

"I have to," I said. "You and Reynolds are tied up downtown, and Parker had to stay back. We're hearing the venue may be changing, so he needs to be ready in case Mulvaney calls him back with further details."

"It is changing; Mulvaney just called me. He told us to hold off on putting any more effort into the perimeter; he's not sure where the new location is going to be, so we're standing down for now." I exited the highway and followed the directions the GPS system was telling me. Chris didn't speak for a long moment. Then he said, "If you need anything, just call me. Even if I have to ignore Mulvaney's orders, I'll help you."

"Thanks," I said, and I told him I'd be in touch as I disconnected the call and turned onto a dirt road.

I looked at the map on the GPS system. It said I was one mile out. My heart was beating hard in my chest. I thought about Jami being beaten. I thought about the last thing she'd said to me, telling me there were two men inside the warehouse where she was being held. The sniper would make three. Three of them and one of me. I didn't like the odds, but I'd come against odds worse than that before. So had Jami. She'd risked another beating by relaying what she knew to me. I thought about the odds again. The truth was I'd go in to get her even if there were a hundred guys inside.

My thoughts drifted back to my first wife, Maria. She'd been killed on the streets of Chicago in what I first thought was nothing more than a random act of violence and later understood was an intentional killing. I'd long since found and taken care of the people responsible, but the pain never really left. Even after I met Jami, and even after we were married. There was and always would be a nagging feeling in my gut, a feeling that I could have stopped it from happening somehow. I never had a chance to save her. I thought about that as my mind raced, and I planned what I'd need to do when I got to the warehouse. I looked at the GPS as it announced I was half a mile out from my destination. My phone rang, and I answered it.

"This is Jordan," I said, seeing it was Simon calling me.

"They're on the move," he said. "They're headed right toward you, Blake. Two of them got into a car."

I stepped on the brakes. "There's nowhere to go, Simon," I said as I looked out through my windshield.

"Well, you need to do something. I can see both of you on my screen. You're stopped now, and a black car is heading straight for you. And it's moving fast. Hang on, let me zoom in a little and see what you can do."

"I can't do anything except pass them or drive backwards half a mile."

"Hang on. Okay, there's a little alcove about twenty yards ahead of you. You need to turn right into that."

I pressed the phone against my ear and let my foot off of the brakes. My vehicle didn't move. I tapped the gas gently and felt the tires spinning on the mud, but nothing was happening. I put it in reverse, and somehow, that worked. My vehicle rolled backward; then I slammed it into drive. There was a brief hesitation as the tires reversed; then I lurched forward. Up ahead I saw what looked like a small opening. I turned the wheel to the left and made a wide right turn into it. As I did, I caught a glimpse of the black vehicle Simon was telling me about up ahead. I pulled in through an opening between an overgrowth of trees and bushes. I heard scratching all around my SUV as I squeezed in slowly. Then I hit something in front of me, and I couldn't go any farther. The vehicle wouldn't move. I tapped the accelerator gently, then I pushed down harder, but nothing happened. I kept the phone pressed to my ear and turned to look over my shoulder and said, "I'm in as far as I can go. There are tree branches covering the back of my SUV."

"It's not enough," he called. "I can see the back of your SUV still. They're going to pass you soon, Blake."

I faced forward and set the phone down. I put the gear shift in reverse and backed out a few feet. Then I slammed it into drive, and I stomped on the gas pedal. The wheels spun for a brief moment over fallen leaves and mud and underbrush, then they caught and my SUV moved forward and thumped over what must've been a small fallen tree, because my two front tires cleared it with the added speed, and I was able to drive another five or six feet farther into the brush. Branches completely covered the back window. I moved the gear shift to park and killed the motor and waited. I couldn't see anything but faint daylight.

Then it happened. I saw the car pass through the rearview, left to right. Nothing but a dark shadow. Then I heard Simon calling for me. I picked up the phone, and he said, "I think you did it; they just passed you."

"Is that other vehicle still on the north side?"

"Yes, it is."

"Do you have the infrared going? I need to know where to go when I get inside." No response. "Simon?"

"I'm working on it," he said. "I'll have to call Morgan, I guess. Stay on the line, and I'll patch him in."

The line went quiet and, as I waited, I saw another call was coming through. An unknown caller. The kidnapper. Either the guy in the building half a mile north of me, or one of the guys in the vehicle half a mile south. I tapped my thumb on the button to take the call and brought the cell to my ear. "Yes?" I said.

"Mr. Jordan, my sources are telling me the peace treaty signing is no longer happening downtown."

I said nothing.

"If that's true, then we're going to have to speed things up. I want you to meet my associate in thirty minutes. He's going to deliver something to you. Something instrumental to your next assignment."

I thought about the timing. I turned my head left, instinctively, in the direction of the warehouse. It was hidden from the brush and overgrowth from where I sat inside the alcove. "I can't do it in thirty minutes."

"You will," he ordered, but I didn't respond. "Mr. Jordan, I don't need to remind you that you're not in a position to negotiate with me. I have your whole life in the palm of my hand. At any time, all I have to do is clench my fist and you'll have nothing." He paused. "Head downtown. I'll call you soon."

30

"YOU STILL THERE, MATE?" ASKED MORGAN AS I SWITCHED back to the other line, and I found a Bluetooth earpiece and put it in.

"Yes," I said as I adjusted the earpiece and slid my phone into a pocket and reached for my Glock.

"While you were gone, I helped Simon apply the infrared filter to the satellite feed. We can see three people inside the warehouse. Two on the south side and one closer to the north, near the parked vehicle."

Simon added, "The two on the south side are stationary. Morgan and I think one of them may be Jami."

"Two prisoners," I said, thinking it through. I thought about the surveillance footage from outside my home that I'd watched. I figured they were right; one of them was Jami, and after another moment I realized the other was the delivery guy I'd seen in the video. "Do we know anything about the UPS driver?"

Simon said, "Actually, I looked into that the moment I left the conference room earlier. Before I had the idea of the satellite and using it to track down the sniper." He paused.

"His name is Bob Miller. There's nothing on him. The guy's totally clean. No record at all, no questionable known associates or affiliations. Seems to have just been in the wrong place at the wrong time. The company already contacted authorities. Metro PD visited the facility to talk to the manager. They found the GPS dumped on the side of the road."

I drove on. I had initially thought I'd leave my SUV in the alcove. Half a mile wasn't far. I could get to the warehouse in five or ten minutes if I hurried. Then I thought about the car that had driven by me. I wasn't sure if Jami's kidnapper was sitting in the vehicle and had left one of his men behind to keep watch, or if the man who called me was in the warehouse and had sent two of his henchmen out to meet me. I decided I'd be better off taking the chance with driving up next to the warehouse and being out in the open than leaving my vehicle all the way out here, hidden, a long way back. Plus I'd have Jami with me. Plus we'd have to trek through mud and the rain. I started the motor and put the gear shift in reverse and asked Simon and Morgan to keep their eyes out for me. I didn't want to be caught off guard if the men in the car changed their minds and came driving back toward me.

I stomped on the gas, and my wheels spun like they'd done before. But this time, instead of struggling to catch onto the dirt road with all of the mud everywhere, they were spinning on dead leaves and fallen branches and underbrush. Then they touched the log I had run over, and they caught, and my SUV bumped over it. I moved backwards fast. The hanging branches scraped my vehicle again as I reversed back onto the road, and I jerked the wheel to the right to straighten out. Then I slammed the gear shift into drive and stepped on the gas. Simon said he could see me again and talked me through the approach to the building.

There was a large fence surrounding the place. I pulled up tight against a gate and noticed a padlock on it. For a second I considered backing up and ramming through it. Then I thought about the noise I'd make. I didn't want to run the risk of alerting the guy on the north side of my arrival. So I put it in park and cut the motor and stepped out into the mud. I climbed onto the hood and climbed over the top and then dropped onto the ground. I stayed crouched and looked up at the large complex as rain hit my face. I took one look behind me, back toward the road; then I turned back. Then I stood and sprinted toward the side of the warehouse.

A flash of lightning lit up the sky as I moved. Three seconds later I heard the thunder. Thirty seconds after that, I made it to the building and put my back against the wall. There was an overhang shielding me from the rain. I looked back and saw my SUV tight against the gate, somewhat hard to see with the dark sky overhead and rain coming down in thick sheets.

"Um, Blake, we have a problem," said Simon. "The person to the north is now closer to the two who are stationary. I want you to hang back a minute. Maybe they're making their rounds and will leave soon."

"Copy," I said as I checked the time. "Guys, is one of you tracking that vehicle to see where it's headed?"

"I'm doing that," said Morgan. "That way Simon can stay focused on keeping a visual on the warehouse."

"They're going to arrive in twenty-five minutes," I said, checking my watch. "They're expecting me to be there. When I don't show up, it's going to be a problem."

"It won't matter," said Simon. "If you're able to find Jami and get her out, that is."

I nodded to myself and grabbed my phone and put it on silent. I dropped it back into my pocket as Simon told me that the person who had walked to the south side of the warehouse where I was standing was now making their way back up to the north side. I moved around the perimeter, looking for a way inside. But there was nothing on the south side of it. Simon told me he'd seen them climb into their vehicle near the southeastern corner. So I moved toward the side and found a steel door and several large bay doors all along the eastern side. Simon told me the guy was still moving north but was slowing; then he said they'd stopped completely, like maybe he was sitting down at a desk or a table, working on something. I tried the door. It was locked. I raised my Glock and thought about sending two bullets into where I thought the locking mechanism would be. Then I thought about the guy on the other side of the building. Lightning struck again. Closer this time. I thought about trying to time it; maybe I could fire a round into the locking mechanism with the next strike. Maybe it would act like a silencer in a way. But I waited through two long minutes, and nothing happened. Then I noticed something. A thick string protruding from underneath the bay closest to me.

The rain was still coming down hard. I stepped out into it and hustled toward the rope and picked it up. I pulled upward, and the bay door moved a little. I looked to my right and saw another rope on the right side of it. I imagined two men were supposed to lift it open due to the size and weight of the bay door. I bent down to get more leverage and gripped the rope tighter than I had before, and I stood up tall, pulling up as hard as I could. I groaned as I strained, and the rope started to slip a little, but I gripped it even tighter. The bay door lifted slowly a few inches, then a foot, then two feet. I kept the rope in my right hand and reached down with my left to grab the bottom. Then I grabbed it with two hands and lifted the bay door up until there was about three or four feet of clearance. Then I crouched down and let go, and then I rolled inside.

The bay door fell hard, but since it was only a few feet, the sound wasn't as loud as I thought it would be. I reached for my Glock and got into a crouch. I leveled my weapon and looked all around, but I saw no one. To my right I saw the other two bays. In the middle was a UPS truck. To my right, a parked van, backed in. "Where do I go?" I asked quietly as I scanned the interior, left to right, as my heart beat faster.

"Straight ahead," said Morgan in my earpiece, and I assumed he was now monitoring both satellites.

"The tango is to your right now," added Simon. "He's still stationary. I'll let you know if he moves."

I stood and moved slow, in a crouch, two hands gripping my Glock, headed toward the western interior. For a brief moment, I considered the two people Morgan and Simon were seeing on the infrared could be two bad guys, and the person to the north might be someone else periodically checking in with the two. So worst-case scenario, three bad guys. Best case, Simon was right—it was Jami and the UPS guy. There was an exit door straight ahead of me along the wall. To the left of that, in the corner, were two offices. Both doors were closed. I got to the first one and stood next to it and looked north. I saw nobody there. So I turned the handle with my left hand and gripped my Glock with my right. I turned the handle slowly. It was unlocked. I raised my weapon as I pushed it open. There was a man in a brown uniform on the floor, bloodied and beaten and zip-tied to a desk. He looked up at me defeatedly, just a slow, labored movement. Then his eyes grew wide. I put a finger up to my lips; then I held my hand out. *Stay quiet; wait here,* I was telling him, and the man nodded his understanding. I closed the door quietly and glanced back to the north. Still nobody there. Simon asked if it was Jami. "No," I said in a low voice.

Then I went to the door of the second office. The one in the corner. It was larger, that was clear. I repeated the same process. The door was unlocked. I pushed it open, and I saw my wife. "I got her," I said.

31

President James Keller sat alone inside the Oval Office. He was holding a pen with red ink and a printout of the speech he was planning on giving at the signing. As he marked up a few sections he wanted reordered and made some notes, there was a knock at the door. It startled him for some reason. "Come in," he said as he held onto the loose papers and looked up over his reading glasses and stared at the door.

The door opened, and a man in a dark suit looked inside. "Ethan Meyer needs to see you, sir."

"I'm a little busy right now; I thought I told you, I need an hour uninterrupted to go through this speech."

The agent looked at him with an expression that said: *You're going to want to talk to him*. Keller sighed heavily and dropped the papers onto the *Resolute* desk and removed his glasses. "Alright, send him in."

The agent nodded and disappeared from view. Five seconds later Keller's chief of staff stepped through, and the agent reappeared for a brief moment to grab the doorhandle and pull the door closed.

Keller was still holding onto his glasses. He said, "This better be important, Ethan. This is a very important event. I don't want to be fumbling over words. I want to be articulate and precise in what I say."

"Yes, Mr. President," said Meyer. "This is important, and it can't wait."

Keller stared across the desk for a brief moment; then he tossed his glasses onto the printed speech and pointed at the chairs opposite where he sat. Meyer nodded his appreciation and sat down in one of them.

"Mr. President, we cannot have the signing take place in that building."

"The hell we can't."

Meyer held two hands out in front of him and lowered his head and said, "Please, just let me explain."

Keller made no reply. Just maintained his cold stare, waiting for Meyer to get into the details.

Meyer said, "I've been made aware of a threat the intelligence community has been looking into. A serious threat."

"Ethan, if you're referring to the overseas phone call with the vague, empty threat, then—"

"It's more than that," Meyer said, interrupting his boss while trying to figure out what words he could say that would convince the man to listen to him. Then after several long moments of silence, as much as it pained Meyer to go there and bring any legitimacy to his predecessor, he said, "I spoke with Emma Ross."

Keller furrowed his brow. "Emma?" he asked curiously. "Explain."

Meyer took a deep breath, thinking about it and deciding the best way to spin the excuse. "Mr. President, she has more details than the FBI or DDC or even DHS for that matter. And you know your Secret Service team isn't going to talk to you about any threats in play. They never do that. They don't share active threats with protectees. They'll move you from one place to another if situations change; they'll rush you away if you're in imminent danger; they'll refuse to take you places they warrant are not safe. They are aware of the threat in play but do not believe you are directly in harm's way, so they're remaining silent."

Keller leaned forward and lowered his head slightly. He maintained his stare. "And you know differently?"

Meyer nodded slowly.

Keller lifted his head and took a deep breath. He looked away and let it out. "Fine," he continued. "We'll do it here, at the White House, on the South Lawn. Let President Stepanov know."

32

PARKER CHECKED ON SIMON HARRIS, WHO WAS STILL SITTING alone inside the conference room. He stood in the doorway and asked for a status update. Simon told him they'd just found Jami. Parker nodded his relief and said to give him an update once they got out of the warehouse and were on their way back to the NAC. Simon nodded his understanding and kept his eyes glued to the laptop screen and the live feed coming from the satellite circling the Earth from a thousand miles overhead and explained to his boss that he had to keep watch for the vehicle that had left the compound in case they decided to come back unexpectedly.

Parker slapped the inside of the doorway twice. *Good work*, he was telling Simon as he stepped away and let the conference room door close on its own. Then he walked across the warren of cubicles, all of them empty and waiting for new hires of analysts, which Parker needed for his new division at DHS. Then he walked past Simon's space and saw his desk lamp still on and an open soda can left there on the desk. He smiled to himself, proud of the work Simon had done without having to rely too heavily on DDC's

Morgan Lennox out of Chicago. His smile faded as he approached his office and saw through the open blinds his daughter and the woman named Miriam Hassan sitting inside. He knocked on the door twice and entered.

Emma Ross was sitting in his chair on the opposite side of a large wooden desk. Hassan was in one of the two chairs opposite Ross. Parker stood awkwardly as the door closed and pulled out the other chair.

Parker said, "I'm glad you're okay."

Hassan nodded vaguely but made no reply.

He shifted his eyes to his daughter. "Emma, what are we going to do about the CIA men and the video footage at the safe house?"

"I've already taken care of it."

"How?"

"I made a phone call," she said. "No corner office yet, but I have good people who work for me."

Parker nodded and looked away.

"We were just talking about what happened down on P Street. I'll catch you up."

Emma filled in the gaps for her father. She explained to him the phone call Hassan had overheard, the loud, tinny voice with the order her husband would disobey, the disappearance. Parker understood the connection immediately. A phone call from overseas into the United States threatening the life of one if not two presidents. He knew threats came in all the time, all day every day. Many were ignored. Some were looked into, at least on the surface. A few required nothing more than sending a few agents to the person's home to knock on their door to shake them up and maybe scare them a little.

But this was something different.

When Emma finished telling her father everything she

knew and Hassan confirmed the details of the story, Parker cleared his throat and turned in his seat a little. He said, "Mrs. Hassan, forgive me if this is too direct, I know you've been through a lot so far today, but why would these people want you dead?"

Miriam Hassan said nothing. Parker shifted his eyes over to Emma for a brief moment, then moved them back and added, "I assume the whole point of moving you to the safe house was because you feared for your life. Which is perfectly understandable. I'm sure the US government would've given you a new identity and a place to live, for a little while at least. Did anyone know you were in that house on P Street?"

She shook her head slowly. "No one. We have no family here. No close friends. I told nobody."

Parker leaned back and sighed and turned to face his daughter. "Why would anyone want to take her out?"

THEY SAT THERE ANOTHER MINUTE, NOBODY SPEAKING, Hassan staring at Emma and Emma staring at her father and Tom Parker staring out at nothing at all. He didn't understand how anyone would even know about the safe house let alone why they'd try to kill the woman sitting next to him. Emma asked Hassan if she wanted something to drink. She nodded that she did, so Parker stood and gestured for Hassan to go with him, and he took her to the kitchen area of his forgotten building at the Nebraska Avenue Complex. Parker got Hassan a water. She told him she was feeling ill and wanted to rest. So he took her to a small conference room within view of Parker's office and told her to take it easy and he'd check on her later. Parker returned to his office and closed the door. He twisted the blinds to the windows that had been closed off so he could see the room Hassan was resting in. He turned back, and Emma was looking at him. She said nothing. He stared across at his daughter. "Can I sit in my own chair, in my own office, Emma?"

"Sorry," she said and stood and let him pass. Then she remained standing as Parker took a seat and looked past her, through the blinds, and kept his eyes on the door leading to the smaller conference room. Emma looked at her watch, then followed his gaze to the small conference room; then she sat down in the seat Hassan had been in. There was a moment of awkward silence. Then she said, "About this morning..."

"Forget about it," he said.

"No," she replied. Then she thought for a long moment and added, "You and I have had a rocky relationship. And it's gone on like this for many years. Way before Elizabeth was born. Before Mom left."

Parker said nothing. Just moved his eyes back from the conference room across the hall to his daughter.

"You were gone a lot. Mom used to tell me that you were away on long business trips in faraway places."

"I was."

Emma shook her head. "Not all the time." She took a breath and let it out. A long sigh. A conversation she didn't want to have, but she had things bottled up inside that needed to be said. "She left us. She left both of us. I was a kid still. Seventeen years old. My senior year of high school. I needed her then more than ever, but she just walked away." Emma paused and turned back to her father. "And I blamed you. As I should have. I didn't know why she left. I thought that was when you started drinking. But it wasn't. She left because of the drinking. I real-

ized that later when I tracked her down and confronted
her."

Silence filled Parker's office as he thought about Emma's
words. He could see the pain in his daughter's eyes. Pain
from years of built-up frustration and built-up resentment.
Years neither of them would ever get back. Parker said,
"What I told you this morning was true. I haven't had a
drink in over a year now." Parker stood from behind the
desk and pulled out the chair next to her and sat down. He
thought about those last couple of months when his little
girl had been home before she left for Yale, before the
empty house he still lived in, before his daughter had gradu-
ated and gotten married and had Elizabeth and then gotten
divorced. A lot of life had been lived in a short amount of
time. His daughter had grown up way too fast. Elizabeth
didn't even know who he was for the longest time. "I don't
expect you to believe me," he finally said. "To be honest, I
don't think I'd believe me, either, if I were you. All I can tell
you is this, Emma: I was young and stupid. I messed up." He
held up his hand and showed her the wedding band he still
wore. "You know why I don't take this off? It's not because I
wish your mother would come back. It's because I know
she's not coming back. Not now, not ever." He lowered his
hand. "It's a reminder, Emma. A reminder of what I had and
of what I lost. I lost her, then I lost you, and I never really
had Elizabeth. Not until after what happened in Chicago.
Ever since you moved back to DC, you've kept your
distance."

"Because I want to protect her from the pain I felt.
Because I feel like I have to break the cycle."

Parker nodded. "Believe me, I understand." He lowered
his gaze and opened his hand and played with his wedding
band. He held his open palm out to her, but she wouldn't

take it. He dropped it back into his lap and said, "Emma, second chances aren't about happy endings. They're just a chance to end things right."

TWO MINUTES PASSED IN SILENCE. THEN PARKER GAVE IT UP, and Emma got back to business. Parker stood and paced his office, running a hand across his face and thinking hard as he occasionally glanced across to the small conference room where Miriam Hassan was resting. Then he said, "It doesn't add up, Emma."

"What do you mean?" she asked.

"Something's off. I don't know what it is, but I don't like the thing at the safe house."

"Go on."

"Why would a sniper try to take her out? I don't understand why they'd want to kill her. Because of what she might have overheard? Why didn't they come for her at her house after killing her husband? When it was easy? Before she called the cops and Metro PD looped in the Bureau and your people? Don't you think that would've been the best time to get her? When she's home alone, waiting on her husband to return?"

Emma said nothing.

"Just think about it for a minute. *That* was when they should've done it. Not now."

Emma did think about it. She said, "They didn't know yet. They found out later. Somebody told them."

"Who?"

She said, "I don't know."

Parker looked at her seriously and said, "I think she does."

"She doesn't."

"How do you know that?"

"Didn't you see her when she first walked in here? She was shaking like a leaf. Plus we vetted her story."

Parker crossed his arms and looked away. "Someone's lying," he said. "Maybe not her. But someone."

Emma thought about that for a long moment. Then Parker's phone rang. He walked around the large desk and remained standing and punched a button to answer the call on speakerphone and said, "Tom Parker."

"Tom, this is Peter Mulvaney," said the FBI director from across town. "I just got off the phone with Agent Rivera. It's official, the White House is moving the venue for the peace treaty signing. New location TBD."

Emma Ross smiled and looked away.

Parker said, "Best guess?"

"Rivera seems to be pushing for a small venue, like inside the Oval. Keller wants it on the South Lawn." Mulvaney paused for a moment. "I'm moving my men over that way; we're banking on the South Lawn." Parker said nothing. Mulvaney added, "Tom, that's not the only reason why I'm calling. That phone call from overseas that the NSA intercepted, we now believe it originated from a small town in Russia. We've been working with the CIA, and we confirmed the call came from a terror cell we've been watching."

Parker thought about that for a moment. "What does that mean, Peter?"

"It means the order came from inside the Kremlin. From someone with power. Someone who isn't aligned with Stepanov and his agenda." Mulvaney paused. "And it means if they pull this off, it'll be an act of war."

33

I CLOSED THE DOOR BEHIND ME AND STEPPED INSIDE. I holstered my weapon and crouched down slightly. "Are you okay?" I asked.

Jami nodded.

I reached into a pocket and found Mason's knife and used it to cut her zip tie. She brought her wrists forward and massaged them. Then she stood, and we embraced.

"I was wrong," she said. "There are three of them, Blake. Not two."

"I know," I said. "The third guy's a sniper."

Jami furrowed her brow and looked away briefly. Then she said, "We need to hurry before they find us."

"Two of them left. They're heading downtown. They think they're meeting me. There's only one guy still here, on the other side of the building. Morgan and Simon are keeping an eye on him with the infrared."

Jami shook her head and studied me. "Why would they be meeting with you?"

I put the blade away and reached for my gun. "I'll explain later. Right now we need to get you out of here."

Jami nodded vaguely. "There's another man here some-where. A UPS driver. We need to get him out, too."

"He's in the next room."

Jami nodded again. I opened the door slowly and looked out. Nobody was there. "Guys, how's our tango?"

"Still on the north side," answered Simon. "The guy's stationary."

I turned back and looked at Jami. "You ready?"

But Jami said nothing. She just stared across at me with a serious look on her face; then she turned away.

"What's wrong?"

She shook her head. A slow little movement at first, then a more definitive gesture. "I can't go with you."

"What are you talking about?"

Jami took a step backward and put her hands up to her temples with fingers extended, trying to focus, trying to think quickly. Then she repeated, "I just can't go. The guy who was here, he told me things. Blake, he's planning some-thing. He said he has someone on the inside who will take out President Keller."

"Then let's go stop it from happening."

"You don't understand. His man is already there. And he has access to the president. No one can stop it."

I thought about that. "Then we'll take out the tango on the north side, and we'll wait here for them to get back. We'll take them all out. Or we'll keep the guy who kidnapped you alive, and we'll force him to talk."

Jami shook her head again. A defeated gesture. Like she knew there was only one way to move forward. My phone rang. I heard the call coming in from my Bluetooth. I pulled it out of my pocket. It was the guy.

"He's calling me," I said. "He's probably getting close and wants to tell me where to meet his man."

"You need to go," Jami said. "Whatever it is you're doing, keep doing it. Keep the ruse going for now."

"No."

"You have to. Listen to me—I know the guy. We worked together while I was with the Bureau. I don't know his name, but he was with the HIG team. He did interrogations. They'd bring him in whenever the CIA picked up someone from a Russian terror cell from around the country. Because he was Russian, too."

"I'm not leaving without you, Jami."

She took two steps closer to me and put her hands on my shoulders and looked up at me. "You have to."

"Blake, our tango is stirring," I heard Simon say in my earpiece.

Jami said, "I just need a little more time with him. For an interrogator, the guy likes to talk. He's told me a lot of his plan already. He told me his target is definitely President Keller, but I sensed there was more to it than that. Maybe he wants to take out both presidents. And he told me the attack is happening today. At a surprise peace treaty signing he said is taking place today." She paused a moment. "I think I can push his buttons and get him to talk more. I think I can get him to tell me who he has on the inside."

"No," I said again.

"Blake—listen to me—if it were anyone else, what would you do? Would you keep an agent in place here?"

I said nothing.

"You already know the answer to that." Jami turned and went to a drawer and pulled out a zip tie and sat back down in her chair and tossed the tie to me. "You need to put the tie back on me. Just keep it loose."

"Blake, our guy to the north is starting to move," Simon said in my earpiece.

Jami stared up at me, but I made no reply. She said, "You know where I am now. You told me that Morgan and Simon are watching with the infrared. I'll be fine. I just need a little more time, okay? Tell Lynne May what I'm doing. I promise, she would agree with me on this. In fact, if she knew, she would insist on it."

I said nothing.

"Please, you have to go. Set the tie and get out of here while you can. As soon as I learn who his man on the inside is, I'll find a way out of here. Then we'll know who we need to go after. You have to trust me."

I looked away for a moment, deciding. Then I stepped behind her and placed the zip tie around her wrists. I kept them loose. Then I pulled Mason's blade out of my pocket. "Use it," I said as I held it out for her to see. She refused. She didn't want to get caught with it. I stuffed it into her pocket anyway and stood back.

"Blake, our tango is on the move," Morgan said in my earpiece; then he told Simon to zoom in some.

I went to the door and reached for my Glock. I cracked it open and looked out into the bay. I saw nothing. "I love you," I whispered and turned back to look at her. She mouthed *love you* but no words came out. Her mouth quivered as she formed the words. I stepped out and closed the door. Along the far wall were the bays. To my left was a side door.

I stood there, thinking.

Then I stepped outside and left Jami behind.

34

THE RAIN WAS STILL BEATING DOWN HARD. I DUG MY WALLET out and found a dollar bill and folded it twice and left it in the door jamb. I turned and saw there was less of an overhang along the western side of the building where I stood. I ran south and turned left and found cover. I stared across the grass at the fence and my SUV parked up against the gate. Lightning struck somewhere close by. I flinched, and two seconds later, thunder rumbled loudly, and I put my hand to my earpiece. "Did you guys get all of that?" I asked.

"We got it, mate," said Morgan with a somber tone.

"Simon, I need you to keep the satellite in place. Keep an eye on Jami at all times. I want to know the moment anything changes—if someone arrives or leaves, I need to know about it. Don't lose sight of her."

"Okay," said Simon.

"Morgan, call Lynne May and tell her what happened."

"Will do." There was a long pause on the line. Morgan was thinking. "What are you going to do, Blake? The kidnapper thinks his guy will be meeting you any minute now. How are you going to handle that?"

I said nothing.

I DISCONNECTED THE CALL AND STOOD ALONE, THINKING about it, watching the rain fall at a slant, coming down in sheets, beating hard against my SUV. My phone buzzed. "This is Jordan," I said, answering it.

"Mr. Jordan, I have my man approaching the downtown area. Are you ready to meet him?"

"Yes," I lied.

"There's a café on Tenth just north of L Street. He will be at a table, waiting. He'll have something for you."

"What is it?"

"He will give you further instructions when you see him." The kidnapper paused. "You have ten minutes."

I looked at my watch. "I can't get there in time."

"You told me you were ready to meet him."

I said nothing.

"I'll give you fifteen. Be there or the girl dies."

The call was disconnected. I pulled my cell phone away from my face and looked at the screen for a moment. Then I lowered my hand and thought some more. I felt the urge to go back inside the building. The urge to take down the guy keeping watch over Jami. If it was the kidnapper, I'd make him talk. And if it wasn't, if the kidnapper was in the car with the sniper, then I'd take them both out when they arrived. I'd keep the kidnapper alive long enough to force him to talk and tell me who his man on the inside was.

Then my thoughts drifted back to Jami and what she had said: *His man is already there. And he has access to the president. No one can stop it.* If that was true, if the guy who took Jami really had a man on the inside, then he wouldn't talk to me. He wouldn't have to. His man would most likely already have his instructions. He would've been told if something happened, if they lost contact, to proceed accordingly. "Damn it," I said as I dialed the number for the only person who could help with the little time that I had.

CHRIS REED ANSWERED ON THE FIRST RING. HE SAID, "HEY, man, is Jami okay?"

"I need your help," I replied. "Where are you right now?"

There was a brief pause, and then he said, "Reynolds and I are still at the Pullman House."

"There's a café on Tenth just north of L. How far away is that from you?"

"I don't know; maybe ten or fifteen minutes' walking distance from where I am now."

I checked my watch again. Then I gave Chris Reed the summary of what had happened with Jami and the kidnapper's demand that I meet with his man so he could give me something and how much time we had.

"What are you saying?" he asked.

"You need to meet him for me."

"You want me to pretend to be you?"

"Chris, I'm in Bethesda. It's a twenty-minute drive and that's if I run the lights. I don't know if I'll make it."

"You can do it in fifteen." He paused, thinking. "How do you know he doesn't know what you look like?"

"He's not meeting me; he's sending one of his guys to meet with me."

"He'll probably have a description."

"Then come up with something."

"And if he doesn't buy it?"

"I don't know," I said. "Chris, please. You told me earlier if you could help me in any way, you would do it. I need your help now. I can't let this guy wonder why I'm not there. I can't miss this meeting."

Chris grew quiet as he thought it through. "What about Reynolds? What do I tell him?"

"I don't know," I said again. "Come up with something. Make up an excuse."

"I can't, Blake. We both report to Mulvaney. We're both here, waiting on him to give us our new orders."

"Tell him you have to take a call." I paused. "Listen, I'm on my way now. Call me when you're done."

I didn't give Chris a chance to respond. I disconnected the call and dropped the phone back into my pocket. I looked across the field and saw the rain wasn't letting up at all. It was still coming down hard. Thunder continued to rumble seconds after far-off lightning strikes. But the storm was moving to the east. I stood for another long moment; then I sprinted across the wet field. My shoes sank into the mud as I moved. I slowed as I got to the fence, and I grabbed hold of it and climbed up. I came up over the top and lowered myself down slowly onto the hood of my SUV, which was still parked tight against the other side of the gate. I hopped down and climbed inside and wiped water off my face and stared across at the distant building. I felt sick to my stomach. I started the motor and sat there, wanting to go back inside.

But Jami was right. If it were anyone else, I wouldn't have second-guessed them. So I backed out and I threw it in drive and I left.

35

Morgan Lennox told Simon to give him a call the moment anything changed. Simon said he would, and Morgan disconnected the line. Then he stood in his cubicle in the Chicago DDC field office and looked all around. Nobody else in his department was still there. His boss, Roger Shapiro, was in his office down the hallway. Probably the same scene that was taking place at the Washington field office where Lynne May worked. But neither Shapiro nor May could help him. Or Tom Parker with DHS for that matter. He paced around the other workstations in a wide circle, hearing Shapiro's voice booming from the other end of the hallway, on the phone with someone. Morgan put his hands on the back of his head and stopped and just stood there for a long moment. He'd overheard the conversation between Blake and Jami. While Simon focused on the satellite and the infrared, Morgan had done a quick search using the parameters he'd overheard from the conversation. Jami had mentioned a man, a Russian, an interrogator with the Bureau, back before she'd left to join DDC. He typed in the information and ran a search and stared at the results.

He had to do something. But he couldn't talk to Shapiro about it. And that meant he only had one option. Morgan nodded to himself and walked back to his cubicle. He stared at the landline phone sitting on his desk and thought through what he needed to do and what he'd have to say. Then he picked up the phone and paused as he tried to recall the phone number he needed to dial; then he punched it in with a finger. The line rang once. A switchboard operator answered, and Morgan asked for a name. There was a moment of awkward silence, and the operator gave an excuse about the man having left for the day. Morgan lied and told her that was poppycock, they had just spoken a minute earlier, and his call had dropped, and he simply wanted to be reconnected. After another moment of awkward silence, Morgan heard music come on the line for fifteen long seconds. Down the hallway, he heard Shapiro wrap up his phone call quickly. A rushed ending to a conversation. Then silence. Then Morgan heard two loud rings.

"Peter Mulvaney," said the Bureau director as he answered.

"Mr. Mulvaney, my name is Morgan Lennox. I work at DDC, out of the Chicago office."

"I know who you are. I was just speaking with Roger Shapiro." There was a pause. "How can I help you?"

Morgan lifted in his seat two inches and looked over the cubicle wall and down the long dark empty hallway. "I need your help. I know I'm supposed to go to Shapiro first, but I can't."

Mulvaney was thinking about that. "Why not?" he asked.

"Because I need to call in a favor for someone. Someone Shapiro wouldn't be happy about me helping."

There was a pause on the line. Mulvaney was curious, so he said, "Who?"

Morgan lowered himself back down into his chair and leaned back in his seat, stretching the phone cord as he did, keeping a visual past his cubicle wall and on the long hallway. "Blake Jordan," he finally said. "I believe you're aware of an initiative going on at the moment to track down an overseas phone call."

"Yes, I am. And we've handed everything we know so far over to the CIA."

"That's the thing, sir. You haven't."

"I'm sorry?"

"There's a man who worked for the Bureau. Maybe he still does, I don't know. He was part of an FBI HIG team and worked with then-FBI agent Jami Davis during the brief period of time she worked for you all." Morgan paused. "He was of Russian descent. He helped out whenever Russian interrogators were needed."

"Mr. Lennox, I don't know where you think you're going with this."

"Sir, I'm trying to help you figure out who the person from that overseas call contacted here in the States."

There was another pause on the line. Longer this time. Mulvaney asked, "You think it's connected?"

"Pretty bloody sure."

"How so?"

Morgan peeked around his cubicle wall again. *All clear.* "Here's what I think happened, sir. I believe someone used a burner phone to make a secure call into the United States. The call was answered by this man. The guy who was—or maybe still is—a part of the Bureau's HIG team. The caller gave his man a simple order. It didn't need to be long; it had all been explained beforehand. The guy over here was just waiting for the go-ahead to proceed with the previously agreed upon plan. And now the plan is in motion."

"Lennox, what are you saying? The HIG guy is our person of interest?"

"I'm saying I think he's the one who took the phone call. And he's got a guy on the inside. I need to—" Morgan sensed someone approaching. He pulled the phone away from his ear and peeked around his cubicle wall and saw Roger Shapiro walking toward his desk. Morgan gently placed the handset back onto the cradle, disconnecting the call, and brought a random screen up on his monitor. Shapiro arrived at his desk and knocked twice on the wall. Morgan acted like he was startled and turned and looked up at him.

"Mr. Shapiro, I didn't realize you were still here."

Shapiro nodded vaguely and looked around the almost empty floor. A few random analysts in another department on the other side of the building were still working on their assignments while Shapiro's field agents were out and around Chicago. There was always some issue to be dealt with, some threat to be looked into. But he didn't need someone like Morgan sitting around collecting overtime on a Friday night. He said, "What are you working on, Lennox?"

"I'm helping Lynne May with something," he lied.

Shapiro nodded and said, "I assume you're up to speed with what's going on out there? In Washington?"

"Yes, I saw that Keller is moving the location of the ceremony. Most likely to the White House."

Shapiro nodded again. He said, "Need you on standby, should anything go down."

With that, Shapiro slapped the top of Morgan's cubicle and told him to have a good night and headed out. Morgan kept his eyes glued to his computer screen and pretended to be typing something as Shapiro left. Then he turned and watched as Shapiro got to the exit and said good night to DDC security. Then Morgan stopped working and just sat there for a moment, wishing he could be honest with his boss; but knowing how much he disliked Blake, the man who had Shapiro's job years earlier, that was never going to happen. Morgan was thinking about the differences in management style from Jordan's when his desk phone rang. The sound was shrill and jarring in the otherwise quiet office. Before the third ring, Morgan answered.

"This is Peter Mulvaney," said the voice on the other end of the line. "I believe we got disconnected."

Morgan said, "I'm very sorry about that." He was going to explain his lack of trust with his boss, then he decided he'd better not get into it with Shapiro's colleague, so he simply said, "Sir, I need you to help me—"

"Identify the interrogator," said Mulvaney, finishing his sentence. "We hired the man. So yes, I can help."

36

CHRIS REED HURRIED ALONG THE STREETS OF DOWNTOWN Washington and turned the corner at Tenth Street. Up ahead he saw in the center of the street a café. The rain had let up some and had turned from a straight-up downpour to a pathetic drizzle in a matter of minutes. The lightning wasn't as close as it had been, but he could still hear the occasional thunder boom to the north somewhere. Probably out near Bethesda. He'd hung up with Blake and just stood there for a long minute, trying to come up with some kind of excuse to give Agent Reynolds. Mulvaney had sent them there as a pair to head up the efforts of establishing a perimeter around the Pullman House and help Metro PD wherever they needed it. But once it was clear the venue was moving, and knowing he and Reynolds were just standing around waiting for Mulvaney to get back to them with further details, he had decided the best path was the simplest path.

So he told Reynolds he needed to get something to eat. They had time to kill, and there was a café a few blocks away. So he asked Reynolds if he wanted anything. Reynolds said to get him a large coffee, black. Reed nodded and slapped his partner on the back and told him he'd be back in a few minutes, and he left.

There was nobody sitting outside the café. There were five tables with a large umbrella planted in the center of each of them. They were doing a good job keeping the chairs dry. The sky was gray and so was everything else because of the dreary day. He could see lights were on inside, and as he approached, he checked his phone and set it to silent, then dropped it back into a pocket.

Opening the door, he saw nobody inside except for an older couple sitting together and three employees working behind the counter. One was in charge of taking orders, another was taking payments, and another had barista duties. All three looked at him as he stepped inside, and a bell chimed above him.

"Welcome in," the employee taking orders said as he stepped inside. "What can I get started for you?"

He eyed the older couple briefly; then he scanned the interior. He saw nothing and said, "Large coffee."

"Room for milk?" she asked.

"Black," he said. Then he stood there and waited as the woman grabbed a to-go cup and turned around. Thirty seconds later she was done and had carried the coffee down to the register where he was waiting to pay. He checked his watch. Eighteen minutes had passed. He turned and looked out the door and saw no one. The lady at the register rang him up. He asked if they were normally busy, and she said no, they were dead this time of day and apologized if the coffee was stale. He asked if there had been anyone else in there before he arrived. The clerk shrugged and pointed at the older couple sitting behind him. Chris told her to keep the change and took Reynolds's coffee and went back outside, where he pulled out a heavy chair and sat down. To his left, in the direction where Reynolds was waiting, he saw nothing. To the right, he saw a car park and the driver kill the headlights. And far beyond that, he saw a black, muddy SUV park.

THE PASSENGER DOOR FROM THE FIRST VEHICLE OPENED. A man wearing black stepped out and looked all around; then he passed between two other parked cars and glided across the wet street, unfazed by the lingering rain. He moved toward Reed and furrowed his brow as he looked him over. As the man approached, he looked inside the café and saw the older couple; then he slowed and stopped by the table.

"Jordan?" the man asked.

Chris Reed nodded but said nothing in return.

The man in black pulled out another one of the heavy chairs opposite Reed and sat down. He stared across, looking him over again. "You're not him," he said as he looked around briefly. "You don't fit the description."

"What was the description?"

The man paused and said, "The man named Jordan has brown hair. Yours is darker. Almost black."

"Undercover assignment last week," he lied. Then Chris added, to deflect the questioning, "You're late."

The man studied him a moment longer; then he nodded. "The FBI and Metro PD have a perimeter set up. We didn't expect that. We had to figure out how to drive around them without stopping at a checkpoint."

Reed said nothing.

The man said, "In a few hours, the two presidents will be meeting to sign the treaty. We understand the venue is changing. But Mr. Jordan, the venue does not matter. We need you there, on-site, wherever it takes place. You need to have a visual of the presidents at all times. You will be our eyes and ears on the ground. We have a man in place who will make sure the peace treaty is not signed today."

"Who is it?"

The guy smiled and shook his head slowly. "You will meet him soon enough. And when you do, your job is to remove every roadblock, every obstacle in his way so he can do what we need him to do—on live TV."

"Which is kill one if not both presidents." Reed tilted his head to the side. "Is that right?"

The man said nothing in reply. Just stared.

Reed took a deep breath and let it out. He moved his gaze to the left and looked down the glistening street. The light rain fell at an even pace, hitting the canvas umbrella at their table. Reed turned to his right and glanced down the road. He saw the two cars still there. The clean one and the muddy one. Nobody was out on the street. Nobody he could see right then, at least. He faced forward and leaned in and said, "You need to understand something. I've spent my whole life protecting this country. President Keller is a personal friend of mine. I've known the man for over twenty years."

"Which is why you were chosen. We knew you had carte blanche, Mr. Jordan. As you've told us, you have unique access and privileges. There is nobody better to make sure our man on the inside stays on course."

"If you think, after knowing my history with the president, that I'd ever let anything happen to him—"

"Let me ask you a simple question; would you allow your president to die if it would save your wife's life?"

Reed said nothing. He put himself in Jordan's shoes and thought hard about it. He didn't know for sure.

"Nobody will know your involvement, Mr. Jordan. And provided you have kept your end of the deal and not discussed this with anyone on your side, either, you should have nothing to worry about. Correct?"

Reed nodded vaguely but did not reply. He saw movement out of the corner of his eye, but he didn't look. He just kept his gaze forward, focusing on the man at the table sitting across from him and his question.

"You could've told me all of this with a phone call. So why are we here? What's the point of this meeting?"

The man wearing black reached into a pocket and pulled out a phone. He reached across and set it down. "Take it," he said as he kept his eyes on Reed's.

"I already have a phone," said Reed as he heard two muffled pops from somewhere down the street.

The man nodded. "It is not for you, Mr. Jordan. It's for our man on the inside. You need to give it to him."

Reed furrowed his brow. "He doesn't have a phone?"

"Not a secure one. He needs this one." With that the man pushed his chair back and stood. Reed must've had a confused look on his face because the man answered the question he had without having to ask it. He said, "Do not worry, Mr. Jordan. You will not have any trouble locating our man on the inside. We will be in contact with you soon with further instructions." Then the guy turned and hustled across the street.

37

THE SNIPER CROSSED THE STREET AND TURNED TO HIS RIGHT and headed north, hustling along the sidewalk. The guy chanced a glance over his shoulder to look back at the man named Jordan. He was still sitting there at the table, watching him move. Then Jordan stood and turned left and headed south along the sidewalk on his side of the street. The sniper faced forward and saw the driver in the idling vehicle parked tight against the sidewalk, waiting for him. He could barely make out the driver as he sat there waiting on him. The driver looked like his face was turned to the left. Maybe resting his eyes after a long grueling day.

He didn't blame him. He was ready for the day to be over, too. The sniper reached into a pocket and found his cell phone and placed a call. Five seconds later the line started to ring, and five seconds after that the call was answered. His message was short and to the point. "It is done," he said. Then the man on the other end of the line told him he'd done well and said to return to the warehouse so they could regroup. He clicked off and stopped moving and glanced back one more time and saw no sign of Jordan anywhere. Therefore no sign of imminent danger. The man was gone. He'd already turned the corner somewhere behind him. He stood there remembering the circuitous route they'd taken to avoid the various checkpoints set up by the FBI and Metro PD and figured Jordan didn't have to worry about such things.

Not yet, anyway.

He turned back and kept moving toward the vehicle. The rain had slowed from a very light drizzle to a very fine mist. His driver had the windshield wipers on low. He saw them move left, then right, then a long pause before they moved again. The driver didn't notice him yet. The big guy was still looking away, still resting. The sniper looked all around as he moved to the passenger door. He smiled as he approached, pleased with himself and the work they had done thus far to thwart what the American and Russian governments were planning later.

He grabbed the door handle and looked back one last time. Still no sign of Jordan. He pulled the door open and slid inside, then pulled the door shut and buckled his seat-belt. "Let's go," he said to the driver.

But the driver did not respond. He just stayed there motionless, his head tilted to the left, resting against the window. The sniper dug into a pocket for his phone, and annoyed, he said, "Wake up. We need to go."

Then his eyes grew wide. He sensed the presence of someone else inside the vehicle. Then a muzzle was pressed against the back of his neck. He could feel its warmth from the weapon being discharged recently. He just sat there, stunned, his mind racing, suddenly remembering hearing two muted pops earlier.

Then a low, menacing voice from behind said, "Show me your hands, or you'll end up like your friend."

. . .

FIVE SECONDS PASSED BEFORE THE MAN OBEYED MY COMMAND. I kept constant pressure on the trigger, ready to act the moment the man tried anything. But he didn't. He just needed a little time to make his decision. He slowly let go of whatever he was digging into a pocket for and brought two hands up so I could see them. He turned his head slightly, maybe to check the seat behind the driver to see how many of us there were. Or maybe out of instinct, trying to catch a glimpse of my face, knowing he couldn't from where he sat. Maybe trying to figure out who I was. Then he did. "What are you doing, Jordan?" he asked.

"I want you to slowly reach for your phone and toss it into the back seat."

The man hesitated; then he lowered one hand and dug back into his pocket. He grabbed his phone and tossed it back. It landed on the seat next to me. I grabbed it and slipped it into my pocket along with the driver's phone I'd already taken.

"What are you doing?" he asked again.

"Leveling the playing field. There were three of you and one of me. Now there are two. Soon, one."

"If you kill me, you'll give up all hope of finding your wife."

"You mean the warehouse in Bethesda?"

The man said nothing.

"I've already been there. Try again."

The man went quiet for a moment. Then he said, "I have information I can give you if you let me live."

"I'm listening."

He shook his head and said, "First I want immunity."

"For what? A kidnapping?"

"For what is about to happen to your president if you don't act fast."

I said, "How about if I like what you have to tell me, you get to live."

He said nothing.

"Start talking."

The man remained silent as he thought through what he was going to tell me. Then he said, "It will happen live on television. Just before the two presidents sign the document. That's when they'll be killed."

"Who's going to do it?"

The man said nothing. I pushed my Glock forward against the back of his neck. The man reflexively leaned forward but made no reply.

I said, "Why'd you try to take out Miriam Hassan?"

"Try?"

"That's right. She's alive and well. She's sitting inside one of our federal buildings at this very moment."

"Impossible."

"Is it? You know, I was a sniper, too. In the Navy. I was a SEAL, a long time ago. I'd always aim for a headshot unless I was instructed not to." I paused a moment, and then I added, "So who told you not to?"

The sniper said nothing.

"Why'd you need to meet me at the café?"

"To give you a secure phone to give to the man we have on the inside." He turned his head left again. He was looking at me out of the corner of his eye. My Glock was now pressed against his temple. Then I saw his eyes shift. He stared at the driver next to him. Then his eyes moved again. They lowered a degree and grew wide as he saw what I'd done to his friend. "I have more information you might find valuable."

"I don't think you do."

"You already killed one of us. What is my boss going to think when he learns you took both of us out?"

I glanced right to look over my shoulder. I stared out the tinted window and saw nobody out on the street. I turned left. Clueless drivers buzzed by us. I lowered the Glock and pressed it tight against the back of the seat like I'd done earlier. I squeezed the trigger twice. Two muted pops. I said, "I guess we'll find out."

38

I SAT IN THE BACK SEAT ANOTHER MINUTE, WAITING TO SEE IF anyone from the shops to my right would come out. Nobody did. I felt the sniper's neck for a pulse; then I stuffed my Glock into my holster and leaned forward, crouching awkwardly, feeling around the guy's pockets for anything else he might have on him. But there was nothing else. No identification, just a gun I didn't need and the phone I already had. I sat back and looked around one more time. Then I pushed the door open and climbed out. I shut it hard and walked back to my SUV parked thirty yards behind theirs and climbed inside. I checked the side mirror and pulled out and drove around until I got to a checkpoint. I showed the officers my DHS credentials, and they let me through, and I drove some more until I found Chris and Mark Reynolds standing together. Reynolds was on the phone, holding a coffee in his free hand. Chris Reed noticed me and walked up to me.

"Hey, man," he said as I climbed out. "I saw you pull up as I was talking to the guy. Did you follow him?"

"No," I said. "But they're no longer a problem."

Chris narrowed his eyes, studying me. "What about Jami?"

"I left her at the warehouse. She insisted on it. She told me she recognized the man who kidnapped her. She thinks he worked for one of the Bureau's HIG teams back when she was still at the FBI. Morgan's trying to find out who he is. And Simon's keeping an eye on the warehouse to maintain a visual for me."

"You need to call Lynne May," he said. "Tell her about Jami so she knows what's going on."

"We called her." I stood by the open door and looked all around. Police lights were flashing from MPD cruisers parked all around the perimeter they had set up. Windshield wipers set on low moved every few seconds to handle the mist. "You got the phone?" I asked.

Chris nodded. He reached into a pocket and found the device and handed it over. I took it from him and inspected it. It was a bulky older model but clearly a burner phone. Chris told me the guy had said it needed to be given to their man on the inside as a way for them to communicate securely with him.

"Any idea who it is?" asked Chris.

I briefly ducked into my SUV and set the phone on the armrest next to the driver's seat. "No," I said.

"The venue is changing. Reynolds is on the phone with Mulvaney now. I got the feeling from talking to the guy that wherever it takes place won't matter that much. Their guy on the inside would still be in place."

I said nothing as I wondered who the kidnapper's man might be.

"What are you going to do when you find him, Blake?"

"Their guy on the inside?"

Chris nodded.

"I'll hand him the phone. I'll play along. Then I'll take him out."

"Seems too easy."

"I know."

Chris looked over his shoulder and saw Reynolds still talking on the phone. He turned back and asked, "What if the phone's something else? Like a red herring? Or a homing beacon for a drone strike maybe?"

"It's not," I said. "Unnecessary. A drone would take out half the White House."

He thought about that for a while, and then he said, "So where does all of this leave us?"

I rested both arms on my open door as I stared out at nothing and thought through everything so far. "Jami's safe," I said. "As safe as she can be. The guys I took out weren't her kidnapper. That much was clear. It was just a driver and the sniper. That means he's in the warehouse. She's there alone with him."

"You trust her to be able to handle him herself? If she needs to?"

I ignored the question. I didn't trust anyone. I said, "The venue's changing, and I assume the new location will be at the White House. So I assume Mulvaney will have you and Reynolds take up a position there and help MPD set up a new perimeter outside. I'll be on the inside. I'll wait for the kidnapper to call and tell me who to give the phone to. Whoever it is, I'll take him out then and there. Game over, Chris. And if the phone thing is a red herring, or if I don't get another call from the kidnapper and he goes dark, I'll send someone to get Jami. I'll tell Rivera everything, and we'll secure both presidents. See any gaps?"

My friend thought about it. "Other than not trusting Jami? No."

I said nothing. Then I noticed Mark Reynolds in my peripheral vision. He was walking toward us. He spoke something into his cell phone, wrapping up his conversation with Mulvaney; then he ended the call and dropped his phone into a pocket and slowed. I stepped around the open door and stood next to Chris.

"It's official," said Reynolds as he stopped moving and eyed us both. "It's happening at the White House."

"Inside?" asked Chris.

Reynolds shook his head. "South Lawn. The president isn't budging on the guest list, so they have to have it outside." He pointed at the building behind him with a thumb. "Word's out. The media's packing up and heading over. Metro PD's moving out shortly. We need to help them set up a perimeter along Fifteenth and Seventeenth. We've got natural barriers to the north and the south, so we don't need to worry about any other streets." He paused. "There are reports of a shooting outside one of our safe houses, but the agents inside are denying it happened, so we're moving forward."

Chris shot me a sideways glance. I said nothing.

Reynolds turned and studied me for a moment like he could tell something was up. "You coming with us, man?"

"Parker wants me close to the president," I said. "So I'll be on the inside, not on the perimeter with you."

Reynolds nodded. "Sounds like a plan." He looked at Chris. "Ready to head out?"

Chris said that he was. Reynolds and I bumped fists, and Chris joined him, and they walked back toward the building. I guessed they needed to alert the others and discuss logistics with MPD before heading over to the streets bordering the South Lawn. I climbed back into my SUV and watched them move and sat there for a moment, thinking about Jami. Then I reached for my phone and dialed the number for Rivera.

He answered on the first ring and confirmed the change in venue and said his team was scrambling to get in place. I told him I didn't want to distract him and what they were trying to do, but I needed to meet him and be there on-site. Agent Rivera pushed back some. I reminded him of Parker's conference call from earlier in the morning. I told him Parker wanted me there and so would the president. There was a brief moment of silence as Rivera considered it; then he said he'd make sure I was on the guest list at the gate. He said one of his men would come out to get me and bring me inside. Then Rivera disconnected the call.

I pulled out and got on the road. One of the two men's cell phones rang as I drove. I ignored it, and it stopped. Then the other phone rang. I didn't answer that one, either. I checked the time and decided I had a few minutes to spare, so I headed south and west. When I got to Independence, I pulled to the side of the road. I stepped out and tossed the phones into the Tidal Basin. Then I climbed back in and drove off.

39

I arrived at the White House ten minutes later. I parked at the Ellipse and stuffed the phone the sniper had given Chris into my pocket, and I walked up to a checkpoint inside a covered guardhouse. There were two agents inside and many others visible all around the periphery, and I was sure many more not visible, monitoring every square inch. I showed one of the agents my identification and told her Agent Rivera was expecting me. As I waited on the woman to check the guest list, my phone buzzed in my pocket.

I answered and Tom Parker said, "Where are you, Jordan?"

"At the White House, waiting to get inside."

"I'm pulling up now. Wait for me."

The agent at the gate didn't see my name on the list, so she made a phone call. She listened and nodded and set the phone down. "You and Tom Parker are clear to enter." She looked all around. "Where is he?"

"On his way," I said.

She nodded again and handed my credentials back to me as I waited on Parker to arrive. Five minutes passed. My cell buzzed again, and I saw UNIDENTIFIED CALLER on the display. "This is Jordan," I said.

"Mr. Jordan, my people said they met with you at the café."

I held up a hand and motioned to the agents inside the covered guardhouse that I needed to take the call in private. I stepped out and walked slowly toward the Ellipse. "They did," I answered. "I have the phone you want me to give to your man on the inside."

The kidnapper said nothing.

"So who am I giving it to?"

"Not yet," the voice said. "I'll tell you soon."

I looked ahead and saw Tom Parker far in the distance, climbing out of his Crown Vic. "If not now, when?"

The kidnapper paused. "Mr. Jordan, I am not a stupid man. If I tell you who my man on the inside is now, you will be eyeing him the whole time. You will cause suspicion. And that would jeopardize the mission."

Parker looked up and noticed me standing there. I said, "What's the next task? Besides the phone thing?"

"To make sure there are no impediments to the plan."

"When will you release my wife?"

"Once it's done."

"And what if your guy doesn't do it? What if he changes his mind at the last minute?"

"You will make sure it is done. And I still have people in the area to make sure you do your part as well."

"Do you?"

There was a pause on the line. A question, followed by a sudden realization. "What did you do to them?"

"I need to go; I'm about to enter the White House," I said and clicked off.

Parker walked up to me. I dropped my cell into a pocket and shook his hand. "You doing okay?" he asked.

As we walked to the guardhouse, I told him about the men I'd taken out. Parker asked who they were, and I said I wasn't sure, aside from what I knew, which was that one of them was a driver and the other was the sniper who tried to take out Miriam Hassan and that they both apparently worked for the guy who kidnapped Jami. I asked Parker where Hassan was. He said she was still at the Nebraska Avenue Complex with Emma. He said Hassan was extremely frightened. Emma had tried to convince her to go to Langley with her where they could discuss next steps, but she didn't like how exposed we were at the NAC and refused to leave. Parker said he'd left them with Simon until he could get back. Now that he knew the sniper was dead, he'd be able to convince Hassan that it was safe to leave. He said he would deal with it when he got back.

"I understand Morgan Lennox is trying to figure out who the guy is," Parker added.

"Jami said she knew him," I said. "They both worked at the FBI at the same time. He was on a HIG team."

"The president called me a little while ago. Keller said he wanted me here. He insisted on it. I guess with everything our two countries have been through over the years, he wanted his friends to see this historic signing live and in person. Not on TV." He paused. "I told him you were most likely going to be here, too." Then Parker grew quiet. I saw concern on his face as he looked up at the White House.

"What's wrong?" I asked.

Parker looked at me seriously. He was thinking hard. "You okay with Simon watching the warehouse?"

"I'd feel better if we had someone on the ground nearby," I said as we moved.

"That's what I was just thinking."

"I don't think the guy's going anywhere."

"And if he does, Simon will be able to track him."

I nodded and told Parker about the café and the cell phone the sniper had given Chris Reed. Parker asked if he could look at it. He held it in his hand and turned it all around, inspecting it. The phone was locked. There was no way to view the call history or even place a call. It could only be used to receive a phone call.

Parker handed the phone back to me and asked, "So what's next?"

"This is the last task. That's what he's telling me, at least. He wants me to get inside, and before the peace treaty is signed, his man on the inside will approach me. Then I hand the phone over to him."

"Then what?"

I thought about it. "Then I stop it from happening. We'll know who the guy is, and we take him down."

"Then the guy in the warehouse kills Jami and escapes."

I said nothing.

"Simon uses the satellite and follows him. We track him down and arrest him. Keller lives, and Jami dies. Is that really what you want?"

"Of course not," I said as we stepped up to the guardhouse.

Parker nodded vaguely and looked around, thinking some more. "Then we need a better plan, don't we?"

40

MORGAN LENNOX MOVED THE PHONE TO HIS OTHER EAR AND cradled it against his shoulder as he listened to the FBI director typing frantically on his side of the line as he tried to look something up. "You sure you know who this guy is, mate?" Morgan asked as he toggled his screen back to the satellite to check on it.

"I'm positive," answered Mulvaney. "His first name was Viktor. If we're talking about the same guy. We hired him years ago, back when Bill Landry was still here. We needed more interrogators who spoke Russian. He seemed like a good hire at the time. I'm accessing the personnel records now to look him up."

"How do you spell the first name? With a *c* or a *k*?"

"Viktor with a *k*," the Bureau man answered. "Russian descent, mid-thirties, dark hair, dark features."

"You don't remember his last name, Mr. Mulvaney?"

There was no response. Just frustration and maybe a sense of embarrassment coming from the man.

Morgan heard more typing, and he pulled up a database as he searched himself. Even though DDC didn't have direct access to HR records within the FBI, there were plenty of interagency documents he could sift through. There was a search bar. Morgan typed "Viktor" AND "interrogation" and came up with nothing. Then he tried "Viktor" AND "HIG," but the search yielded no results. Then he simply tried "Viktor."

Five results were returned. Mulvaney said he needed to put Morgan on hold for a minute. The line went silent, and Morgan kept the desk phone cradled with his shoulder as he scrolled through prior bulletins and interagency notifications until he got to result number four and saw the date from three years earlier. There had been intel gathered from the CIA and shared broadly amongst the various government agencies around a man who had been picked up in the US and interrogated by a HIG team member. The author of the bulletin was someone with the name Viktor. Morgan stared at the last name and whispered it to himself as he looked away, trying to decide if it rang a bell or not. He decided it didn't and read on.

The CIA had stepped in and used the HIG team to find out what the Russian was doing and how he'd shown up on American soil. The HIG team member named Viktor had been the lead interrogator. Simply because they had no other Russian language experts available. After several hours across several days, Viktor had debriefed the CIA and explained that the man he'd interrogated wasn't talking. But he seemed to pose no imminent threat. So they decided to hold him another week; then they sent him back to Russia.

Morgan reached the end of the document when Mulvaney came back on the line. "Still there, Lennox?"

"I'm here, mate," he said as he ran a separate search using the man's full name.

"I'm working on the last name."

Silence as Morgan waited for the results. When he got them, he said, "Mr. Mulvaney, let me ask you a question— was this man whom you all hired involved in an interrogation approximately three years ago? With a Russian man picked up stateside whom you all questioned before letting him go a week later?"

There was a pause on the line. "Yes," Mulvaney answered curiously. "How do you know that, Lennox?"

The results came in. Morgan stared at them and said, "If we're talking about the same man, then I found one of the reports he filed. And if that's him, then we have his last name. And if that's his last name, then we have a major problem." Silence on the line. Morgan spoke the last name. Mulvaney said that was it. Morgan breathed. "Mr. Mulvaney, the guy's supposedly dead. But I can assure you, he's very much alive."

41

JAMI JORDAN WAITED FOR OVER AN HOUR BEFORE SHE SAW HER kidnapper again. After Blake left, she sat in her chair, wrists loosely held together with the new zip tie her husband had placed on her, listening to the patter of hard rain hitting the aluminum roof overhead. She could hear the man in the next room groaning every so often. Jami imagined he'd been beaten, probably just as much as she had. With every minute that passed, Jami grew more concerned that she had made the wrong decision. If she couldn't get the Russian to give her the name of his man, what would she do? And if he did talk, how would she relay it in time for Blake or her boss, Lynne May, to do anything about it? Could she really get away from him?

Long after the rain died down and things seemed to grow quieter, she heard movement outside her room. She heard footsteps getting closer; then her door opened. Her kidnapper stood in the doorway and stared.

"Was he here?" the man asked.

"Who?" she replied.

Viktor's eyes narrowed as he studied her; then he looked

all around the room, trying to decide if anything was different. Then he stepped farther inside and said, "Your husband has taken out the two men I sent. Mrs. Jordan, you and I are fully aware of what I am capable of. I don't think you want to lie to me." Viktor paused a long moment and added, "I will ask you again: was your husband here? Are we being watched?"

Jami narrowed her eyes and stared back at him. "I hope so."

Viktor smiled to himself, his training as an interrogator taking over. He was expecting the woman to answer no. He'd learned over many years that detainees would adamantly and wholeheartedly respond negatively if they were guilty or if they knew something they didn't want the government to know. And because she had not done that and had answered almost defiantly, Viktor believed truly she did not know. Still, he had come too far to take any chances. He was close to succeeding. So he decided to move anyway.

Viktor stepped farther inside and walked behind Jami and grabbed her arm. He helped her to her feet and brought his weapon out from behind his back and gestured for the door. Jami stared and did not move. "We need to go," he said. "I'm giving my men five minutes, and if they do not call me back, we will leave."

"Why?" asked Jami.

"This location may have been compromised. Your government may be watching us as we speak." He shoved her hard, and Jami stumbled and fell onto the floor. She got to her knees and looked up at him. Viktor racked the slide and aimed his weapon at her. "I'm losing my patience with you. Get to your feet."

Jami took the opportunity and the small amount of

leverage that she had and decided this was her chance. "I'll go with you, and I won't give you any trouble. But first, I want to understand what you're doing here."

"You know what I'm doing," he said, staring down at her.

"You said you have a man on the inside, someone already in place who will stop the peace treaty from happening. You're using my husband to make sure it happens. I want to know who he is. I want a name."

The man named Viktor kept his weapon in his hand but crouched down low to get eye level with Jami. Then he cocked his head to one side and studied her closely. He told her she knew the man, too. A lot of people knew the man. But that wasn't good enough. Jami was persistent. She told him she wanted a name. She demanded it. So he paused a moment, weighing the pros and the cons in his mind.

Then he told her.

SIMON HARRIS HAD BEEN STARING AT THE LAPTOP SCREEN FOR what felt like hours. He needed to use the restroom, and his mouth was dry. So he went to the conference room door and pulled it open. He used his foot to lower a small metal kick-stand and kept it propped open. He looked across the large open space. Parker wasn't there. Nobody was there except for someone inside his boss's office. He saw it was Emma.

Simon walked back to his laptop screen and saw nothing change. No new vehicles had arrived. The lone car parked to the north was still in the same spot. The infrared showed the one tango roaming the building and the two captives, Jami and the UPS driver, still stationary. So he chanced a quick break.

Emma Ross looked up and noticed him and waved at him through Parker's office windows. She was sitting behind her father's desk, on the phone. He waved back. On his way out of the men's room, Simon went to the vending machine and got a cold Mountain Dew and stepped back into the conference room. Simon left the door propped open. He didn't want to bother Parker with a phone call but still wanted to know the moment his boss returned so he could get up to speed with the latest on the peace treaty signing.

As he walked around the conference room table, he popped the tab on his soda and took a quick drink. Then Simon found the remote control to the flatscreen TV mounted in the corner of the room and turned the power on. He found a cable news channel and kept his eyes on the screen, reading a banner that scrolled across as he sat down in his chair. The banner read KELLER AND STEPANOV TO SIGN PEACE TREATY. Simon shook his head in disgust, wondering who had tipped off the media, thinking about how the president had likely wanted to make the surprise announcement when the press conference started.

Then he noticed something out of the corner of his eye: movement.

Simon lowered his gaze and stared at his laptop screen, and his eyes grew wide. The screen was moving.

"No, no, no, no," he repeated over and over again in a low voice as he watched the aerial view of the warehouse slowly moving. The center of the warehouse had been in the dead center of his screen when he'd gotten up. Simon had been zoomed out enough for him to see not only the warehouse but also most of the dirt road that led to the warehouse. But now the vehicle parked at the north side of the building was in the upper left-hand corner of the screen as the view panned to the south and the east in a slow movement.

Simon's heart began to race. He tried typing in a series of

commands to stop the satellite from moving. He watched in horror as nothing he tried worked. Simon picked up the phone and called Morgan Lennox, but the call went straight to voicemail. Morgan was on the phone. He cursed under his breath and tried typing a new set of commands, but nothing worked. The screen continued its slow awful scroll to the southeast as the aerial view of the car parked to the north disappeared; then the warehouse itself disappeared; then the dirt road leading to it moved offscreen. Then Simon sensed movement outside the conference room. He looked up and saw Emma Ross appear in the doorway, brow furrowed, eyes narrow.

"Is everything okay?" she asked.

"No, it's not," he answered.

"What's wrong?" Emma asked as she stepped inside the room and looked at his laptop screen.

Simon pointed at it. "I've lost control of the satellite for some reason. I've lost the visual we had on Jami."

He turned and looked up at the woman as she hovered over him, staring over his shoulder at the screen. Emma reached into a pocket and fumbled for her cell phone. Simon asked, "Who are you calling?"

"My father," she said in a soft voice as blood drained from her face, and she looked more concerned than Simon had ever seen. "He just called me; he's headed there now and needs to know he's going in blind."

AFTER TEN MORE MINUTES WAITING INSIDE THE COVERED guardhouse, one of Rivera's men came for me. They asked me to check my Glock and leave it with the agents in the guardhouse. I thought about what I was getting myself into; I would be the only person inside the White House grounds with the knowledge that someone was going to take out one if not both presidents. Chris Reed would be with Reynolds outside along the perimeter. Unable to help me. Which meant I was the only person who could stop it from happening. I tried to argue with the two agents. I explained that I was with DHS and a personal friend of President Keller's. I told them about the active threat, which they were all aware of but only had a vague notion of, but it was no use; if I wanted to get inside, I had to leave my weapon behind.

So I checked my weapon with them, and a woman agent used a hand wand and moved it up and down my body. It went off around my waist. I presented both cell phones and car keys and dropped everything into a small basket, and she waved the wand again. This time I passed. After stepping through and collecting my things, they asked about Tom Parker. I said he couldn't make it. He'd arrive later. Then I followed the agent down a long winding path inside the gate. A minute later, I entered the White House.

Simon Harris watched helplessly as his screen continued to pan slowly, away from Bethesda and toward Washington, DC. Emma Ross called her father. He answered, and she put the call on speakerphone and explained what was happening. Parker asked Simon how he could've lost control of the satellite, and Simon said he didn't know. Parker told him to keep trying to get a hold of Lennox. Emma asked her father what the plan was. He said he was going to wait close to the dirt road leading to the warehouse. Blake would call him when he learned who the assassin at the White House was. They would then simultaneously take down the assassin at the White House along with the man inside the warehouse.

Simon grabbed his cell phone and thumbed through the contacts list and found the number for Morgan Lennox. He tapped it with his thumb to place the call, and then he pressed the phone to his ear.

"This is Morgan Lennox," he answered on the third ring.

"It's me," he said. "We have a big problem."

"What is it, mate?"

"The satellite's moving. It's panning southeast, towards DC. Morgan, I don't know how to stop it."

"Simon, I need you to calm down. We'll figure this out. Go to the task bar and select override, and I want you to enter the following command." Morgan walked him through it. Simon entered it in. "Did it work?"

"No," he said, putting the call on speakerphone.

"What error code did it give you?"

Simon read it to him. There was a long period of silence on the line. Morgan was busy looking it up. Emma Ross stared at Simon. Parker listened. Simon watched helplessly as the slow scroll continued.

"Bloody hell," Morgan finally said.

"What does it mean?" asked Parker from Emma's phone, overhearing everything.

"It means the satellite has been retasked by the FBI. And it means it'll be a while until we can get it back."

The Secret Service agent took me to their command post on the ground floor of the West Wing, directly below the Oval Office, room W-16. I told the man that I needed to see the president. He said we'd all be seeing him shortly. There was a massive bank of monitors stacked ten high and ten across, showing feeds from hidden cameras located all over the White House grounds. I saw President Keller emerge from the Oval Office with President Stepanov. Some kind of last minute meeting. Maybe Keller was offering a preview of the remarks he was going to make while on camera. Maybe Stepanov was doing the same. They disappeared from one of the monitors and reappeared in another. An agent stepped up next to me and watched along with me. I turned to look over my shoulder and saw the man who had brought me in step outside. I turned back and continued to watch as the two presidents entered and exited different feeds.

Then I noticed another view. It was of the South Lawn. There were endless rows of chairs set out. Television crews were being admitted inside and meeting their press corps counterparts. Things were moving fast. I saw movement on another monitor, and the two presidents reappeared exiting an elevator on the bottom floor, underground, and they hustled to the Presidential Emergency Operations Center. I saw Agent Rivera greet them at the door. He ushered them inside, and I asked the agent standing next to me if there was a problem. He said there wasn't, yet. Rivera needed to brief the men on what to do should there be one. Then I turned back to face the monitors as I wondered, myself, if there would be one or not. Then I scanned every monitor and studied every face and wondered which one was going to take the shot.

MORGAN LENNOX SAID HE NEEDED TO GO. HE EXPLAINED HE had just spoken with Peter Mulvaney and had his direct number saved from the caller ID on his desk phone, having just spoken with the Bureau man. There was a moment of brief silence. He figured Emma and Simon were wondering why he had called him. Morgan heard the tinny voice of Tom Parker speak from Emma's phone, saying he had Mulvaney's personal cell number and would try calling him, too. Emma asked how far out Parker was from Bethesda. Parker answered twenty minutes. Then Morgan clicked off and placed his cell phone on his desk and leaned forward to get a better look at the landline. He touched the screen and saw Mulvaney's office number on the caller ID. Morgan pressed a button to call the number back. There were four long rings.

"Come on, pick up," he whispered to himself through each of them. But the call wasn't answered and went straight to voicemail. Morgan left a brief message; then he tried again. Same result. Then he thought long and hard about what he could do and realized there was nothing he could do. Out of options, he dabbed the cradle and heard a tone. He looked away, trying to remember Simon's number. Morgan hovered a finger over the keypad, but before he dialed, he thought of one more option. Maybe the only real option he had. He listened to the tone a moment longer, and it timed out and started pulsating, a harsh tone repeating itself over and over again. Morgan dabbed the line one more time, then dialed another number. After one ring it was answered. "Mr. Shapiro, this is Morgan Lennox." He paused. "Sir, I need your help."

FIVE MINUTES PASSED. THEN TEN. I CHECKED MY WATCH AND grew impatient as more Secret Service agents stepped inside the command post. They huddled together and allowed me to join them. They confirmed what the agent by the monitors had assumed—that the two presidents were being briefed by Rivera in the PEOC. They needed to understand what a quick evac would look like and where they'd be rushed off to and how it would all go down. And Rivera needed to understand what Keller had in mind in terms of how long they'd be out on the lawn and potentially exposed. The agent doing the talking looked past me. I turned back to the monitors and saw Rivera emerge from the PEOC and head to the elevators. He had left the presidents there with his men, I guessed. Rivera disappeared into an elevator, and I turned back and listened to the agents huddled together discuss their plans. They spoke of the vague threat they were all aware of. They discussed how agents would be on the rooftops, watching everything below and all around the White House grounds. Agents would be watching every corner of the South Lawn and around both presidents. They spoke of the FBI and MPD officers covering streets to the east and to the west. I stood in silence, waiting on Agent Rivera, wondering how the kidnapper's man expected to make it out of here alive.

TOM PARKER EXITED THE HIGHWAY AND NAVIGATED HIS BLUE Crown Victoria onto a surface street. He kept his eyes on the road and brought his cell phone to his face and scrolled through his contacts list until he got to the *M*s and found Peter Mulvaney's personal cell number. He tapped on the number and pressed the phone against his ear and waited through two long rings. Then the Bureau director answered, "Tom?"

He said, "Peter, we have a situation we're dealing with."

"I have a situation of my own."

"I know," said Parker. "Listen, we had one of our interagency satellites positioned over a warehouse."

"The one in Bethesda?"

Parker said nothing.

"We saw that, but it didn't show it was being used officially."

"That's because we weren't using it officially. Peter, I'm on my way to that warehouse. I need it there."

"Why?"

Parker heard his GPS tell him to make a turn, and he obeyed the command and said, "It's a long story, but the short of it is, we have a kidnapping situation underway, and we need to keep monitoring that building."

Mulvaney said nothing for a moment. Then he said, "We thought with the change in venue for the peace treaty signing, it would be wise to have extra coverage to help monitor the area around the White House."

"Is it absolutely necessary?"

Mulvaney paused again. "No, it was just a precaution. We have more than enough manpower down there."

"Can we have it back?"

"Yes, but you'll have to wait until it locks into the location we programmed. Then you can move it back."

"How long will that take?"

"Twenty minutes. Thirty, tops."

Parker asked Mulvaney to make a call and tell his people to yield control of the satellite to DHS. Mulvaney said he would. Then Parker called Simon back with the update. Simon asked his boss how close he was to the warehouse. Parker glanced down at the GPS as he drove and answered, "Less than fifteen minutes."

"There's a dirt road you'll be turning right onto when you make your final approach. You need to hold off on making that turn. When you see it, just pull off to the side of the road and wait. It's a narrow road, and it leads to a locked gate. We don't know if they're back yet or not. I don't want you getting pinned inside."

Parker said he understood. Simon told him that Morgan was working on getting Roger Shapiro to authorize the use of another satellite, but there was a problem—Emma spoke up and said she got a tip that the peace treaty signing was happening in twenty minutes. Parker told Simon to keep his eyes on the satellite and, as soon as it locked into place, to retask it back over Bethesda and to stay in contact with Lennox in case he had better luck. Parker clicked off. Ten minutes later, he approached the dirt road and pulled off to the side. He killed the motor and sat in silence, watching the road, and he glanced at his watch. *There's not enough time to move the satellite*, he thought as he checked his revolver and settled in to wait.

43

PRESIDENT JAMES KELLER SAT ACROSS FROM THE RUSSIAN president inside the PEOC. Agent Rivera had given them the room to talk privately and headed upstairs to meet with his agents in the command post. Rivera left a few of his men stationed outside the soundproof doors and along the hallways to the elevator. The two men were alone. There were no advisors present. No interpreters needed. Not yet at least. Not until the Russian president would speak to the people of his own country on camera and Keller would listen to the translation on a delay in an earpiece. Keller asked Stepanov if he had any reservations. But the man made no reply. He just looked downward and shook his head slowly. Keller didn't believe him.

"President Stepanov, are you concerned about security?"

Stepanov looked up and took a breath. "Mr. President, you need to understand something. Half of the citizens of your country will be upset with today's announcement. The other half will praise your decision. There will be experts and talking heads on cable news for a week arguing both sides of the issue." Stepanov gestured with one hand in a waving fashion. "Then it will all be over. The people of America will move on to the next big issue, the next controversy to be argued. This will be old news in a week's time."

Keller furrowed his brow and tilted his head to one side. "Go on," he said, trying to understand.

The Russian president paused a moment longer, then said, "My people will not treat me as well as you."

Keller said nothing.

"This is why I spoke only to my most senior leaders before leaving my country to meet with you. Mr. President, in a few minutes the people of my country will be hearing about this peace treaty in real time. This will be the first time they're learning of this." The man shook his head. "They may not be too happy with me. In fact, should they choose to do so, they very well could retaliate. They could try to overthrow my government. They could try to oust me." He paused again. "They could even try to kill me."

Keller lowered his gaze. "I understand."

Stepanov shook his head. "You don't," he said. "Not really. This is one of the most secure buildings on the planet. You are completely safe here. This threat you have made me aware of, we both know there is nothing to be concerned about as long as we're on these grounds. Even if we weren't, your Secret Service team would make sure nothing would happen to either one of us." The man paused one more time. "Please understand, once I leave the US, when I head back to my home country, my future is uncertain."

President Keller nodded solemnly. "I see. I did not know you had only conferred with your top leaders."

"If I had discussed my true plans outside of that small, inner circle, I might not have been permitted to leave. It is not like your country, where you can make an unpopular decision and the worst that can happen is impeachment. Our government follows the will of the people. I only hope they side with me."

Silence in the room. Keller took a breath and let it out. "And if they don't?"

Stepanov said nothing. He didn't need to.

President Keller understood. He asked, "Are you sure you want to go through with this?"

Stepanov nodded; then he forced a smile. "As sure as I have ever been about anything, Mr. President."

Keller stretched out his hand across the table. Stepanov took it and grasped it firmly as they shared a moment. Either the start of a new diplomatic relationship between two countries at odds for decades, or the death sentence for a man from a completely different upbringing but the same worldview of freedom. The two presidents stood, and Keller gestured for the door. They exited the PEOC, and the Secret Service agents stationed outside the door escorted the men down to the elevator at the far end of the long hallway. The elevator doors chimed open, and Keller's chief of staff emerged. Ethan Meyer said, "Ten minutes, sir."

44

I WAS STANDING OUTSIDE THE CIRCLE OF AGENTS WHEN THE door to the command post opened. Agent Rivera stepped inside, and the huddle broke. His men stepped aside, creating an opening like a team of football players who were letting their coach step into the circle to call a new play. Rivera noticed me and nodded once, then said to his guys, "Listen up. The two presidents will make their way to the South Lawn shortly." Rivera paused a moment and glanced at the monitors. I followed his gaze. I saw Keller and Stepanov appear in the East Colonnade, heading toward the White House's south exit with two of Rivera's men following them at a distance, wearing dark suits, speaking into wrist mics. Rivera continued, "Same plan we had for the Pullman House. Same general assignments as before. If you were to be outside there, you'll be outside with me here. If you were to be within earshot of the presidents there, same assignment here. Only we have a more controlled environment here. This is our house. Nobody knows it better than us. But don't let your guard down. We know about the intercepted phone call that's being looked in to. The Bureau has people along the east and west perimeters and a satellite they've positioned overhead. MPD is out there assisting them. Our focus is getting through this peace treaty signing without incident."

I studied the faces of Rivera's men. I tried using what I'd learned as a SEAL years ago, looking for microexpressions, any sign that one of them could be the man on the inside Jami's kidnapper had said was in place. The man I was supposed to give the cell phone to. The man who would make an attempt on one if not both of the president's lives. But none of them offered any facial expressions that seemed concerning to me. None of them seemed stressed. None of them seemed distracted. None of them were eyeing me or each other, assessing who would give them problems, who wouldn't. My eyes scanned back and forth, looking for the one I should be worried about. The one Jami's kidnapper would need me to make sure took the shot. The one I'd have to make sure *didn't* take the shot, if Parker could save her first.

But they all looked the same. No major differences in their appearances. Just a dogged determination to get through their assignment without any issues. They all seemed to be on the same page, listening to their coach, ready to break the huddle and go out onto the field and get the job done. Then Rivera clapped his hands twice and pointed at the door behind him with his thumb, and his men moved past him and left the room. Everyone left except for Rivera and one other man. He was to stay back and watch the cameras. He moved past me and stood in front of the massive bank of monitors and studied each one in turn. Rivera got a call and answered it and stepped to the other side of the room. The agent near the monitors took his time looking at the different screens; then once he got through them all, he focused only on the ones that showed people he wasn't familiar with. Video feeds from hidden cameras showed press corps members taking their seats along with Vice President Mike Billings and others from Keller's administration.

Rivera wrapped up his call and pocketed his phone and walked over to where I was standing. I offered my hand, and he shook it and glanced over at the man watching the screens. Rivera said, "Anything new?"

"You tell me," I replied. "Has the Bureau shared anything new regarding the threat?"

Rivera shook his head and stared at the monitors. "No. It's just an empty threat as far as I'm concerned."

I followed his gaze and turned around and saw the two presidents walk toward the south entrance. They hung back and spoke to each other. Keller nodded and checked his watch. Then he lowered his hand and brought it forward and placed one on top of the other as the two leaders waited to exit the White House. My phone buzzed in my pocket. I dug it out and looked at the screen. *UNKNOWN CALLER.* I silenced the call and dropped it back into my pocket. I couldn't talk to the guy. Not yet. "I need to get out there," I said.

I turned back and saw Rivera shift his gaze away from the screens and over to me. "I can't let you do that."

I narrowed my eyes.

"Empty threat or not, I have to contain the area. I don't need anyone on the South Lawn unless it's absolutely necessary. Stay with Agent Bryant. I'll come back for you after the ceremony."

. . .

AGENT RIVERA STEPPED OUT OF THE COMMAND POST AND LEFT in a hurry. Agent Bryant and I were the only ones left in the room. Bryant took a seat in front of the massive deck of monitors, moving his eyes from screen to screen, completely focused on the task at hand. My cell phone buzzed in my pocket again. I checked the caller ID and saw it was Parker. "Excuse me, I need to take this," I said.

Agent Bryant nodded vaguely but made no reply and kept his focus on studying each of the monitors in front of him.

I stepped to the back of the room and said, "This is Jordan."

"What's the latest?" asked Parker.

I turned and stared across the room at Bryant. In a low voice I said, "He tried calling a few seconds ago."

"You couldn't take the call?"

"No."

"Figure out who the guy is yet?"

"No," I said again, eyeing Bryant. "I thought it might be one of Rivera's men, but I was wrong."

"Who else could it be?"

"I don't know, Parker. There are a lot of people here. It could be anyone." I studied the monitors from across the room and watched as countless government officials and reporters moved across the screens. "When the guy calls and tells me who his man is, I'll take him out and I'll call you. Where are you now?"

"Sitting at the end of a dirt road about a mile away from the warehouse. We lost control of the satellite. Which means we no longer have a visual. Which means I'm going to have to go in blind to get Jami back."

"How'd you lose control of the satellite?" I asked. Parker started to reply as my phone buzzed in my hand. I brought it

to my face and look at the screen. *UNKNOWN CALLER.*
"Parker, he's calling me right now."

Parker said, "Take it."

I clicked off and answered the incoming call. "Yes," I
said.

"Mr. Jordan, I assume you're in position?"

I stared across the room at Bryant. "Yes," I said again in a
low voice. "I'm in the Secret Service's command post."
Bryant turned his head slightly. He'd picked up on some of
the conversation from across the room.

The kidnapper said, "You need to get to the South Lawn
as quickly as possible."

"Who is your man?"

No response.

I glanced across the room. Bryant was focused on the
monitors again. The people in the crowd were all seated. I
watched as the two presidents stepped outside and made
their way to a podium. Bryant tracked them as they walked
across the grass, studying everyone around them.

"Who is he?" I asked again.

The kidnapper breathed. "You," he said. "You are my
man. Now get to the South Lawn. I'll call you back."

THE LINE WENT DEAD, AND I STARED DOWN AT THE SCREEN.
"How could I have been so blind," I whispered. Agent
Bryant stood from his chair and pressed his hands flat on
the desk in front of him and leaned forward. He was more
focused now. The presidents were making their way,
offering periodic waves of the hand, Keller reaching the
podiums, gesturing for his Russian counterpart to step
forward along with him. My heart was beating hard in my
chest. My breathing grew faster but was shallower. My

fingers were shaking. I steadied them and tapped on the number for Tom Parker and pressed my cell phone to my ear.

"What do you got?" he asked, answering on the first ring.

"It's me," I said.

"I know."

"No, Parker," I whispered. "I'm his guy on the inside."

Parker said nothing. I pictured him sitting inside his Crown Vic, on the shoulder of the road, furrowing his brow, wondering how he hadn't seen it either.

I looked across at the screens and saw the ceremony about to begin. "Parker, you need to go in right now."

TOM PARKER CLICKED OFF AND STARTED THE MOTOR AND made the turn onto the dirt road. He thumbed his call log and pressed his phone to his ear. Simon answered, and he asked, "Any progress on the satellites?"

"Yes," he answered. "The one we were using locked into position in DC, so I was able to retask it back to Bethesda. And as a backup, Morgan somehow convinced Roger Shapiro to authorize temporary use of another one through DDC. So both are going to lock into their new coordinates at roughly the same time."

"Which is when?"

There was a pause on the line. "About ten minutes."

"I don't have ten minutes."

"I can't make it go any faster, Mr. Parker."

Parker drove faster along the dirt road that was in reality very muddy and very hard to steer on. His Crown Vic fishtailed as he drove. He regained control and said, "Tell me what I'm dealing with up here."

There was another pause as Simon closed his eyes and

thought about it. "Okay, so the dirt road extends east about a mile and dead-ends at the warehouse. The gate is locked. Blake had to climb over the fence."

"There's no way in hell I'll be able to do that."

Simon said nothing back.

"What else do I need to know?"

"There was a car parked on the north side of the building. We think it was the kidnapper's. Mr. Parker, are you sure you can't just wait a little bit longer? We're coming up on nine minutes until we'll have a visual."

Parker saw an alcove up ahead. "I can't. The bad guy's expecting the assassination to take place now."

Simon made no reply. He just hung on the line as Parker pressed his foot harder against the accelerator. He passed the alcove to the right of him and navigated a wide curve, then the road straightened out, and up ahead he could see the gate, closed tight. Parker told Simon what he was going to do. He said he had to go and asked his analyst to call him back as soon as he got one of the satellites in place. Then he set the phone down and gripped the wheel with both hands as he straightened out and stepped down on the gas.

45

I DUG INSIDE MY POCKET TO FIND THE BLUETOOTH EARPIECE, and I put it in as I moved closer to Agent Bryant. The two presidents were standing side by side, ten feet apart, at two identical podiums. Half of the crowd seated before them were on their feet and clapping. The other half were seated with arms crossed, looking unconvinced that this was a good idea. Keller raised a hand briefly to end the applause from his supporters, and the clapping slowed, and those who were standing took their seats. My phone buzzed in my pocket. I looked at the caller ID and saw it was Parker calling. I tapped my earpiece and said, "Yeah."

"I'm moving in now, Jordan. Made a hell of a lot of noise ramming the gate. What's the best approach?"

"Go to the western side. I kept the door from locking so we could get back in."

Parker said he was headed there now. I listened to his labored breathing as he moved into place. He told me he saw the door. I told him I'd left a dollar bill between the jamb and the latch so it wouldn't lock. I waited, listening to him breathing while I watched the president make his remarks. I figured once he was done speaking, his Russian counterpart would say a few words. I had a little bit of time before the signing. But not much. Parker whispered and told me he was inside. I told him the tango would be to his left, on the north side. The first room to his right was where Jami was being held. The room next to that had the UPS driver. I felt my heart racing faster as I watched the monitors behind Bryant and listened to Parker head in. I could see him moving in my mind's eye, making sure the area was clear, making sure the tango to the north wasn't heading his way. Parker whispered that it was clear, and he was entering the first room.

There was a long pause. Then he whispered, "She's not here."

"Check the other room," I whispered back.

I waited through thirty long seconds; then he said, "Not here, either."

"Then you need to head to the northern section. The guy has them up there somewhere."

I heard another call coming in. I checked the ID. *UNKNOWN CALLER*. I ignored the call and waited. A full minute passed. Then two. At three minutes, Keller was well into his speech. I couldn't hear the words, but the man was animated and clearly speaking with conviction, and I figured he was explaining why they were there and what it meant. The Russian president looked out over the crowd, then turned to Keller as he smiled and nodded. Parker whispered that he was making his approach. He said there were two more rooms. They were identical to the ones on the south side. I turned and headed to the back of the room as I listened and heard him clear each of them with the same result. "Nobody's here, Jordan," he finally said.

"Is there an exit door anywhere?"

"Yes, just like on the south side."

"Check outside, see if the car Simon saw is still out there."

Parker checked. He came back and said, "I'm sorry. There's no vehicle out here. They're gone."

MY HEART SANK IN MY CHEST. I STOOD IN SILENCE, NOT believing what I was hearing. Parker called for me, but I didn't reply. I just turned back and thought through what this meant. Parker called for me again. He asked what our options were at this point. When I didn't reply, he asked me what I was going to do now.

Another call was coming in again. The same words showed on the phone's display: *UNKNOWN CALLER.* "I don't know," I said, clicking off and answering the incoming call. "Where are you, you son of a bitch?"

"I had a feeling," he said. "You didn't play by the rules, Mr. Jordan. You were watching me, weren't you?"

"Where is she?"

"Here with me. She's safe, for now." I could hear Jami in the background. Her voice was muffled, but she was trying to speak. She was letting me know she was still there and still alive, just unable to tell me more. "You're running out of time. President Keller will finish his remarks soon. Then Stepanov is going to speak. Then they will take a seat and sign the treaty. Mr. Jordan, you are to kill them both before they do."

"You know I could never do that."

"You wouldn't kill a president to save your wife?"

I said nothing.

"Because that's your choice, Mr. Jordan. Right here, right now. Hours ago, I said when someone tells you who they are, believe them. You seem to have forgotten that. I'm the guy who's going to make you feel the same pain you felt when your first wife was killed. Only this time, you will have to live the rest of your life knowing you were the one responsible for her death. Not me. Because you had a chance to keep her safe. It's your decision. It's your choice."

I said nothing back. Just stared at the monitors, my chest heaving up and down as I processed his words.

"I will call you back in five minutes. That will be your last chance to comply and save her life. Choose wisely."

THE CALL ENDED, AND I MOVED FORWARD, TOWARD AGENT Bryant. "Everything okay?" I asked as I moved.

Bryant nodded. "We're about five minutes away from the signing. Then fifteen more minutes of exposure. Within twenty minutes, the presidents should be back inside. Rivera insisted that the ceremony be quick."

I glanced down and saw his gun holstered on his hip. I came up fast and wrapped my arm around Bryant's neck and grabbed my wrist with my free hand, and I squeezed hard. "I'm sorry," I whispered as Bryant struggled for twenty long seconds. Then after his body went limp, I took his sidearm and checked the mag. It was fully loaded. I found his handcuffs on his belt and cuffed the man to a heavy cabinet door. Then I glanced back up at the row of monitors and studied the landscape, trying to figure out where I should go.

I HID THE WEAPON IN MY WAISTBELT AND EXITED THE command post and headed upstairs to the south exit. There was still a scattering of Secret Service agents posted along the corridors and doorways. They eyed me as I approached, and I nodded as I moved past them. I hurried out the southern exit and stepped along the path I had seen the presidents walk through, toward the reporters and their cameramen. Keller was still speaking as I approached. He noticed me, and I caught a smile as he watched me move. The Russian president was standing next to him, nodding in agreement with what Keller was saying, preparing to give his own remarks at any moment. I looked across the folding chairs and saw they were all occupied. A few people held onto black umbrellas even though it was no longer raining. I stood in the back, watching, thinking, my heart beating hard, my chest still heaving, oblivious to whatever words Keller was speaking, just deciding what I was going to do. Then there was an awkward moment of silence. I became fully present again and saw Keller gesture toward Stepanov. Then the Russian president began speaking. He kept his comments short. He wanted to speak in English. Through a heavy accent, the man said he agreed with everything Keller had said and urged the people of both nations to support their efforts. Then he spoke in his own language, saying what I decided was the same message, just translated for his people. As I watched, my cell phone buzzed in my pocket. "Yes," I said, answering the call using my earpiece.

"You must do it now," the voice said as I saw the two presidents exit the podium and move toward a table.

To my right I saw two Secret Service agents stepping out from the White House. One of them was Bryant. He was speaking into a cuff mic. I shifted my eyes and studied the agents standing behind Keller and Stepanov. In unison, they put a hand to their ear, listening, acknowledging, then scanning the crowd. Jami screamed. A muffled sound, her mouth gagged. Maybe her loose zip tie hadn't been loose enough.

Then the kidnapper said, "Something's wrong. They know about you. Take the presidents out right now."

"I can't," I said in a low voice.

"Do it and I'll let her go. Don't and you'll find her body dumped on the street. You'll never find me."

"I'm too far away to take the shot."

"You were a sniper, Mr. Jordan. You have unique access. You can walk right up to them. This is why I chose you. You are the only one who can stop the signing. Take them out now, or I swear the woman dies!"

I rested my hand on the weapon in my waistbelt. My fingers were shaking. My palms were sweating. Adrenaline was surging throughout my entire body. I gripped the weapon tight. I was estimating the distance and the trajectory of the bullet and how much I'd have to compensate. Not much. Thirty yards. Aim for the head. No, the chest. There was movement to my left. I turned and looked behind me. Agents from the far end of the lawn were jogging in my direction. I faced forward as the two presidents sat down.

"Do it now!" the voice screamed in my earpiece.

Keller reached for a pen. Stepanov did the same. Then Keller reached for a black portfolio and opened it.

"Take the shot!" the voice screamed.

I gripped the weapon even tighter. Could I take the shot? Could I take out both presidents? *Yes*, I thought.

"Go to hell," I said as I pulled the weapon out of my waistbelt and dropped it on the grass.

I looked to my left and saw Agent Rivera running toward me. To my right, Bryant and another man were approaching fast. Behind me, footsteps were growing louder. I put my hands up and interlaced my fingers and set them on the back of my head. I got down on my knees and waited. I saw Keller sign the document. Then he handed it over to

Stepanov. As the Russian president signed it, Keller faced forward, looking out across the many faces, smiling broadly. Then he noticed me. His smile faded. The people seated at the folding chairs in the crowd noticed. They turned around and watched curiously as the agents approached.

"You know who you are?" asked the voice. "You're the guy who just signed your wife's death warrant."

"No," I replied. "I'm the guy who's going to find you. And I'll be the one who kills you."

The kidnapper said nothing.

"When someone tells you who they are, believe them," I said, repeating his own words back to him. Then the call disconnected. Rivera and Bryant reached me at the same time. They grabbed me from each arm and lifted me to my feet and escorted me away, back toward the White House's south entrance. Back to their underground command post, I assumed. I looked over my shoulder and saw the people seated watching us. The other agents walked back to their posts. The media captured the scene from a distance. I turned and faced forward as I moved. Jami was missing, her kidnapper got away, and I was under arrest. I had failed. As we approached the south entrance, I heard a faint, high-pitched sound, growing louder. "Bomb!" I yelled as I broke free from the men, found the phone in my pocket, and I threw it away from us.

46

THE EXPLOSION WAS DEAFENING, AND WHEN I OPENED MY eyes, all three of us were on the ground. Rivera yelled something to his agent, who drew his weapon and aimed it at me as Rivera turned, patted me down, and then turned me over on my stomach and placed handcuffs on me. I lifted my head and saw Presidents Keller and Stepanov being rushed away and the people who were seated in front of them scatter. Rivera and his agent got me to my feet again, and they pushed me forward, faster this time, toward the entrance.

I half thought I'd be whisked away in one of the Bureau's or MPD's vehicles. But instead, I was escorted back inside the White House and was marched down long corridors, past the agents posted along the wall. When we got to the command post, Rivera's man opened the door for us, and Rivera shoved me inside.

"Leave us," Rivera said to his man. The agent who had opened the door for us left. "You too," Rivera said, and Agent Bryant stared back for a long moment, then he stepped past us and left the room.

There was movement on the monitors. I watched as

government officials and the media were being directed to a safer place. The presidents were no longer visible on the screens. "Agent Rivera," I began.

Rivera pointed at a chair. "Sit down and start talking."

I nodded and moved to the table in the middle of the room. I used my shoe to kick a chair out, and I sat down on the edge with my wrists still handcuffed behind my back. Then I looked up as Rivera stepped closer to me. He grabbed a chair and pulled it out and set it directly in front of me. Then he sat down. "You know why you're here and not downtown at the Hoover Building? Because this is my house, Jordan."

I said nothing.

"You and I go back a long time. And because of the threat we prevented together on inauguration day, I have you to thank for President Keller entrusting me to lead my team of agents." Rivera shook his head slowly. "But make no mistake, Jordan. I don't owe you any favors. Not when it comes to keeping the president safe." He pointed away. "What the hell was that about? Start talking, now."

I lowered my head and stared at the floor. "You're right," I said. "Agent Rivera, I have my reasons. But I don't believe you'd help me even if I told you. Would you?"

Rivera made no reply.

"I'd be wasting my breath. All I can tell you is someone I care about is in danger. She might not even be alive now. I was being blackmailed. In the end, regardless of what you saw, I made the right choice. A choice I have to live with."

"Is that all you're going to tell me?" Rivera nodded to himself once and looked away. "You're in a lot of trouble, my man. Nobody's going to help you here, and now the media's all over this. Guess you accomplished one thing—" Rivera stood "—you've shown the people of both countries that, even with a peace treaty, terrorism is alive and well, even within the sacred grounds of the White House."

Rivera walked to the door and stepped out into the hallway. I heard muffled conversations for less than a minute; then Bryant and another agent stepped inside. Bryant went back to the monitors and took a seat. He pressed a few buttons, and the view changed. No longer was he monitoring what was going on outside. Now he was looking at the main corridors within the White House, studying faces, watching for any movement. The other guy remained standing at the door and crossed his arms and just stared at me.

My thoughts drifted to Jami's kidnapper. I imagined him driving, and I thought through what I would do if I were him. I'd pull off to the side of the road, and I'd verify if there were any casualties from the device his man had said was a phone. A device meant to kill me to cover his tracks. Or maybe a backup plan if I had been standing closer to Keller and Stepanov.

Then I'd kill Jami, and I'd flee the country, or I'd go into hiding until the news cycle changed to something else. I closed my eyes and thought about the last time I saw Jami. She was sitting behind a table in the warehouse, beaten, tears in her eyes, telling me to trust her and mouthing the words *love you* to me as I made the decision to leave her there alone. I opened my eyes and asked myself a question: *Am I a patriot? Or a terrorist?* Then I hung my head and closed my eyes again because I knew the answer: I was neither.

I WAITED INSIDE THE COMMAND POST FOR CLOSE TO AN HOUR. With every passing minute, I imagined the kidnapper getting farther away and the chances of Jami still being alive getting worse. I called out to Agent Bryant and pleaded with him to help me. But he made no reply and just kept his eyes fixed to the screens, monitoring the hallways inside the building. Then I heard muffled conversations outside the door. Two familiar voices. Then a third. The door opened, and President Keller himself stepped through. Keller looked at me; then he turned back to the agents and said, "I need the two of you to give us the room."

The man at the door left. Bryant turned from the monitors and said, "Mr. President, I'm supposed to—"

"You're supposed to keep me safe. I'm in this room. Therefore you know my exact whereabouts. I'm safe."

Agent Bryant glared at me for a long moment; then he moved to the open door and closed it behind him. President Keller moved closer and pulled out the same chair Rivera had sat in and took a seat. He rested his elbows on his knees and brought his hands together as if he were going to pray; then he leaned forward. "I spoke with Tom Parker about your situation. He walked me through it all. How did we get here, son?"

I stared back and said, "These people knew that I could get close to you. They took Jami to blackmail me. They threatened to kill her. They wanted me to take you and Stepanov out before you signed the treaty."

"Did you consider it?"

"Of course not."

"Then explain what happened. You took Agent Bryant's weapon. I saw you out there on the lawn, waiting."

"I was extending the play. I was buying time; I was trying to come up with something."

Keller tilted his head to the side as he listened. "Agent Rivera thinks otherwise."

"I don't care what he thinks."

Keller narrowed his eyes.

"Sir, with all due respect, I have known you for over twenty years. My father was your best friend. And I'd like to think I've proven my own loyalty to you. In fact, I know I have." I paused. "Sir, I have saved your life countless times. I have put my own life on the line to keep you and the people you care about safe by doing whatever this country has asked of me."

Keller said nothing.

"These people chose me because I have unique access. They knew I could get to you. And sir, you and I both know that I was a pretty good shot in the Navy. I was a sniper. I won awards. Mr. President, trust me—if I wanted to kill you, you wouldn't be sitting in front of me right now. If not with a pistol, then with the explosive I was carrying around in my pocket that these people tried to kill me with." I paused a long moment and looked away. "Mr. President, they knew about Maria. They tried to use it against me. They knew if I didn't go through with their order to take you and President Stepanov out, it would mean a death sentence for Jami. For all intents and purposes, I was the only person who could pull it off."

Keller said nothing.

"I had a chance to save her. We found her, but she refused to go with me. Her kidnapper had already told her that you and Stepanov were the targets. She thought if she stayed, she could get a name. She didn't realize it was me. Neither did I. If we knew, none of this would've happened."

Keller nodded to himself. He placed his hands on his knees and said, "Blake, in my experience, when a woman you love tells you to trust her, you should probably listen." The president grew quiet for a spell. "You can't blame yourself, son. She has a job to do, too. She'd be expected to stay back and get any information she could if it had to do with national security. You were doing your job; she was doing hers." He paused again, longer this time. Then he looked me over and said, "Do you think you can get her back?"

I lowered my gaze as I leaned forward and said nothing. "Very well." Keller stood and patted me twice on the back. Then he went to the door and stepped out, where muffled conversations picked back up again.

47

THE DOOR OPENED AGAIN, AND JAMES KELLER STEPPED INSIDE, followed by Rivera, followed by Tom Parker. Parker must've used the hour to finish clearing the building and drive back and enter the White House. Keller pointed at me and said, "Take off the handcuffs." Rivera hesitated for a beat, and Keller said, "Now."

Rivera walked over to where I was sitting and fished a key out of his belt and removed the handcuffs. I brought my hands forward and rubbed my wrists. I remained seated and looked up at the three of them.

Keller said, "Agent Rivera, I want you to transfer custody to Tom Parker and Homeland Security."

Rivera said, "Mr. President, Jordan took out one of my men and stole his weapon. He could've killed you."

"You have it wrong," replied Keller. "Blake was made aware of a possible assassin inside the White House. He had every reason to believe it was one of your men. Who else would be able to get to Stepanov and me?"

Rivera thought about that and said, "Then he should've told me."

"What if it was you?"

Rivera said nothing.

"Agent Rivera, you locked him up in this room, impeding his ability to respond. The very reason Jordan was here was to coordinate the DHS response to keep me safe."

"Which is my job."

"Which is also his job," added Parker, referring to me. "It's all of our jobs, really."

The president continued, "As soon as Jordan learned the threat was over, he gave himself up. Did he not?"

"You expect me to let this guy go after what just happened? He had a bomb on him. It detonated, sir."

Keller took a step forward and lowered his voice. "I know this looks bad, but there's more at play here. A lot more than I want to share at this time. Agent Rivera, I need you to work with me. I will explain the rest to you when I am able to—now drop this issue and move on."

I stood up and stepped forward, toward the three men, and joined them in the semicircle they'd created.

Rivera's eyes moved from Keller to Parker, then to me. "What about the cameras?" he asked.

Keller said nothing.

"There were reporters out there recording the whole thing, including the explosion. Have you turned on the news, sir? It's all over the networks. How do we explain this away? What do we tell them?"

"That's not for you to worry about."

"It is, actually. My job will be on the line. They may not have captured Jordan's face, but the media knows a man was on White House grounds with a gun, and when he was led away, a bomb went off." Rivera shook his head and looked at each of us in turn. "That's an issue. That's not something that will go away."

Keller thought about that for a long moment and turned to Parker. Parker nodded vaguely and said, "I'll call Emma as soon as we leave. Knowing her, she already knows about it. And given her history with your administration, Mr. President, she's already thought about what she'd do if she'd still been your chief of staff." Parker shifted his eyes to Keller and asked, "Where is Ethan, by the way? Why isn't he helping us?"

"With President Stepanov, I assume." Keller turned to Rivera. "What's your answer, son. Will you help?"

AGENT RIVERA ANSWERED BY TAKING A STEP BACK AND gesturing to me with an open hand while eyeing me. Parker nodded his appreciation, and President Keller reached for the door handle and pulled it open. Parker led me outside, where Agent Bryant and a few other agents were gathered and talking in low voices. They grew quiet as we passed. Parker kept a hand on my back for a long moment; then when we turned a corner, he lowered it. I heard footsteps and turned back and stopped moving. Keller was catching up to us.

He looked at me and said, "Son, five minutes ago, I asked if you could get Jami back. You didn't answer me."

I nodded vaguely. "I don't know where she is. I don't even know if she's still alive."

"I didn't ask if you knew where she was. I asked if you could do it. Trust yourself. Are you following me?"

I nodded again. "Yes, sir."

Keller's eyes moved to Parker, and he said, "Tom, I want you to help Blake any way you can. I'm giving you and your department whatever you need." Keller paused. "I've known Blake a long time. And son, you're right—you have saved my life more times than I can count. The threat here is over." He caught my gaze and said, "Go and get your wife back."

I LEFT THE SAME WAY I HAD ENTERED, BUT IN REVERSE ORDER. Keller had one of his Secret Service agents escort us out. There were reporters and news crews parked all around the perimeter of the White House with cameras rolling. We managed to get to the guardhouse and collect our weapons before they noticed us. Then Parker and I entered the Ellipse and found his Crown Vic and my SUV parked close to each other. Parker dialed Emma and pressed the phone to his ear, and as the line rang, he asked, "So what's the plan?"

"We look for the guy. If Jami's still alive, he'll have her with him, or we'll make him tell us where she is."

Parker nodded and looked away, and then he furrowed his brow. Emma wasn't answering. He left a brief message for his daughter, and then he dropped the phone into his pocket. "Where do we start?" he asked.

"We think like him," I said as I tried calling Simon Harris, but he didn't answer, either.

"If I'm thinking like him, then I'm thinking I failed. I'm thinking the peace treaty was signed, so the only hope he had of stopping it didn't pan out; I'm all alone now, so I'm cutting my losses and fleeing the country."

I said nothing for a long moment. I just turned my head and stared at the White House in the distance, thinking. Then I said, "That's what I thought, too. But we're wrong, Parker." I paused. "Where is Emma?"

"Back at the NAC with Simon."

"Why is she there?"

"She's keeping an eye on Miriam Hassan. And she's keeping her safe. The woman was really shaken up."

"Why?"

"Because someone tried to kill her. Because she knows something. Something having to do with today." Then Parker thought about it some more, and I watched his eyes grow wide with panic. "Let's go, Jordan."

48

PARKER AND I DROVE SEPARATELY, BUT I PULLED OUT FIRST, SO I led the way. Parker must've called ahead because as we approached the entrance to the Nebraska Avenue Complex, I saw the man inside the guardhouse craning his neck, waiting for us, and he pressed the button to open up the gates as we arrived.

We parked our vehicles and ran inside. Parker took the elevator, and I took the stairs, and we arrived in the lobby of the second floor at the same time. Parker looked at me and nodded a question: *Ready?* I drew my weapon and nodded back: *Let's do it.* He swiped his badge and pulled the door open, and I stepped in, swinging my Glock left to right and back again. Parker followed me inside with his own gun drawn. I moved to my right and entered the conference room where we'd met earlier in the day, but Simon wasn't there. I stepped out and saw Parker up ahead, passing Simon's desk, glancing inside his office briefly, then heading toward the smaller conference room. I jogged across the open space and joined him at the door, and we followed the same procedure as before: two nods asking and confirming that we were ready, the door pulled open, Parker and I stepping inside and finding another empty space. No sign of Simon or Emma Ross or Miriam Hassan. The space was empty and silent and lifeless. Nobody was there but us and the guy at the guardhouse. We stepped out of the small conference room and regrouped at Simon's desk.

"Where the hell are they, Jordan?"

I said nothing.

JAMI JORDAN OPENED HER EYES AND BLINKED SEVERAL TIMES as she tried to understand where she was. She felt her wrists loosely zip-tied together. She blinked again and lifted her head slightly and saw another man next to her, arms behind his back, staring at her. Fear in his eyes. They were back in the vehicle that had brought them to the warehouse originally. The man's UPS truck. The engine was humming, and the floor was vibrating as the driver moved the vehicle at a high speed. Jami decided they were on a highway somewhere. She closed her eyes and listened carefully, and then she felt a terrible pain in the back of her head. Then she remembered what had happened. She had been sitting inside her cell, her wrists loosely bound, waiting for the kidnapper to reappear and give her another opportunity to ask more questions about his man on the inside. But when her kidnapper finally returned, he simply opened the door to her cell and the cell next to hers and gestured with his weapon for both of his prisoners to stand and step out.

As Jami obeyed and stepped out of the room, she saw the UPS driver again for the first time in hours. Their kidnapper gestured with his weapon for the two of them to turn to their right and walk toward the truck. The back door was opened wide, and they moved toward it. The packages had all been removed and were stacked high along the wall. Jami followed the UPS man, watching him from behind as he kept turning his face to the left to look back with his peripheral vision as he moved onward. Jami followed his gaze and noticed the vehicle she'd seen earlier. A van, parked inside, with two men working. A younger one and an older one, working hard, loading fertilizer and something else into the vehicle. She got to the truck, and their kidnapper ordered them inside. First the man, then her. Then her kidnapper stepped inside. She heard a thud, and the driver fell to the floor. Before she could react, he struck her in the head.

And now she was awake and so was the UPS man. She looked back at the guy and noticed the expression on his face. It had changed. No longer was it full of fear and dread. Now it was different, like he'd decided this whole nightmare was close to being over. But not in a good way. Like he was resigned to his fate, and his fate was likely certain death.

"Hey," she whispered, loud enough for the man to hear her but soft enough to be cloaked underneath the hum of the loud engine and the road noise. The man looked at her. "We're going to be okay. I promise." Jami nodded reassuringly, but the man just looked away, unbelieving, still resigned to his perceived fate.

PARKER TRIED CALLING EMMA ROSS AGAIN, BUT SHE DIDN'T answer. Neither did Simon. Parker called his daughter's boss at the CIA as I called Morgan. Emma's boss didn't answer, so Parker left a message for the man to return his call. Morgan answered immediately and told me he hadn't heard from Simon in a while, but he still had control of one of the satellites and asked me what I wanted him to do with it, if anything. I asked Morgan about the warehouse. He said it was empty, according to the infrared. No sign of Jami. No sign of anybody. He said that Simon's satellite was still positioned over the White House, but the FBI was requesting it. I conferred with Parker and told Morgan to give it back to the Bureau on Simon's behalf and then reposition his acquired satellite over DC again, since I knew it would take some time to move it back.

"Anywhere in particular, mate?" Morgan asked on speakerphone.

"Put it back over the safe house," said Parker as he stepped closer. "Until we figure out if we need it."

Morgan said he'd do it soon, but he needed to go because he had Peter Mulvaney holding for him on the other line. They had just identified the kidnapper. I asked for the name. Morgan said, "Viktor Babushkin."

IT TOOK LESS THAN A MINUTE FOR JAMI TO PULL HER RIGHT hand through the loose zip tie her husband had set. Which was thirty seconds longer than she thought it would take. It had been the perfect length. Not so loose that it had come undone when she had been suddenly struck and collapsed on the bed of the truck. Not so tight that she was unable to free herself. The man noticed her struggling through it, and she watched his eyes grow wide as she managed to free her right hand, then grabbed the tie and pulled it off her left and set it on the floorboard. Jami felt something in her pocket, large and bulky and painful after it had pressed up against her for however long she had been in this position. Jami remained flat and kept her eyes on the man and watched his face, weary but now full of wonderment and possibilities. She raised a finger to her lips for the man to understand that he had to be completely silent. She pointed toward the cab of the truck and cupped a hand behind her ear. *We have to be quiet or he will hear us*, she was saying. The man nodded. She again pointed toward the cab and wiggled her fingers like two legs walking slowly. Then she pointed at him and then pointed toward the floorboard. An exaggerated movement, making it clear he was not to help but to remain where he was. The man nodded again, reluctantly but in agreement.

Then the noise from the motor changed. It no longer howled with a high-pitched wail as the driver pushed it to the limit out on the highway. The truck was now coasting. Jami pressed her hand flat against the floor and steadied herself as she and the man next to her felt their bodies being pulled to the left side of the truck. They were exiting. If she was going to do something, she'd have to do it now. Jami pushed herself up and reached into her pocket and found the knife. She pulled out the blade and moved over to the man. Jami reached behind him and quickly cut the tie from his wrists. The man leaned back and rubbed his wrists as Jami leaned in close and whispered into his ear, "I need you to stay here. Don't make a sound."

The driver stepped on the brakes, and they both leaned forward, toward the cab, and steadied themselves. Then they came to a complete stop. The truck rocked forward, then backward; then it grew almost completely silent. The road noise was gone. All noise was gone except for the hum from the idling engine. Jami gave the man a stern look: *I mean it, don't move.* He nodded his agreement: *I won't make a sound.* But he crouched and quietly positioned himself so his left foot was on the bed of the truck and moved his right knee next to it and put the flat of his hands on the floor, and he nodded again: *But I have your back.*

Jami stood quietly and slowly stepped forward, rolling her feet as she moved, steadying herself by grabbing hold of the empty racks where packages would've been. She got to the front. The metal door to the cab was closed. She moved her left hand and gripped the handle and held the blade with her right. A tight grip on both. She slowed her breathing, closed her eyes, and waited. The vehicle lurched forward. The light had changed. Physics pulled her right as the driver turned left. Then Jami pulled open the door.

49

Emma's boss called Parker back. He asked the man about his daughter's whereabouts. He said he knew nothing. The last time he'd seen her, Emma was in her office in the Original Headquarters Building. Then she'd had a meeting with a man named David Malone, then returned to her office to make a few calls. Then she had to go to meet with someone. Emma never returned. Her boss decided she had left for the day and would return on Monday. Parker asked what the meeting with Malone was about, but Emma's boss said he didn't know. It was private. She was summoned to his office; he took her there; then he left. Parker thanked the man and clicked off and looked away. "What are we going to do now, Jordan?" he said.

"Let's go to her apartment," I said. "Maybe her phone's just not working."

"You think she'd go there? With Miriam Hassan?"

I thought about it. "I don't know what to think. But something happened here. They're all gone." I went to a window and looked outside. "Simon's car is still in the parking lot." I turned back. "Something's wrong."

Parker thought about that for a long moment. "She probably has a neighbor looking after Elizabeth. That's what she normally does. We can start with her apartment, but what about the safe house?"

WE TOOK THE ELEVATOR DOWN TO THE FIRST FLOOR AND stepped out into the lot. My SUV was parked next to Parker's Crown Vic. Simon's hatchback was farther down. There weren't any other vehicles around us. I said, "They took Emma's vehicle." Parker nodded vaguely, and then I said, "You want to take your car or mine?"

But before he could answer, I heard the rumble of an engine close by. I looked right, and Parker looked left. We both stared across the small lot and watched as a vehicle turned off Nebraska Avenue and pulled into the entrance to the NAC. A dark brown vehicle. A UPS truck. Parker and I looked at each other for a brief moment. Two confused expressions, trying to process what we were seeing. We turned back, and I watched as the driver stopped at the guard shack for a moment; then the black wrought-iron gate opened.

The driver accelerated. I heard the idling engine start to roar for a moment as the driver entered, and then the truck slowed to make the turn toward where we were standing. There was another burst of acceleration, followed by hard braking. The truck hissed and bucked to a halt ten feet in front of us. Then the engine was cut. Parker and I stepped forward and glanced at each other again for a brief moment. Then I turned back and walked to the driver's side with Parker following. I squinted as I moved and held a hand up to block the sun as it broke free from the clouds. Then a figure stepped out and stared across at me. Then Jami ran towards me.

She gave me a hug and wrapped her arms around me. I pulled her in and asked, "Are you okay?"

Jami nodded that she was, her head tight against my chest.

I looked up and saw movement. Another figure. I raised my hand to block the sun again and saw a man step out from the passenger side. I stared at him as I held on to Jami tight. Parker stepped around and walked toward him. Jami loosened her grip and turned to look and said, "It's okay. He's with me, Parker."

The man stated his name to Parker but didn't say much more. He looked really shaken up. And concerned. And conflicted. Like he knew he should be glad to be safe, but there was something else on his mind. I recognized the guy immediately. It was the man who was in the cell next to Jami's at the warehouse. The man who knocked on my door. The one who coerced Jami into coming out, somehow. Jami said he had to get home to check on his daughter, and I understood why he looked so concerned.

Then I asked Jami how she got away. She motioned for us to follow her around to the back of the truck. Parker and I followed her back and watched as Jami grabbed onto the handles and pried open the doors. Lying on his back was a large man surrounded by a pool of crimson that had run along the floorboard and had collected along the back of the truck. Jami turned back to look at me and said, "I told you to trust me."

I looked at how she'd done it and said, "I told you to take the knife."

Jami shot me a look, and then her expression changed as she looked away. "We have a problem," she said.

"Tell us," said Parker as I grabbed the knife, wiped the blade on my jeans, and dropped it in my pocket.

"In the warehouse, when they forced us into the truck, I noticed something. There was a van parked. There were two men loading it. I caught a glimpse of it as I moved from the cell they were keeping us in."

"What were they loading?" I asked.

Jami turned to look at me. "It looked like fertilizer. And other material. My first thought was explosives."

I furrowed my brow. "Explosives?"

Jami shrugged.

"Why would they do that? How would they use it?"

She looked away again. "I don't know." Then she had another thought. "Blake, is the president okay?"

"Yes," I said. "They both are. They signed the treaty already. It's a done deal."

"So we're good," added Parker. "The threat against the presidents is over. And Jami's safe. Whatever this thing with the explosives is, it's separate from the assassination attempt. Maybe they were trying to cover their tracks. Maybe they set it on a timer to go off later, to destroy any evidence they may have left behind. Maybe they want to blow the whole damned warehouse up. We can have someone go back to check it out."

Jami nodded vaguely but said nothing back.

Parker said, "We're leaving to go to Emma's apartment. To check on Elizabeth and see where Emma is."

Jami narrowed her eyes and looked at me, and I said, "She's missing. We came straight here from the White House. Emma's car was gone. She was going to stay here with a woman she had in protective custody at a safe house down the road. They're both gone. So is Simon. We don't know what happened."

Jami thought for a long moment. "That doesn't feel right. Maybe they went back to the safe house."

"That's what I thought," said Parker. "But I still want to check on Elizabeth just to make sure she's okay."

Jami glanced at the UPS driver standing by himself. "I'll call Lynne May to let her know I'm okay. She can send over some DDC agents to take him home and process the guy in the truck."

I nodded and said, "Parker, you go check on Elizabeth and see what you can find. We'll call you later."

Parker agreed with the plan. He hustled over to his blue Crown Victoria and slid inside the driver's seat. Parker reversed quickly and accelerated past us. The gate opened, and I watched as he turned onto Nebraska and disappeared from sight. The UPS guy said he'd wait in the cab. We climbed into my SUV and I turned the ignition as Jami called Lynne May. She got her voicemail and left a message saying she was okay and to send someone to the NAC. Then she clicked off and turned to me. Concern in her eyes. Jami said, "The dead guy in the truck; I didn't recognize him, Blake. It wasn't the guy who kidnapped me."

"And that's a problem?"

"Yes," she said. "It means there are more of them out there. And we don't know how many there are."

50

JAMI AND I MADE OUR WAY TO THE SAFE HOUSE, AND I CALLED Chris Reed as I drove. He said he had just left his post with Reynolds and had been asked to head back to the Hoover Building to meet with Peter Mulvaney for an after-action report. I brought him up to speed on the disappearance of Emma, Simon, and Miriam Hassan, and I told him we needed his help. Chris said he'd meet us in twenty minutes. I clicked off and drove on. Jami got a call back from Lynne May. She brought her up to speed and told her about the truck parked at the NAC. May said she'd send some of her people out to meet the driver and ID the dead guy.

We pulled up to P Street and parked half a block away. I put my SUV in park and left it running and stared out through the windshield and spent the time waiting on Chris to fill Jami in on everything that had happened over the last several hours. The file her kidnapper had wanted to be deleted, breaking Hassan out of the safe house, the sniper, the meeting at the café, how Chris Reed had pretended to be me while I took out one of the men in the vehicle, and how I'd then taken out the sniper after he'd met with Chris.

I talked through all of it as quickly and with as much detail as I could.

"Tell me about Miriam Hassan," Jami asked. "Who is she?"

I checked the rearview and side mirrors and watched as vehicles passed us as I thought about it. "I don't know much other than she was picked up by the Bureau a week ago and was being kept at the safe house."

"Why?"

"Because her husband went missing, and she thought she was in danger."

She thought about that and said, "Talk to me about the husband."

I turned back and faced forward and stared at the safe house. "She thought he was caught up in something. She overheard a conversation. Someone called and asked her husband to do something for them. He refused and ended up missing. She called Metro PD, who called the FBI, who called Emma Ross."

"Why?" she asked again.

"Because she told them something concerning. Her husband was running with the wrong people. Specifically, the guy who kidnapped you. The guy who tried to get me to assassinate the presidents today."

Jami went quiet for a long moment. She said, "You think something's off with Miriam Hassan, don't you?"

I thought about it some more and said, "I can't put my finger on it, but yes, something's not right." I turned and saw Jami narrow her eyes as she stared at me, urging me to continue. "There was a Kevlar vest near the entrance to the safe house. Just sitting there on the coatrack. What are the chances?"

Jami said nothing.

"I was ordered to break her out. She said she was scared, and I was on a deadline, so I had her put the vest on underneath her jacket. I had under two minutes to break her out. She was adamant that someone wanted her dead and would make an attempt on her life. But I didn't agree. It seemed unlikely."

"But they tried."

I nodded. "And it wasn't a drive-by, which would've been easier. It was a sniper from across the street." I pointed up and to my left to show her. Jami craned her neck and took a long, hard look at the distance. I followed her gaze as it moved in the slanted direction the bullet had taken to its target on the ground. Jami glanced back at me, confused. "Two things were wrong. One, the sniper didn't go for a headshot."

She furrowed her brow. "That's a problem?"

"A big problem," I said. "I was a sniper, Jami. And the first thing they taught us was to go for headshots."

"Maybe they were inexperienced."

"They shot her right in the chest. Dead center."

Jami furrowed her brow again. "And two?"

I turned to face her. "She followed my instructions perfectly." Jami made a face, like she wasn't following. "I had less than two minutes before I had to break her out. I put the vest on her, and she asked me what to expect. I wasn't following. She said, if she was shot, she wanted to know what it would feel like. So I told her. I said it all depended on how close the shooter was to her. Either way it would feel like taking a full-on swing with a baseball bat to the chest, if that's where she was shot. She looked at me, Jami. Her next question should've been, what if I'm not shot in the chest, but it wasn't. Instead she asked what she should do. So I told her. I said the wind would be knocked out of her. I said she needed to fight the urge to gasp for air. I said I wouldn't be far; if it happened, I'd come back for her, but she had to remain perfectly still."

"And she followed your instructions?"

"Perfectly. I was walking back to my SUV, expecting someone to pick her up and take her away. Not shoot her. But I heard a shot fired, and I turned back and saw her collapse onto the sidewalk in front of the safe house. I looked up and saw a sniper on the rooftop. I glanced back, expecting to see her gasping for air. But she wasn't." Jami said nothing. Just nodded for me to continue, so I said, "I ran back to my vehicle and pulled up tight against the curb, right next to where she was. I got out and looked, and the sniper was gone. I thought about going after him. I hesitated for a moment. But I wasn't sure if we were being watched, so I went and picked her up. She was perfectly still. I got her in here. She was sitting right where you are now. I put the seat all the way back, and I drove away and told her to stay down until we were out of the area." I paused and looked straight ahead as I thought about it some more. "She did everything perfectly. To a T."

"So what are you telling me? That Miriam Hassan is in on this somehow? What, do you think she kidnapped Emma and Simon? You think they're inside the safe house right now, being held at gunpoint?"

I noticed a vehicle pull up and park in one of the spots behind us. Chris Reed flashed his lights twice. "Let's find out," I said as I pushed the door open and climbed out, and Jami did the same thing on her side.

Chris Reed climbed out and stared at us. He looked at Jami and said, "I'm glad you're okay."

Jami said nothing. Just nodded and looked away.

Chris turned to me and said, "So what are we dealing with, man?"

I explained the situation to my friend. I walked Chris through what I was thinking. That we needed to get into the safe house and see if Emma, Simon, and Miriam Hassan were inside. I told Chris and Jami about the two CIA men. I brought them both up to speed on the issues I was having with them. If I was right, and Hassan was keeping Emma and Simon hostage, they were likely part of it. We'd have to assume the CIA men were hostiles and would need to be neutralized. Chris had concerns. Major concerns. He said he couldn't take action against a CIA agent. If he was fired upon, he'd fire back. He could call Peter Mulvaney and ask for his support and have him send some of his men down here, but Chris couldn't do what I was asking him to do on his own. But he agreed to follow me inside and provide cover for us should we need it.

Jami didn't have a weapon, so Chris opened his hatch and tugged on a drawer and found a Glock. He loaded it with a mag and asked if I needed ammo. I told him I had a mag in my pocket already. Cars buzzed past us, oblivious to what was about to happen. Chris closed the hatch and stared. I said, "Ready?"

Chris looked at Jami, then glanced at the safe house. Then he turned to me and nodded once. "Let's roll."

51

I STEPPED FORWARD AND LED THE WAY TO THE SAFE HOUSE. Cars buzzed by on the street in both directions as I glanced up at the rooftops of the buildings across the street. I saw nobody up there. Twenty paces later, we approached the entrance. Jami was to my left, and Chris was on my right. "Plan, boss?" he asked.

"We know the back is sealed off. So the only way in and out is through the front door. Chris, you'll enter the code, and I'll storm the building. I want both of you to hang back until I clear all of the rooms."

"I'm not hanging back," said Jami.

I glanced left to look at her, then I faced forward, and I nodded once.

"I'll watch the exit," said Chris. "Mulvaney wouldn't want me to be a part of this. He's expecting me to arrive at the Hoover Building any minute now. But if you need help, I'll have your back, man. Promise."

I nodded again. We got to the entrance and stepped up to the door. I saw the camera in the corner facing us. If someone was monitoring it from inside, we wouldn't have much time to act. "Enter the code," I said.

Chris punched the digits into the keypad. He drew his weapon and crouched down and looked up at me. Jami had her Glock gripped tight in her small hands and put her left shoulder against the side of the building and aimed the weapon at the ground. I pulled my Glock out of my holster and turned the handle.

I pushed the door in, then moved my left hand so it wrapped around my right, and I looked inside the open space. I expected to see Miriam Hassan standing in the center of the room, aiming a weapon at a couch where Emma and Simon would be seated. But what I found was the complete opposite. Through the foyer, past the entryway, Miriam Hassan was seated on the couch next to Simon, and Emma Ross was standing.

"Emma," I called in a loud voice as I stepped through and glanced left and right, "are you okay?"

"Yes, we're fine," she called back. "Put the guns down."

I paused, I looked to my left, and Jami gave me a look and lowered her weapon. I turned back even further and saw Chris Reed at the door, looking in. He lowered and then holstered his weapon and stepped inside. I turned back and waited another moment; then I lowered my own weapon and slid it into my holster. "Emma, what the hell is going on?" I said as I moved closer. "We thought you and Simon were in trouble."

"We might be," she said.

Jami and I stepped into the room as Chris hung back in the foyer, watching the door. "Explain," said Jami.

Emma said, "We were waiting on my father to get back. Miriam was still nervous about leaving after what happened outside this building earlier. She was terrified, and I had promised her we'd stay at the NAC until we figured out what was happening and until I was sure it was safe to leave. Then I got a phone call."

"Who called?" asked Chris as he stepped into the room and stood at my side.

"This man I work with at Langley. One of my superiors." Emma glanced at me and anticipated my next question. Then she turned her gaze to Hassan and added, "I was told to bring her back. It was an order. He knew what had happened outside this building. So I pushed back. I told him that Hassan didn't feel safe here, and I didn't blame her. I was reprimanded. He said I was already on thin ice. I had no choice."

Jami said, "Simon, why are you here? And why didn't either of you call Parker or answer your phones?"

Simon looked up from his laptop, which was set on a coffee table where he was working from.

But Emma answered on his behalf and said, "I told him to come with us. And my superior told me not to use my phone. So I turned it off, and I told Simon to do the same. He said he'd call from the landline here later to check in." Then Emma turned to me. "Blake, what happened to the two agents who were here?"

"They're missing?"

"I don't know if they're *missing*, they're just not here. The place was empty when we arrived."

I stared at Miriam Hassan. She stared back for a brief moment, then looked down at the floor. I had been so sure that something was off with her, but I was wrong. My phone buzzed in my pocket. It was Parker. I answered and told him Emma and Simon were safe. I gave Parker the address for the safe house, and he said he was on his way as I saw another call coming in.

"This is Jordan," I said, ending the call with Parker and answering Morgan Lennox's call.

"Listen, mate, I have some information to share with you."

"Go ahead," I said, stepping away from the others.

"I had some downtime after we last spoke. So I started working on that file you were told to delete from the FBI's instance of the database. The one Chris Reed transferred to me. Just trying to figure out what the hell it was and why it had no pictures associated with it. They had encryption on it, so I basically had to treat it not as an interagency file but like a file we might find on a random laptop we needed to decode. I ran it through a cleansing process, and I got in."

"What did you find?"

"Someone tried to delete the file a week ago, but they couldn't. They didn't have the proper access. But they were able to change the last name and encrypt it to hide the associated image."

I turned back from the kitchen and looked over my shoulder and heard low conversations from the others. "I don't understand," I said, speaking softly so I wouldn't be heard.

"The last name on the file was originally Bortnik. Not Babushkin. They changed it. Not sure why they didn't bother changing the first name. So they are one and the same." He paused. "That's not all, mate."

My heart was beating hard in my chest. I said, "Tell me."

Morgan said, "There's a linked file. I see it now that this one's decrypted. Blake, the file is on Miriam Hassan."

52

I CLICKED OFF AND DROPPED THE PHONE INTO MY POCKET AND moved back toward the living room. Miriam Hassan kept her eyes on me, tracking me as I moved. Emma and Jami stopped talking and turned to look at me. Chris stepped aside for me to pass by him, and Simon looked up from his laptop as I approached. I looked at each of them in turn for a moment, then I stared down at the woman, and I said, "Who are you?"

Miriam Hassan furrowed her brow. She looked at Emma Ross. "I'm sorry?" she asked, glancing back.

"I'm not going to ask you again." Then in an exaggerated manner, I repeated the words, "Who—are—you?"

Hassan shook her head slowly and narrowed her eyes. "I don't understand. You already know who I am."

"I know what you've told us." I raised my hand and pointed at Emma Ross. "And I know she had you in protective custody and kept you here for your own safety." I lowered my hand and stepped closer to her. "And I know your husband was caught up in something he shouldn't have been, and then he disappeared."

Hassan nodded slowly. "That's right." She glanced at Emma again. "Mr. Jordan, I am not following."

I made no reply and just stared at her. Jami put her hand on my back and whispered, "Blake, stop. She's not involved in any of this."

I turned to look at Jami. She was biting her lip, tugging on my arm, trying to pull me away. Emma Ross stood to the side, arms crossed, head tilted, a curious look on her face, waiting to see where this was going. I heard a text message come through. I reached for my phone and thumbed the screen and saw what Morgan had sent me. I looked up at Hassan. "Does the name Viktor Bortnik mean anything to you?"

Hassan swallowed hard and said, "No."

Then Chris's phone chimed. I turned and watched as he dug it out of a pocket and read a message. "A person of interest has been identified," he said. "The Bureau's Cyber Division just confirmed the voice from that overseas phone call the NSA intercepted. The voice of the man who took the call. Same name."

My phone chimed again in my hand. Two images from Morgan. One of a man and one of Miriam Hassan. Jami put her hand on top of mine and turned it so she could see the screen. "That's him," she said softly. "That's the man who kidnapped me. The man I worked with when I was at the Bureau. The guy in charge."

I took a step closer to Miriam Hassan and turned my phone around so she could see the image for herself.

I watched as she looked it over. I studied her reaction. The blood drained from her face. There was a mix of shock and confusion as she looked at the image. Then she looked away, focused on nothing at all, trying to make sense of what she had seen. "Let me guess," I said. "You're going to tell me you don't know him."

Hassan blinked hard, then looked up at me. Eyes wide. "I do know him." She paused. "That's my husband."

—————

53

I stood in silence, studying Miriam Hassan's face, watching her closely, checking her body language. She stared at the image with disbelief. Then she looked up at me again and shook her head slowly. "Impossible," she said. "I don't believe it. You have the wrong person." She looked away again, thinking. Trying to reconcile what I had told her. Unable to do it. "I knew him as Viktor Babushkin. Not Bortnik."

Simon lowered the lid of his laptop slightly and leaned back in his seat, taking in the news. Thinking hard about what this meant. Chris's phone rang. He looked at the caller ID and said it was Mulvaney calling. He stepped away and answered the call and listened for a moment; then he stared at me and nodded once. *Same message from Mulvaney*, he was telling me. *Viktor Bortnik is the person of interest. He's our man.*

Chris pulled the phone away from his face. He said, "Mulvaney wants me back. You okay with that?"

I nodded. "Yeah. Thanks for your help here."

Chris stretched out his hand and met mine, and we shook. "Need anything else, just give me a call, man."

I nodded again and watched him walk past us as he brought the phone back to his ear to talk to his boss. Emma and Jami took a seat on another couch adjacent to where Miriam and Simon were sitting. I crouched down to get eye level with Hassan. "Your husband is still alive," I said. "He faked his death."

"No," she replied. "I told you, that's impossible."

Jami said, "If that's your husband in that image we showed you, then it's not. I can promise you that."

Hassan said nothing.

"Tell me about him. Does he have family nearby? Brothers, sisters. Any children?"

"No. It's just us. We didn't have children."

"Why would he fake his own death?" I asked. "Why lead you to believe he was killed?"

Miriam Hassan grew quiet for a long moment. Like the concept was foreign to her. Like the premise was faulty. But she eventually answered, "If it is true, then—" she paused a moment "—I guess to protect me."

"From what?"

Hassan blinked hard and took a breath and said, "I guess whatever he may have been caught up in."

"There's got to be something you can tell us," I pressed. "Did you know he worked at the FBI?"

She shook her head. "He said he was a teaching assistant at Georgetown. We met at a campus overseas."

"Are you from Qatar?"

She nodded.

"So you married a Russian and kept your maiden name?"

She nodded again. "He encouraged me to."

Emma Ross excused herself. I watched as she moved toward the restroom and closed the door. A moment later it opened back up again. She called for Jami as I dropped my phone back into a pocket and started pacing. Thirty seconds after that, Jami called me over. She picked up a small steel trash can as she and Emma stepped out, and Jami handed it to me. I looked inside. There were charred pieces of paper and black ash underneath. I looked up, and Jami said, "Why would somebody burn papers? What could it be?"

I stepped away and walked back into the kitchen and set it on the counter. I dug my hand inside, and my fingers came out covered in ash. I used the light from overhead to get a better look inside. There was one small piece of paper still intact. I brought it out and held it up to the light and flipped it back and forth.

There were markings. Handwritten notes in blue ink. Burn marks in the corners and a line from a red marker, going from left to right and a partial line from top to bottom, cut off from ripping or from burning. Like a cross.

"What is it?" asked Jami.

"Something they didn't want us to find," I said.

"Who?" asked Emma.

I looked up from the burned scrap of paper. "The guys you had in here watching Hassan."

Emma furrowed her brow. "You think they destroyed some kind of evidence?"

"Who burns paperwork in a trash can? Why even have paperwork? Everything's digital now."

Emma thought about that for a moment and said, "Well then, what could it have been?"

I lowered my hand and set the small square of paper down on the counter. Everyone's eyes followed. Emma stared at it, thinking. Jami shook her head slowly and picked it up and turned it over, looking at both sides of it. I placed the flat of my hands on the counter and closed my eyes and lowered my head.

Hours earlier, I had been inside the safe house, on a deadline, trying to complete my next task of releasing the person being held here. Releasing Miriam Hassan. I had dealt with two CIA men who weren't cooperating. They had their own orders, which a reasonable man would've understood. But I hadn't been a reasonable man. Not when my wife's life was in danger. I had disarmed one of them downstairs and neutralized his friend upstairs, tying them both to heavy pieces of furniture. Using zip ties I had found in the kitchen. I opened my eyes and turned back and looked at the paper Jami was holding up.

I turned and walked over to where I had seen the zip ties. I pulled open a drawer. They were gone. There was nothing inside. Then I looked to the right. There had been something else there. Something folded over. I had seen it but hadn't given it much thought. Until now.

"What is it?" called Jami.

I said nothing.

"Blake?"

I pointed at the counter. "There was something here earlier. But it's gone now."

"What?" said Emma.

I turned back and walked over to them. Miriam Hassan was watching me again. Still seated on the couch. She stood and stepped forward but remained behind Emma and Jami. Simon was back on his laptop, working, looking up from where he was sitting, listening, keeping current on what was happening. Jami was still holding the paper with the horizontal and vertical red marks. I took it back and held it out but turned it forty-five degrees to the right. "It's an X," I said.

I glanced over my shoulder. "This was a map. I saw it here earlier, on the counter. They were planning something and burned it to destroy the evidence."

"What was the map of?" asked Jami.

Emma Ross's eyes grew wide. "A path," she said. "For the president's motorcade. It goes by this building."

54

Emma Ross called the White House while Simon Harris leaned forward in his seat. I said, "Simon, please tell me one of the satellites you and Morgan were controlling earlier is back in position over DC."

Simon hunched over his laptop and typed in a few commands and said, "Morgan's is over us right now."

Emma clicked off and said, "I'm not getting through to anyone. I'm going to have to try Ethan Meyer."

Jami asked, "When is President Stepanov leaving for the airport?"

Emma answered, "Any minute now, I believe."

Jami found a remote control and pointed it at a television mounted on the wall. It came to life, and she changed the channel to cable news. Live footage of Stepanov getting into the presidential limousine played with a news ticker scrolling across the bottom of the screen that read STEPANOV LEAVES AFTER HISTORIC SUMMIT. Jami turned back and stared. "Blake, I think they're going to try to take him out."

"I know," I said as I turned and stared down at Miriam

Hassan. "Get up."

She narrowed her eyes. "I'm sorry?"

"Right now, you're the only leverage I have to stop your husband from doing whatever it is he's planning. So get up. I'm leaving, and you're coming with me."

Emma Ross stepped closer to me. "Blake, I was specifically asked by my superiors to keep her here."

"I'll bring her back when I'm done." I turned back to Hassan. "I'm not going to tell you again. Get up."

Miriam Hassan stared at me, then turned to Emma Ross. Emma nodded slowly. Hassan stood from the couch slowly, cautiously; then she stepped over to where I was standing. I grabbed her by the arm and pointed at the door and said, "Emma, keep trying to contact the White House. Simon, I need you to start scanning rooftops. Start with this one and work your way out. Call me as soon as you find him."

We started moving, and Jami came after me. "And what about me?"

I stopped moving. I let go of Hassan for a moment and turned back.

"Don't you think you could use my help? When are you going to trust me?"

I thought about that and nodded. "You're right," I said. "Let's go."

WE STEPPED OUTSIDE, AND I LOOKED UP AND SAW WHAT I expected to see. Just a small glimpse, less than one second. I waited for a break in traffic and grabbed Hassan's arm again, and we ran across the street. We got to the other side. I forced Hassan to stand against the side of the building opposite the safe house. Jami turned to look at my SUV down the street; then she turned back and stared. "What are we doing?"

I pointed up. "We're being watched, Jami. I saw the guy when we stepped out. He's on the roof."

"The sniper? I thought you killed him."

I said nothing.

"And we're all going up there to get him?"

I shook my head. "I'm going up to get him. And I'm taking her with me." My phone rang. It was Simon.

55

Simon spoke urgently and told me he'd done what I'd asked. He'd started looking at the rooftops, beginning with the safe house, and worked his way out in greater concentric circles. But he'd immediately seen someone on the roof directly across the street, where I'd seen the sniper try to take out Miriam Hassan. I told him they'd been watching for a long time. I said they probably watched Emma Ross bring Hassan back earlier, and they probably watched Chris, Jami, and me approach and storm the safe house, too.

I told Simon that I had looked up right when I exited the building, and the guy had recoiled back to safety. Out of view. I needed to know if he was still there or if I'd spooked him and he was headed down. Simon told me the guy was still there, back in position, crouched low, peering over the side of the building. I handed my phone to Jami and told her to stay on the line with Simon and watch the exit for me, in case the guy changed his mind and tried to leave. Jami said nothing. Just stared at me blankly, a little frustrated. Then she nodded and pressed the phone to her ear as I ushered Hassan to enter the building.

It was an apartment, and the door was locked. Someone was inside. An older man. I rapped my knuckles on the glass, and he turned to look at me. I pulled my credentials out from my pocket and pressed them against the glass. The man stepped closer and came to the door. He looked past me, out at the road, then pushed the door open. I said, "Thanks," and pulled it open the whole way and told Hassan to step inside.

"Is everything okay?" the resident asked.

"Yes," I said. "But you should get back to your apartment and stay inside for a while."

He said nothing back. Just stared as I led Hassan across the foyer and over to a set of elevators. The older man was still staring at us as one of them chimed open, and we stepped inside. Miriam Hassan was shaking. I pressed the button for the top floor. She said, "What are we doing? Why are we going up there?"

I glared at her as the doors closed, and the elevator lurched upward. "I want to know who's watching me."

"Do you think it's my husband?"

"You tell me."

"He tried to kill me."

"Or one of his men tried to kill you."

Miriam Hassan kept her eyes on me a moment longer; then she looked away. "I have no protection."

"You have me."

"In case something happens to you."

The elevator slowed. I studied the woman one last time. Then I dug into my pocket and gave her the knife.

THE ELEVATOR DOORS OPENED, AND WE STEPPED INTO A LONG hallway. Apartments lined both sides of it. I looked left, then right, then ushered Hassan towards the left where I saw an exit sign with a door leading to a stairwell. I reached for my weapon and gripped it tight with one hand; then I opened the door with the other. "Move," I said, and Hassan hustled through the door. Immediately in front of us, the stairs descended to lower floors. To our right was a short staircase that went upward. I gestured for the woman to take the stairs up.

Hassan went ahead of me. She looked back at me, over her shoulder, as she moved. The staircase curved once, then leveled out, and there was a short path of five feet and a door on the other side of it. Hassan walked up to the door; then she turned back to me again. "I'm scared," she said, gripping the knife tightly.

"You need to hide that," I said.

She nodded and slipped the knife into the pocket of her jeans as I quickly explained what was about to happen. I walked her through the next few minutes, just like I'd done across the street hours earlier. Hassan nodded her understanding, but told me once again that I had it wrong, that her husband was innocent. I ignored her. I spun her around and held my weapon tight in my hand. Then I opened the door.

HARSH SUNLIGHT SPILLED INTO THE DARK HALLWAY FROM THE setting sun. I closed my eyes for a second; then I nudged her onward. Hassan stepped forward, and I grabbed the door handle before it could shut, and I left it ajar. There was a man directly in front of us, on his stomach, prone, peering out over the side of the building. We stepped closer. I nudged Hassan with my Glock. Then I whispered for her to stop moving. There had been nothing on the ground, no makeshift tripwire. That was a mistake. First thing they teach you is to have a spotter. Someone watching you while you watch your target. And if you can't have someone watching you, you need to set up a tripwire. String threaded across an entryway, a tin can by a door, a key wedged high into the door jamb. Something that could make a noise and alert you to the danger behind you. But none of that had been set up. Not by this man. Not from what I could tell. But the guy sensed us. He lifted his head slightly, realizing something was off. Then he turned to the right, and he kept on turning until he was looking over his shoulder directly at us. "Stand up and turn around," I yelled.

The guy glanced back at the road; then he stood up slowly. He turned to face us, and my eyes grew wide. "It's you," I said. His face matched the image Morgan had sent. It was Miriam's husband. Viktor Bortnik.

But he didn't have a rifle. Only binoculars and a radio. I stared at him, confused because he seemed to be watching another location—not the safe house across the street.

Then Miriam Hassan did something unexpected. Unlike before, she did not follow my directions at all. The woman came out with the knife, gripping it tight. She raised her hand and brought it down fast. I caught her wrist with my hand and squeezed it tight. She screamed in pain and dropped the blade. It clattered onto the ground. She said, "Viktor, they know about the motorcade." But the man ignored her. He just reached into his waistbelt and came out with a gun, and I realized I'd made a mistake.

Miriam was his spotter.

She was his tripwire.

"You failed us, Mr. Jordan. You failed our cause. I told you why we needed to keep the treaty from being signed. The people of my country do not want it. And I can assure you that yours don't want it, either. That is why both presidents did this in secret. They knew there would be blowback. But the truth is, you were my backup plan." He shrugged. "Today they will die. Both of them. Two countries will be in disarray. Then both governments will consider the treaty null and void."

"How are you going to do it?" I asked.

"We do not want to be at peace with a nation such as yours," he said, ignoring me. "We don't agree with you and your way of life. I'm not acting alone. I am not a radical. I'm here on behalf of my government."

I raised my Glock and pressed the muzzle to Miriam's temple. "Drop the weapon, or I swear I'll kill her."

He smiled. "Mr. Jordan, I'm tired of you making promises I know you will not keep." Then he looked at his wife and said, "You did well." In one swift motion, he raised his hand and leveled his weapon and squeezed the trigger.

Miriam Hassan fell to the ground.

56

Viktor Bortnik said, "Drop the weapon," as he aimed his gun at me. I fought the urge to take him out. His hesitation in not shooting me immediately was my advantage. But then he did fire a shot, just to the left of me, so I changed my mind. Killing him would do no good. That wouldn't stop the assassination. So I raised my weapon slightly, and I knelt down slowly. Keeping my eyes on him, I set it on the ground.

I stood back up as Bortnik smiled broadly. I said, "I want to know how it's going to go down."

His smile faded, and he watched me closely, studying me, assessing what I might do with the information, then understanding that I just wanted to know what I'd been fighting for, what the whole thing was about. Bortnik said, "You took out most of my men. I underestimated you, Jordan. I was warned, but I didn't listen. I didn't think you'd be brazen enough to make such an attempt with your wife's life on the line."

Bortnik paused a long moment as he looked away to check both ends of the street, thinking through what he wanted to tell me, the only audience he might ever have to explain his actions. "According to my sources, Aleksander Stepanov has just left the White House. He's being escorted by Keller's Secret Service detail. My men have placed a van with explosives in a strategic location." He smiled. "Soon they will die."

I narrowed my eyes. "They?"

Bortnik smiled again, studying me. "I understand that President Keller is in the limousine with him. A kind gesture to accompany his friend to the airport. One last act of solidarity to prove his loyalty, maybe."

I stared back in silence and found it difficult to breathe. It felt like the wind had been knocked out of me.

Bortnik's smiled faded. He said, "Your worst nightmare, isn't it? Like what almost happened to your father back in Oklahoma. With McVeigh. I know all about it, Mr. Jordan. My people did their research. You need to understand that there are many inside your government who agree with me. And I don't mean within the FBI and CIA." He paused for a moment. "I mean people very close to your president."

"Who?" I asked, but the man said nothing. "Where is it happening?"

Bortnik thought about that for a spell. Then he walked closer to me. He stood just six feet away from me. He opened his mouth to speak just as I heard something behind me. His gaze quickly moved from me to the right a degree or two as he looked at the access door behind me. I heard Jami yell, "Drop the weapon!"

But he didn't drop his weapon. Instead he raised his hand in one quick motion and aimed it behind me. I lunged forward and grabbed the gun with my left hand and pushed his hand upward. A shot was fired into the air. I balled my right hand into a fist and brought it up and delivered a blow hard against his face.

Bortnik took the punch and stepped backward. Then he lowered his weapon again as I held onto it. He fired two more wild shots. I kept my grip on the weapon, the fingers of my left hand cupped over the gun, gripping the slide. Then the gun jammed. He was squeezing the trigger, and nothing was happening. Nothing at all. I delivered another punch with my right fist, and Bortnik stepped backwards. I pushed him back, and then I noticed that we were close to the edge of the rooftop. I kept pushing him back; then the back of his shoes touched the ledge. He reached back to steady himself but found nothing there. Bortnik started to fall and let go of the gun and made one last desperate attempt to grab onto something, anything.

He reached for me. The man grabbed my shirt as he toppled over, and he brought me down with him. I started to slide. Bortnik was hanging onto the ledge with one hand and holding my shirt with the other. I started to go with him as Jami crouched down and grabbed my chest from behind and held onto me. We struggled through ten long seconds. "Blake?" she called, concern in her voice, telling me she couldn't hold on much longer. I struggled to pull away. The slide continued. I felt loose gravel with my hands as I tried to pushed myself away. Jami grabbed and pulled, trying to keep me from going over.

But it wasn't enough.

57

BORTNIK WAS A BIG GUY, AND THE BULK OF HIS MASS WASN'T doing him any favors. He held onto me tightly. I clutched the rooftop, trying to stop the slide, pushing away, trying to counteract gravity. My face inched closer to the edge of the building, and as I slid closer to the ledge, the street became visible, and I looked down below. "I can't hold on much longer," I said. Jami made no reply; she just kept grabbing and pulling.

Behind us, I heard the door open again. There was a brief moment of silence as someone stood there, orienting themselves; then I heard quick feet on the gravel as they ran over to where we were. Tom Parker said, "Hold on, Jordan," and he got on the other side of Jami and grabbed my arm and joined her.

Then the momentum shifted. I started moving backwards. Bortnik looked into my eyes, and I watched his expression change. Something was different. He saw an opportunity to save himself by grabbing the ledge and pulling himself up, but he decided against it. Then he looked at me and said, "Good luck, Mr. Jordan."

"No!" I yelled as he loosened his grip and let go of me completely. I was pulled back fast without his weight pulling me down. Parker, Jami, and I fell backwards. They let go of me, and I got to my feet and ran back to the edge of the rooftop and looked down, and I saw Bortnik's body on the concrete ten stories below us. I glanced up and saw the safe house across the street. Then I turned around and looked at Parker and Jami. They got to their feet and stared across at me as I said, "The presidents are in danger."

PARKER STEPPED FORWARD AND ASKED WHAT I MEANT. JAMI told him about the van at the warehouse and the bags of fertilizer. Parker was confused by that. He didn't remember seeing a van there. Then I explained to both of them what Bortnik had told me. He'd confirmed they were making one last play to take out the Russian president. And I told them how President Keller had decided to accompany Stepanov to the airport. Unintended consequences, which Bortnik seemed to be more than okay with. I explained how the man had alluded to a bomb being used to take out the presidential motorcade along its route, and Jami answered Parker's next question, saying the motorcade had just left the White House. Parker reached for his cell. He pressed it to his ear and paced the rooftop in a wide circle, glancing occasionally at the body of Miriam Hassan; then he cursed under his breath and clicked off and looked up. "No answer." Then he looked back at Hassan, then back at us and asked, "So why was Bortnik up here?"

I walked to the ledge and picked up the binoculars. "I thought he was watching the safe house," I said. "But you wouldn't need binoculars for that. It's just across the street." I brought them to my eyes and looked through and scanned slowly to the right. I saw nothing. Then I moved left slowly, keeping the focus adjusted where Bortnik had it set, and I noticed something that caught my attention. There was another man lying prone on a faraway rooftop. I scanned left and saw yet another man, farther down, also prone, only his head and shoulders visible as he watched the road. I handed the binoculars to Jami, and she brought them to her eyes to see. "We've got two snipers," I said. "Probably the guys who were watching Miriam Hassan across the street."

That was when I fully understood that the whole thing was a ruse; the CIA guys were probably in on it. They'd put the Kevlar vest out for me to find. They were great actors. So was Miriam Hassan. Bortnik had been using her to keep an eye on me and what the people closest to me were doing.

Jami handed the binoculars to Parker. He brought them to his eyes to look at what we were seeing. "So Bortnik was their spotter? What the hell are they doing there? Is the motorcade passing along this road?"

My phone buzzed in my pocket. It was Simon. He had Morgan with him, and I put it on speakerphone. "There are men on rooftops," Simon said urgently, concern in his voice. "Right down the street from you."

"We see them," I said. Then I heard motorcycles approaching. I craned my neck and looked down at the street. Six motorcycles buzzed past the building down below, in three sets of twos. I glanced left again and saw all traffic stop. The street grew quiet down below. I glanced at Jami and Parker and said, "The president's motorcade is coming."

WE SPENT A MINUTE ARGUING ABOUT WHAT WE SHOULD DO. Parker was confused because snipers couldn't do much. He said bullets wouldn't penetrate the presidential limo in any way. Not even the windows—they were completely and totally bulletproofed along with the rest of the vehicle. Jami asked about the tires. Parker said they weren't anything to worry about, either. They weren't regular tires. They couldn't be blown out. Jami handed my phone back to me, and I found hers on the ground where Bortnik had been lying. We huddled together and conferenced each other's phones in as we stood on the rooftop. We scrambled to make progress toward a goal we didn't understand yet as time ticked on. Two more officers on motorcycles buzzed by down below. We turned and headed for the door. Parker had left it ajar. We jogged to the elevators, and I punched the button to call for them. Two minutes after that, we were stepping out of the building. I saw a group of people crouched next to the body of Bortnik. The MPD officers had cruised right by it. None of them had seen the body yet. I asked if they were residents of the building. They said they were, and I told them to get back inside.

Parker said, "Simon, Morgan, can you hear us?" We heard both analysts confirm that they could. "We're going to go after the men on the rooftops. We'll need you to help guide us to their locations quickly. We won't be able to tell from street level." Parker looked at me and said, "Who are you going with, Jordan?"

"Jami," I said as I put my Bluetooth earpiece in. She gave me a look: *You still don't trust me, do you?*

Parker nodded, and the three of us started sprinting west, in the direction of the men on the rooftops. Morgan and Simon were talking to each other. I could hear Parker and Jami breathing hard as we moved. The three of us ran past five buildings, and when we approached the sixth, Morgan said, "You're there."

Parker split off to the left and slowed as Jami and I ran past him. Far ahead in the distance I saw police lights from MPD cruisers headed our way. Simon said, "Keep going. You're almost there," so we ran faster.

Two minutes passed, and I heard Parker through my earpiece. He was trying to find a way inside. Then he did. I kept moving. I heard him find an elevator, and then he eventually found the access door to get to the roof. Parker was breathing hard and cursing under his breath again. I heard him struggling. Trying to do something. Unable to. "Can't access the roof," he said. "The guy's barricaded himself in. I can't stop him."

Simon said, "Emma wasn't able to get through to Ethan Myer. She can't stop the motorcade." He paused a moment and said to Jami and me, "Guys, you're very close now, just two more buildings and you're there."

We slowed as we approached, and Jami said, "Is this it?" Simon answered that it was. Jami turned left to take a short set of stairs into the building. I stayed on the sidewalk, looking all around.

Then I saw it.

"Blake, come on. We don't have much time."

I said, "Jami, is that the van from the warehouse?" as I pointed across to a black van parked on the curb in front of an abandoned store.

Jami turned and scanned the road quickly and followed my gaze. "Yes," she said. "I think so."

Then Jami's eyes shifted to me. A question: *Are you coming with me? Or are you going to trust me?*

I looked past her at a glass entry door; then I shifted my eyes back to her and nodded. "Go get him," I said.

Jami nodded back. Then she turned and disappeared into the building. I watched her through the glass door. She ran to the elevators and desperately tapped a button to call for them and glanced back at me. I turned and jogged farther up the street. It was strangely silent without any traffic. I looked up at the roof. Then I turned and stared across at the van, and I thought long and hard.

Then another thought occurred to me as I stared at the vehicle. *Think like them.*

I ran through it in my mind. The proximity, the trajectory, the logistics.

Would it work?

Yes, it would, and the result would be catastrophic.

I said in my earpiece, "I know how they'll do it. They're not going to fire at the motorcade." I paused. "They're going to shoot the van."

58

NOBODY SPOKE FOR A LONG MOMENT. THEN FROM FARTHER down the street, Parker said, "You're right, Jordan. They're going to aim for the explosives. That's the only thing that makes sense, since their weapons won't be able to do any real damage to the motorcade as it passes by. So what should we do?"

"We need to take these people out before they take the shot. Is there no way for you to access the rooftop?"

"No, the guy has it locked somehow. And there's no time to find someone who can open the door for me."

I heard a police siren to my right, at the far end of the street where the Metro PD motorcycles had disappeared to. Then they chirped their sirens, warning traffic, or maybe pedestrians, to clear the area.

"Jami, any luck?" I asked.

"Making my way there," she answered from somewhere high above me. "Trying to find the access point."

I glanced left and looked up the empty street. Residents were stepping outside, looking both ways, trying to understand why there was no traffic and what the sirens were for.

Oblivious to the presidential motorcade making its way toward us. Far to my right, a new set of onlookers emerged and were gathered around Bortnik's body. Some of them were crouched low; others were on cell phones, looking at the body from a distance, placing calls into 911.

I looked to my left again and saw movement, far in the distance, as a long series of vehicles turned a corner and headed my way. More MPD motorcycles followed by black SUVs, followed by a long dark vehicle, followed by more vehicles following close. "Simon, was Emma able to get through to anyone else?"

"No," he said. "Ethan Meyer didn't answer his phone. She can't get through to anyone, Blake."

I ran toward the oncoming motorcade, ahead of the parked van, and into the street so I could warn them. But a shot was fired, and I ducked back and stood close to the building, out of view from the gunmen. "They're not going to see me in time," I said as panic set in. I breathed. "Guys, I can't stop them."

TEN STORIES ABOVE STREET LEVEL, JAMI JORDAN FOUND THE access point to get out onto the roof. She had taken the elevator up to the ninth floor and exited but found no immediate way to get to the rooftop. Jami had gone to both ends of the long hallway and came up with nothing. Then by chance a janitor emerged from a door and looked at her. Jami presented her DDC credentials to the man and asked for his help. He ushered her back through the door he had just exited and showed her a retractable set of stairs along the far side of the wall that was used for servicing the many air-conditioning units for the building. She saw the stairs were down. Jami told the janitor to leave and get to a more secure area for a while.

He'd given her a key, but she had no use for it. She found the door ajar, just like the building farther east where she and Blake and ultimately Parker had confronted the man named Bortnik. She spoke quietly into her phone and told the others what she was about to do. At the same time Tom Parker from a few buildings down from her said he was going to shoot the lock to gain access to the sniper at his building. There were repeated pleas by everyone for Parker to hold off, that all he'd do was alert the gunman to his presence. But there was no reply. And the presidential motorcade was approaching fast. Jami knew it would drive by at any moment. And one of the gunmen, either hers or Parker's—or maybe both—would fire at the van with the explosives, and the result would be disastrous: one if not both presidents would die.

Jami dropped her cell into a pocket and reached for the Glock. She took a breath, and she opened the door.

THE PRESIDENTIAL MOTORCADE MADE ITS APPROACH, FAST AND true and determined and relentless. I once again tried to step out, and another shot was fired, just over my head. Based on the sound, it was from the gunman down the street. Parker's guy, not Jami's. I ducked back and looked on, completely helpless.

Then two more shots were fired, loud in my earpiece. I said, "Parker, are you okay?" No response. None at all. My heart sank, and I said, "Jami?" But there was no reply. I called for her again, but neither of them spoke.

I stood alone, realizing that I had made the wrong decision. I should've gone with Jami. She had asked me to trust her. And I finally had. But because of that decision, I might have allowed my wife to die so I could save the president. I called for Parker and Jami one more time as I watched the motorcade grow closer. There was a rustling on the line, and Emma Ross came on using Simon's phone. She said, "Blake, you have to do something."

"I'm trying."

"You have to stop the motorcade."

"The gunmen have me pinned, Emma."

"Where's my father?"

I made no response. I just looked on as the motorcade grew even closer. Adrenaline surged through my veins as I turned and stared at the van. Jami had said it was loaded with bags of fertilizer. Makeshift explosive material. The gunmen on the rooftops would take their shots just as the limousine passed by it. Perfect timing was required. I knew firsthand how critical the timing would be. A shot fired too early and the explosion would happen before the limo passed by it. There'd be structural damage, but not the kind they wanted. A shot fired too late and they'd have the same outcome. The back of the limo would be blown out. Not a direct hit. For a direct hit, the shot would have to take place at the precise moment the limousine passed by the van. And judging by the speed it was moving, it'd have to be timed perfectly. Two shooters ready. A primary and a backup.

Plus Bortnik, their spotter, making sure they took the shot. Or making sure nobody would stop them.

MPD chirped their sirens as they approached, multiple high-pitched noises that echoed along the mostly isolated and silent street. I thought about the bullets. They'd pierce the side of the van easily. No issues at all. There wasn't a timer inside the van. It wouldn't detonate on its own. The bullet would do all of the work. I guessed they were in communication with each other. Just like Parker, Jami, and me. I breathed.

"Parker?" I called. No reply. "Jami?" No response.

Emma said, "Blake, we're running out of time. You have to do something."

There was rustling on the line. Another shot was fired, from above me. Jami came on and said, "Got him."

I stepped forward and looked to my right at the rooftop down the street. Parker's guy appeared by the edge. But he was limping. Something was wrong. As I watched, I decided he'd been shot. Parker had gotten him. But where was Parker? I watched helplessly as the man settled into position. I saw the rifle extend from the edge. Then he turned it my way. I looked up and saw Jami looking down at me over the edge. "Jami, get down!" I yelled. She ducked, and a shot was fired from down the street. I turned back. The motorcade was about to pass. Emma called for me again, but I ignored her and tried to concentrate.

Then I realized what I had to do. I ran away from the van, toward the limo, giving myself enough distance. I turned back. I reached for my Glock and gripped it tight.

I aimed. I closed an eye.

Then I fired at the van.

59

THE EXPLOSION WAS INSTANTANEOUS. THE CONCUSSION WAVE hit me hard and threw me back several feet. I landed on my back and stared up at the sky, stunned, unable to hear anything, unable to breathe. Several moments passed, and then I sucked in air, and my chest heaved up and down as I tried to catch my breath. I still couldn't hear anything. I was totally deaf. I felt intense heat, and I struggled to raise my head.

Black smoke billowed from what was left of the van. Bright flames rose high into the sky. The front entrance to the abandoned store on the other side of the street was gone. There was a gaping hole two stories high. It reminded me of a smaller version of the Oklahoma bombing and Timothy McVeigh and my father's life that was spared. I prayed that the store had been empty and nobody had been inside it. Then my hearing returned. Muffled police sirens were wailing. Officers ran over to me and drew their weapons and aimed them down at me. I could hear engines humming and tires turning hard on the grit.

An MPD cop reached down and turned me over onto my

stomach. I looked up from the ground and saw the presidential limousine, not too far away, fifteen yards or so. Maybe even closer than that. It made a wide turn and disappeared fast down a side street. The cop standing over me handcuffed my wrists together just as I was finally able to take in a deep breath. Then two cops grabbed me, one by each arm, and they got me to my feet as they yelled at me and barked wild orders and put me in a police cruiser. They slammed the door shut and gathered with other cops and argued over what they should do with me.

I sat in the back of the cruiser for five long minutes. Then I saw movement to my left. Jami walked out of the building. She looked left, then right; then she looked forward and saw me inside. She showed her DDC credentials to the cops and the Secret Service agents who were joining them. Then she pointed at me and pointed at the remnants of the van. I couldn't make out the words. It felt like I was underwater. Sounds were still muted, garbled, my hearing wasn't back to normal yet, and the closed windows made it impossible to hear. Then Jami pointed at the door and told them to do something. One of them did as she asked and pulled me out and found my DHS credentials in my back pocket. He looked them over. Then he turned, and Jami turned, and I followed their gaze and saw Agent Rivera park and step out of a dark SUV and walk over to us. The cop tried to hand my DHS credentials to Rivera, but the Secret Service man didn't want them. Instead he just looked at me seriously and said, "What the hell just happened here, Jordan?"

"He just saved the president's life," said Jami. "Both of their lives. Keller's and Stepanov's."

Rivera's eyes darted from me to Jami; then he turned and saw the van burning brightly behind him.

He turned back and stared. Thinking hard. Then he nodded to the cop. "Uncuff him," he said. "Now."

THE COP REMOVED THE HANDCUFFS, AND THE OTHER OFFICER handed my credentials over to me. I took them back and stuffed them in my pocket. I turned to look at Rivera, and I asked, "Are the presidents safe?"

Rivera nodded but said nothing back.

Then I remembered something. "Where's Parker?"

Rivera furrowed his brow and stared back at me. I looked at Jami. Her eyes grew wide. I put my hand to my ear. The earpiece was missing. Down the road, in front of the safe house, I saw Emma Ross standing. Simon was behind her, in the doorway, watching us from a distance. I told Rivera we had to go. Jami and I jogged east, back down the street, past the burning van and past the multiple police cruisers and black SUVs and headed toward the building that Parker had entered. Rivera followed us. Emma Ross stepped across the street and joined us at the entrance. There was a DDC agent who had just arrived. Jami knew the man. The guy joined us, and we entered together as Simon remained across the street. We took the elevator up to the top floor and came out in a long hallway and split up. Jami and I went right as Emma and the DDC man moved left. Rivera hung back, watching. There to help if we needed it. I found an alcove with a door marked ACCESS TO ROOFTOP, and we called for the others to join us. I scrambled up the stairs and found a door left slightly open. I drew my weapon and opened the door and saw two men on the ground. Both were shot. One was dead. The other was still alive.

"I need a medic," I yelled, and the DDC man radioed for help and gave his exact location with instructions.

Emma Ross crouched down and reached for her father's hand and gripped it tight as we waited for help.

An ambulance arrived five minutes later, and the DDC man went to go meet them at the elevator. Two minutes after that, they were hustling down the corridor toward our location. Emma was crying. I told her everything would be okay, but we needed to get her father to the hospital quickly. I watched her let go of Parker's hand and stand. She took a step back, and the medics hustled over to us and helped get Parker down the stairs and onto a gurney. They rolled it fast toward the elevators. The DDC guy followed closely. Emma Ross ran after them. She told them to wait. She said she wanted to ride with them. The medics tried to protest, but she wouldn't listen. Jami, Rivera, and I stood together and watched as they stepped into the elevator and disappeared. Then everything went quiet again. Rivera told us he needed to get back downstairs. He eyed me for a long moment. Then he extended his hand and said, "Thank you." We shook, and then he left.

I waited until Rivera was gone, and I sat back down on the floor. Jami sat with me. She put her arm around me as I dropped my head in my hands. I said, "I should've been here, Jami. Backing up Parker."

"No," she said. "If he had wanted your help, he would've told you."

I said nothing.

"Even if you'd been here, how would you have shot the van? From all the way over here? It's too far."

I raised my head and glanced at Jami; then I looked away and said nothing.

"Hey," she said in a small, soft voice. "He'll be okay. Do you trust me?"

I nodded.

"And do you trust yourself?"

I said nothing.

"You made a call. You listened to your gut. If you hadn't, this whole thing could've turned out differently."

I said nothing. Just sat there for a long moment, thinking. Then I stood and reached down, offering my hand. Jami took it, and I helped her stand. She gave me a hug and said we should head back downstairs. Simon was probably wondering what was happening. We'd need to fill him in on Parker and update Morgan. As we stepped into the elevator and I hit the button to take us to the first floor, Jami turned to face me. She said, "When it came down to it, you trusted me to do my job. Thank you, Blake. I love you."

I looked away. My mind was racing as we headed down to the first floor. "It reminded me of him," I said. "The van, the explosion, the blown-out building. It reminded me of Oklahoma City. And my dad."

Jami nodded. "He would've been proud of you."

60

ONE WEEK LATER

I KNOCKED ON THE DOOR AT GEORGE WASHINGTON University Hospital. A familiar voice said, "Come in," and I stepped through. Emma Ross stood in the corner of the dimly lit hospital room. "Blake, it's late."

I closed the door behind me and looked at Tom Parker in his hospital bed, asleep, his chest rising and falling every few seconds as he rested. "I couldn't sleep," I said. "So I thought I'd stop by to visit him."

Emma nodded and gestured to a set of chairs close to her and said, "Let's sit down." I took a seat in the cold leather chair. She sat next to me. Machines whirred and made strange sounds. A memory washed over me, and I remembered sitting in another hospital room with my father as he fought for his life. Out of nowhere a feeling of anxiousness washed over me, like I needed to do something, knowing there was nothing I could do. I didn't want Parker to end up like my dad. I needed him to fight and to make it to the other side. I looked to my right and noticed that

Emma had the curtains drawn and the shades up. I didn't know what else to do or what to say, so I stood and walked over to the window and looked out at the city in silence. Bright lights glimmered and glinted across the horizon. I got lost in my own thoughts. Neither of us spoke for a long moment. Then Emma took a breath and said, "I hope you don't blame yourself, Blake."

I glanced over my shoulder and looked at her for a moment; then I turned back.

Emma said, "It could have just as easily been Jami. Or Simon. Or you. Or me. You know that, right?"

"Yeah," I said, glancing over to Parker. "How's Elizabeth taking it?"

Emma said nothing. I turned to her.

Then she shrugged and said, "The truth is, we don't have that kind of relationship with him. Not yet."

"Will you ever?" I asked, turning back and staring out the window again.

I heard Emma take a deep breath and let it out slowly. "We didn't get along very well. Growing up, I mean. Just some stuff he did. My mom left. I thought she'd come back, but she never did. I resented him for it."

"If you're talking about his drinking, I know about it. He leaves work early every Wednesday. Know why?"

Emma said nothing.

I crossed my arms as I thought about it. "He goes to an AA meeting across town."

"You followed him?"

"No. He told me about it. He didn't want me asking him about it in front of Simon, maybe."

"He trusts you."

"He shouldn't," I said. "I don't even trust myself."

"Well, you should."

I moved from the window and went to the chair again. I sat down and leaned forward. I set my elbows on my knees and cupped my hands together, one on top of the other, and rested my chin on top of my hands. There was more silence. Then I said, "There are some things in life you just can't do on your own. If you can't do it for you, then do it for Elizabeth. You still have time, Emma. Time to rebuild what you had with him. Time for Elizabeth to really get to know him. All he wants is another chance. If you'll give it to him."

Emma thought about it for a long moment. This time she was the one who stood. She crossed her arms and stepped over to where her father was and looked down on him, watching him sleep. "I looked up to him," she said. "When I was a little girl. He wasn't home a lot. At the beginning, I mean. He traveled a lot. It was just my mom and me for a while. When he did come home, he was never really home. His body was there, but his mind wasn't. It was always elsewhere." Emma turned and glanced at me. "I guess the job did it to him. Stress, long hours, that kind of thing." She turned back. "My mom got sick of it. So she left us."

Neither of us spoke for a long moment. I watched as Emma pulled a blanket up a little higher on her dad. Then she crossed her arms again and looked out the window for a spell. "I can try," she finally said, glancing back at me. "For Elizabeth, I mean. If what you say is true, if my father is serious about quitting."

I nodded. Said nothing.

Emma turned fully and stared at me from the window. "You're not a very trusting person, are you, Blake?"

I made no reply.

Emma shook her head and said, "Men. They all want to change the world but never want to change themselves."

I felt a knot in my stomach. I had heard something like it before. I tried to place it, but I couldn't.

"If I have to work on my issues, then I think you should have to work on yours, too."

I thought about that and said, "It's hard to trust anyone fully. I still don't know why I was targeted, Emma. It's going to bother me until I know how they did it and who within the government was behind it all."

Emma nodded knowingly. "Sometimes we don't get all of the answers we want. It doesn't mean we should put up walls and close others out. It could come back to hurt you one day. If you keep trying to do it all yourself." She paused for a moment and said, "Do you know the best way to start trusting other people?"

I didn't respond.

"Start with yourself."

I looked away, thinking about her words. "And how do I do that?"

"What's a promise you made to yourself that you can keep? For someone who could never repay you?"

I said nothing.

TWO DAYS LATER

I got home early from work. Jami was in the kitchen, watching the small TV on the counter set to cable news. She greeted me as I set my laptop bag on the counter and looked all around. Boxes were piled high. Pictures were off their hooks and leaning against bare walls. We had loved living away from the city and away from our jobs. We'd made this space our home, but neither of us felt safe here. Not anymore. So we started looking and began packing things up slowly so we'd be ready for when we found something better.

"You made the reservations, right?" asked Jami.

"Right," I said with wide eyes as I looked away like I'd forgotten.

Jami gave me a look. It said: *You'd better be kidding.* She stood from the counter and turned to me.

I smiled and gave her a kiss, and we embraced. "Thank you for doing this with me," I said. "It means a lot."

Jami looked up at me. "Thank you for being the kind of person who would want to do this."

WE ARRIVED TWENTY MINUTES LATER. I PARKED OUT FRONT. I cut the motor and stepped around the hood. Jami pushed her door open, and I helped her out. We walked across the freshly cut lawn and made our way into the building. There was an older woman standing in the foyer. The woman in charge of the place.

"Help you?" she said.

"I'm looking for a gentleman who lives here. Name's Nyland. Joe Nyland."

She narrowed her eyes and looked me over. She glanced at Jami; then she looked at me. "No soliciting."

"I'm not soliciting," I said. "Just visiting."

She said, "We don't allow visitors after four unless you're family. So come back tomorrow, nine a.m."

The woman turned and headed into the cafeteria. Jami looked at me. Her eyes said: *What do we do now?*

"We are family," I lied. The woman stopped in her tracks and turned back. "I'm his son. Please get him."

She nodded once to herself and told us to give her a minute. Jami and I watched as she stepped into the cafeteria. Two minutes later Joe Nyland pushed the door open and looked across with hope and smiled. The man used his walker and pushed it over to where we stood and with wide eyes said, "I'll be damned."

"Sorry to get your hopes up," I said.

He nodded. "Only family after four." He narrowed his eyes and studied me carefully. "Why are you here?"

I glanced at Jami, then I looked back at him, and I shrugged. "I thought we could take you to dinner."

He furrowed his brow. Then he slowly raised one of them. A small curious look. "Steak and potatoes?"

"A meal fit for a king." I looked past him, at the cafeteria. "Unless you'd rather have an MRE, that is."

Nyland smiled. He looked over at Jami again. I introduced him to my wife. We made small talk for a few seconds; then Nyland gestured outside. He said he wanted to get out of there as quickly as possible, before the lady I'd talked with changed her mind and reappeared to drag him back to the cafeteria, aka purgatory.

We stepped outside and walked with him slowly toward the car. Me on one side and Jami on the other. Nyland was slow but moving as fast as he was able. I thought about a lot of things in that moment.

I thought about my dad. He hadn't lived long enough to use a walker or to have to depend on other people. I wondered what life would be like if he were still with me. And I thought about what Emma Ross had said: *What's a promise you made to yourself that you can keep? For someone who could never repay you?*

We helped Nyland into my SUV. Jami insisted that he sit in the front, but he argued and said he'd rather sit in the back. I opened the hatch and put his walker inside. Then I came around the front and started the motor. I looked back through the rearview mirror as I pulled out. Mr. Nyland was smiling and looking out the windows, eager to spend time with some new friends, and probably more eager to eat some real food. He struck up a conversation with Jami. But I didn't pay much attention to it as we made our way to the steakhouse. Instead, I thought about my conversation with Emma Ross and the words she had spoken to me about becoming someone who not only could trust others, but someone who could be trusted.

Jami took my hand. She squeezed it tight and smiled as we headed to an early dinner with a new friend. Someone I could learn from, about how to live. Maybe about how to die. *Do for one what you wish you could do for all*, I thought, remembering my father's words. *Thanks, Dad*, I said to myself as I drove on.

WANT THE NEXT BLAKE JORDAN STORY
FOR $1 ON RELEASE DAY?*

*KINDLE EDITION ONLY

I'm currently writing the next book in the Blake Jordan series with a release planned soon. New subscribers get the Kindle version for $1 on release day.

Join my newsletter to reserve your copy and I'll let you know when it's ready to download to your Kindle.

kenfite.com/books

THE BLAKE JORDAN SERIES

IN ORDER

Made in the USA
Monee, IL
01 October 2022

15007945R00184